"To good times

Scott clinked his mu[...]
excellent IPA."

"Told you."

"My patient says you should always listen when a smart woman gives advice."

"He sounds like a wise man."

He watched her bite into one of the quesadilla wedges. Her face morphed into an expression of bliss.

"Mmm." She swallowed the bite. "Try some."

It all felt so familiar.

But here she was, eleven years later, as smart and funny as ever. Not that she hadn't changed. She'd grown and matured. Become more confident. All those changes had only made her more perfect. More Volta.

And once again, he was going to have to leave her behind.

But tonight, he was going to enjoy his time with her.

Because the memories they'd made in these last couple of weeks might have to last him the rest of his life.

Dear Reader,

I'm so glad you've joined me for this fifth book in the Northern Lights series. It makes me happy to share my home state of Alaska with you.

Alaska is beautiful, but it has its own set of challenges. Alaska has about the same population as the city of Seattle, but the people are spread out across a state larger than Texas, California, Montana and Massachusetts combined. Most of the municipalities in Alaska (86 percent) are not connected to the road system. When emergencies happen, it can get tricky to get sick or injured people to hospitals.

Volta is a flight-certified emergency medical technician. That means she might be flying across the state at a moment's notice to help someone who's in trouble. Volta is also a mother, and, as if life weren't complicated enough, the doctor she's paired with is a man she once loved. Good thing Volta knows how to handle emergency situations.

Research is a delightful part of an author's job, and when I was working on this story, I had the opportunity to meet a few of the dedicated people who work emergency flight response. It's an understatement to say I was impressed by their training and preparation. I sleep better knowing that if my loved ones get into trouble, there are people like them who are ready to help.

Thank you for reading my story. I love to connect with readers. You can find me at Beth Carpenter Books on Facebook or @4bethcarpenter on Twitter. Or drop by my website, bethcarpenterbooks.blogspot.com, and while you're there, you can sign up for my newsletter.

Happy reading!

Beth Carpenter

HEARTWARMING

Sweet Home Alaska

—

Beth Carpenter

Recycling programs
for this product may
not exist in your area.

ISBN-13: 978-1-335-51075-4

Sweet Home Alaska

Copyright © 2019 by Lisa Deckert

All rights reserved. Except for use in any review, the reproduction or
utilization of this work in whole or in part in any form by any electronic,
mechanical or other means, now known or hereafter invented, including
xerography, photocopying and recording, or in any information storage
or retrieval system, is forbidden without the written permission of the
publisher, Harlequin Enterprises Limited, 22 Adelaide St. West, 40th Floor,
Toronto, Ontario M5H 4E3, Canada.

This is a work of fiction. Names, characters, places and incidents are
either the product of the author's imagination or are used fictitiously,
and any resemblance to actual persons, living or dead, business
establishments, events or locales is entirely coincidental.

This edition published by arrangement with Harlequin Books S.A.

For questions and comments about the quality of this book,
please contact us at CustomerService@Harlequin.com.

® and TM are trademarks of Harlequin Enterprises Limited or its
corporate affiliates. Trademarks indicated with ® are registered in the
United States Patent and Trademark Office, the Canadian Intellectual
Property Office and in other countries.

Printed in U.S.A.

Beth Carpenter is thankful for good books, a good dog, a good man and a dream job creating happily-ever-afters. She and her husband now split their time between Alaska and Arizona, where she occasionally encounters a moose in the yard or a scorpion in the basement. She prefers the moose.

Books by Beth Carpenter

Harlequin Heartwarming

The Alaskan Catch
A Gift for Santa
Alaskan Hideaway
An Alaskan Proposal

Visit the Author Profile page at Harlequin.com for more titles.

To the first responders: EMTs, nurses, firefighters, police, pilots and all the others who are there for us when we're at our most vulnerable. Thank you.

Special thanks to Sarah Smith Ransom, who patiently answered my questions about emergency flight response in Alaska and invited me in for a glimpse of the planes, equipment and facilities they use. She shared a great deal of information about the challenges of handling medical emergencies in a huge state with few roads. Any mistakes in the story are mine.

Also thanks to Kathryn Lye, my editor, for helping make this book the best it can be.

CHAPTER ONE

IT WAS NEVER a good sign when your normally unflappable pilot suddenly started swearing. Volta looked up from the patient stats she'd been going over with her partner, Bridget, who stared at her in wide-eyed alarm. They peered out the windows. They were still fifteen or twenty minutes from their destination, but the sky ahead was clear. The engines were running smoothly. The wings were still attached. "What's wrong?" Volta asked Mike through her headset.

"Mount Spurr erupted," he growled. "Once we land in Sparks, we're grounded until further notice."

So, nothing wrong with the plane. That was the good news. The bad news was they had a woman in her thirty-fifth week of pregnancy with dangerously high blood pressure waiting to be transported, and they weren't going to be able to get her to a hospital. Worse, Volta knew the patient. Lori was the school secretary and also assisted Daniel, the volunteer health aide at the Sparks village clinic. Lori's husband, Paul, taught secondary school and coached basketball.

Last time Volta had seen Lori was at the hospital in Anchorage when Lori was on her way to an ultrasound. She'd joked to Volta that they'd timed her due date for June 2 so that she and Paul wouldn't have to miss a day of school. But now Lori's blood pressure was spiking, a major complication. And on top of that, Lori was expecting twins.

Mike must have been having similar thoughts. "At least that doctor is there."

"What doctor?" Bridget asked.

"You know. The one who I'm supposed to start flying around with to all the villages next week for some sort of study. He came into Sparks by an air taxi yesterday, and the dispatcher mentioned he'd probably want a ride back with us. Doesn't look like any of us are getting out today, though."

"I guess not." Regardless of why he was there, Volta was glad Lori was under a doctor's care. Daniel did an excellent job, but preeclampsia was tricky. "What kind of doctor is he?" Hopefully not the academic kind, but Mike did mention a study.

"Something about prenatal care."

"That sounds promising." Volta breathed a

little easier. "How long do you think we'll be grounded?"

Mike shrugged. "Depends on how long the volcano keeps blowing, and the direction of the wind. Last time, about twenty years ago, it was two days."

Two days. Assuming the doctor could get Lori stabilized, two days was doable. In three days, however, was her daughter Emma's eighth birthday party. Volta wasn't going to miss that even if she had to hitchhike home, which, considering they were fifty miles from the road system, would be quite a feat. She hoped it didn't come to that.

Emma would be fine sleeping over with her grandparents until Volta could get back. Since they still had ten minutes before landing, Volta did a quick scan of her calendar. Tomorrow was the PTA bake sale, and she'd volunteered to bring four dozen cookies. Mom would be willing to step in, but her antisugar stance meant what she called a cookie wasn't what most people would consider a treat. Volta's brother's girlfriend, on the other hand, was an excellent baker. Volta set a reminder to call Sabrina later. She returned the phone to her pocket and picked up the fax Daniel had sent when he requested transport.

Mike's voice came through their headphones

again. "Look west." Volta and Bridget glanced out the window, where a tall gray cloud was forming.

"Ash plume?" Bridget asked.

"Yep. We're not going to beat it by much."

Up ahead, the tip of the cell tower over Sparks came into view. Shades of yellow green signaled spring on the tundra. A braided river hugged the south edge of the little community and twisted off to the west. It looked peaceful, as though bad things could never happen there, but they did, and that was when they called in people like Volta, Bridget and Mike.

A few minutes later, Mike landed the plane, the tires bouncing once on the airstrip before rolling to a stop. Mike turned and taxied back to the center of the strip to a parking area. Up ahead, a battered Chevy Suburban rattled along the gravel road between the village and the airstrip. It pulled to a stop beside the plane.

Mike and Bridget climbed out of the airplane and attached a ramp to the door. Volta shoved the portable incubator down the rails. Mike and Bridget picked it up and carried the equipment to the SUV, where Mayor Libby was waiting with the tailgate open. "Glad you're here."

Thanks to her good judgment, as well as being related to maybe 25 percent of the local population, Libby was unofficial mayor for life in the village of Sparks. She oversaw everything while running the combination post office, general store and makeshift diner next to the clinic. She also opened her home as a sort of bed-and-breakfast for the occasional visitor and was a one-woman chamber of commerce. And her Suburban doubled as the village ambulance. "Load her up."

Mike and Bridget loaded the incubator, while Volta jumped down, moved the ramp and closed the door to the plane. Everyone climbed into the SUV. Volta hurried to join them. She slammed the passenger door closed. "How's Lori doing?"

Libby put the car in gear and started it with a jerk. "She's in labor. According to that visiting doctor, she has pre-something—"

"Preeclampsia."

"Right, and so he says she's got to deliver now. Sounds like she's close. You might not be able to fly her out until afterward."

"Unfortunately, we're not going to be able to take her at all, at least not today," Mike told her. "Spurr just blew."

"What, when?"

"About twenty minutes ago."

"Augh. I knew they'd had rumblings, but I thought it had quieted down. I was over with

Lori and Paul and didn't hear the warning. I've got to get back to the post office and find out what's going on." Libby whipped around a corner and headed toward the clinic. "Good thing we have a doctor in town. Seems a shame, though. Lori's been on bed rest for a month, trying to keep from delivering early. But I guess that happens with twins."

"Twins?" Mike hadn't read the patient stat sheet.

"That's right. We're all eager to see if they're identical or not. Paul and Lori wanted to be surprised." Libby pulled up between the clinic and the post office. "I'd better go see what's up with that volcano."

"I'll get a progress report," Bridget told Volta. "Can you and Mike get the incubator?"

"Sure," Volta said.

She and Mike carried the portable unit through the door of the clinic while Bridget disappeared into the second room, where they could hear Paul's voice: "That's it, babe. You're doing great. Ouch—"

Volta chuckled to herself. She'd been on the receiving end of some of those hand clenches during labor. Lori was one of the gentlest people Volta knew, but sometimes it took a lot to make it through those big contractions.

"Hi, everyone. Bridget Hickel, flight nurse.

Bad news, I'm afraid," Bridget announced. "Mount Spurr blew its top, and we're grounded."

"The volcano erupted?" Daniel's voice.

"Yes. We were already two-thirds of the way here, so we kept on coming. Unfortunately, we're not flying out again until the ash cloud is gone. But we did bring an incubator. They're carrying it in now."

"Where do you want it?" Mike asked Volta, swinging his end around to fit it into the waiting room.

"Let's set it here for now," Volta suggested, nodding toward a clear space against the wall. "It sounds pretty crowded in the exam room."

They set the unit on the floor. "I'll head over to Zeke's and see what he knows," Mike told Volta. "Unless you need me."

She'd forgotten Mike's cousin operated an air taxi service out of Sparks. "I don't think so since we can't fly, but I'll call if we do. Thanks, Mike."

Volta headed toward the exam room, but before she reached the door, another voice drifted out, reassuring and calm. "Good job, Lori. Not much longer now. Try to relax for a minute. Slow, easy breaths."

Volta stopped in her tracks. She knew that voice, deep and smooth, with just a bit of drawl. But it couldn't be. The owner of the voice she knew was working on the other side of the world. No doubt this was some other baritone-voiced doctor from Texas. The voice continued, "You're at a ten. Doing great. Next contraction, you'll be able to push."

Dilated to ten? Libby was right. They wouldn't have been able to get Lori to the hospital in time to deliver anyway. Good thing they'd brought the incubator as a precaution. Volta entered the room. Everyone looked her way. Paul was wedged into a corner beside Lori, holding her hand. Daniel was on the other side, monitoring her blood pressure. Bridget had moved into position to assist the doctor at the foot of the bed.

A surgical mask covered most of the doctor's face, but he stared at Volta, his eyes wide in shock. Familiar brown eyes. It had been eleven years, but she remembered every detail. She knew if she got closer, she would be able to distinguish the little flecks of green sprinkled through the brown. What in the world was Scott Willingham doing in Sparks, Alaska?

From somewhere far away, Daniel's voice made itself heard. "Dr. Willingham, Volta Morgan, flight paramedic."

Scott tugged the surgical mask from his face. "Volta?"

She met his eyes. "Small world, huh?" She

turned away to flash Paul a smile and touch Lori's hand. "How are you holding up?"

"I'm okay." Lori blew out a long breath. "The doctor says I'm almost ready."

"He should know. Dr. Willingham has delivered a lot of babies." At least that was what she'd gathered from the Doctors, Education and Medicine for All website. DEMA was always posting photos of him somewhere in the world, holding a newborn baby.

Scott stared at her as though he were glimpsing a ghost. She didn't blame him. That was exactly how she'd felt when she'd heard his voice a few moments ago.

"You two know—" Bridget started to ask, but Lori suddenly sat up with a grunt as a contraction started.

"Okay." Scott was back to his take-charge voice. He pulled the mask over his mouth and moved into position. "This time I want you to push. The first baby is in position. Volta, could you take over Daniel's post? He can handle logistics since he's most familiar with the room. Bridget, please have an aspirator at the ready. Paul, hang on. Okay, Lori, now push!"

Lori gave a mighty groan and raised herself off the bed, puffing her cheeks out. Volta watched the monitor. Lori's BP was high, but it wasn't spiking out of control.

"Good, good." Scott always had such a soothing voice. "A little harder if you can. We're making progress."

"Come on, Lori, you can do it." Volta laid a hand on her arm. "Push."

"I'm trying!"

"I know. You're doing great," Volta assured her.

A minute later Scott sat back. "Okay, contraction's over. Good job, Lori. Now rest."

Daniel handed Volta a moist cloth. She used it to wipe the sweat from Lori's forehead and distracted her with a little meaningless chatter. Almost before Lori could catch her breath, the next contraction hit, and they all jumped into action.

Ten minutes later, Scott lifted a wet bundle. "It's a boy." The baby squirmed, a good sign, and let out a cry of protest at the bright lights and sounds. Scott handed the baby to Bridget and cut the cord. Bridget carried the tiny child to a table to clean him up.

Volta peered over her shoulder. The baby was small and on the skinny side, but for a premature twin, he was well developed, with a healthy color. Paul stared. "He's so little."

"Not that little for a twin," Scott said. "We'll want to keep him in the incubator for a bit, but right now, why don't you hold him?"

Bridget wrapped the tiny baby in a soft blanket and handed him over. With a look of wonder, Paul accepted the baby into his arms. Lori craned her neck to see, and the baby stared back at her with solemn blue eyes. Suddenly, Lori stiffened as another contraction hit.

"Okay, Lori," Scott said. "It's time for the second act. Get ready. Push!"

It took several more contractions, but fifteen minutes later, the second baby was born. But this one didn't squirm. Bridget handed Scott the aspirator. He cleared the mucus from the baby's throat and rubbed the baby's back.

Lori reached for Volta's hand, and Volta squeezed it, but she was ready to run for the prenatal ventilator waiting outside the door with the incubator. An eternity passed in the next couple of seconds, but then the baby sucked in a breath and let out a cry. Volta closed her eyes and sent up a silent prayer of thanks.

Scott smiled. "You have a girl. A beautiful little girl."

He beamed down at the tiny baby in his hands. Scott must have delivered hundreds of babies, but he seemed as excited as if these twins were his first. This really was his life's purpose. It had taken Volta a long time to accept that.

As Volta watched Lori and Paul's new little girl, images of Emma as a newborn flashed through her mind. She'd been twice the size of the baby Bridget was swaddling, but no less a miracle. Emma had been born with a red face, a thatch of dark hair and a voice that left no doubt of her opinion on the whole procedure. Almost eight years later, she still held strong opinions and expressed them enthusiastically. Volta was so grateful to have her daughter. Something that wouldn't have happened had Scott not quit their relationship.

Scott handed the baby off to Bridget so that he could deliver the placentas. Bridget cleaned and wrapped the baby and carried her to Lori. "Meet your daughter."

Lori held the baby and smiled down at her. "Hi, little one. You gave us a scare. Don't ever do that again, okay?"

According to the numbers on the monitor, Lori's blood pressure was already down a few points, and now that she had delivered, she should be back to normal soon. Volta relaxed for the first time since she'd arrived.

Scott pulled down his surgical mask. "Paul, you have a beautiful family. Congratulations."

"Thank you, Doctor." Paul seemed to be trying to figure out how to shake hands while holding the baby, but Scott just laughed and patted him on the shoulder.

"You concentrate on that baby. He and his sister are your top priorities from here on out." He rested his hand on Lori's shoulder and leaned over to admire the other twin in her arms. "You did well today, Mom. We'll bring in that incubator to make sure the babies stay warm and we'll keep an eye on your blood pressure, but y'all will be fine."

Lori beamed. Scott shook hands with Daniel and Bridget, and finally he turned to Volta. "Thank you for pitching in." His eyes caught hers and held. "Why don't we step into the other room and see about that incubator?"

CHAPTER TWO

SOME OF SCOTT'S colleagues at DEMA called him Dr. Chill. The more chaotic his surroundings, the calmer he got. Three weeks ago, he'd performed a cesarean delivery in a tent during a tropical storm while the lights flickered and then went out, leaving him to finish the surgery by lantern. A month before that, he'd hiked seven miles over a mountain for a breech delivery. Neither of those circumstances had tested his ability to remain calm. But when Volta had walked into that room, his heart rate skyrocketed.

He'd known she lived in Alaska. In fact, Volta was the main reason he was here. A local health organization had commissioned help from DEMA to study the quality of prenatal care in the rural areas of the state and give recommendations on how it could be improved. Ordinarily, Scott chose assignments where he could work directly with the people who needed medical care, but he'd volunteered for this assessment project in Alaska because he wanted to see Volta one more time.

He'd tried to forget her. After all, he was the one who broke it off. Few marriages survived the sort of life he'd chosen, and with his background, he was a particularly bad risk. Just like his father, Scott was the sort of man who focused on a job and forgot to eat and sleep and spend time with his family. Volta deserved so much better than that.

Once he realized their relationship was beginning to feel serious, he'd pulled the plug, and he'd never seen Volta again.

Scott's life had turned out exactly the way he'd planned. He'd been with DEMA for ten years now, one of only a handful of full-time doctors ready to go wherever and whenever he was needed. Most of their medical staff consisted of volunteers who took a week or two off from their regular practices to volunteer with DEMA, but Scott worked year-round delivering babies and performing surgeries. And yet, even after all this time, Volta still appeared in his dreams.

He smiled to himself. She'd never liked the name her electrician dad had given her, but it suited her, with her electric-blue eyes and high-wattage smile. Not to mention the way his skin used to tingle when she touched him.

He'd figured he would go to Alaska, get a good start on the assignment and then take a day or two off and find Volta. Once she looked him in the eye and told him she'd moved on and was happy, her memory would quit haunting him. At least, that was the plan.

But instead, she'd just walked into the room while he was in the middle of a delivery. In a tiny clinic in a tiny village in an enormous state. Volta. He followed her into the waiting room, quietly shutting the door behind him. She turned back to look at him, her bright blue eyes focused on his face. So many things he wanted to tell her. So many questions. What was she doing in emergency response instead of physical therapy? Did she ever think about their time together in Hawaii? Was she happy?

In fact, he didn't ask any questions at all. Instead, he opened his arms. After only the slightest hesitation, she rushed into them. And suddenly it was years ago, he was holding Volta in his arms, and for a moment, all was right with the world.

VOLTA CLOSED HER EYES, her cheek nestling into that familiar hollow between his shoulder and his chest, just as though it hadn't been years since she'd last held him. She breathed in the clean scent of citrus from his aftershave. It felt so good. But she couldn't do this. Eleven years ago, he'd broken her heart. She'd worked hard to recover, and now she had her dream job and a wonderful daughter. Scott didn't belong in her life.

She stepped away and looked up with what she hoped was a simple smile. "Scott. What in the world are you doing here?"

"I'm on assignment with DEMA. I'm studying prenatal care in rural Alaska, but when Lori went into labor, Daniel asked me to take over the delivery. What are you doing in Sparks?"

"Doing my job. I'm a flight paramedic for Puffin Medical Transport, based in Anchorage."

"When did you go into emergency response? Last I knew, your plan was physical therapy."

Volta shrugged. "Plans change."

"You enjoy your job as a paramedic?"

"I really do."

"I'm glad. So, tell me about yourself. What have you been up to for the past few years?"

"Oh, the usual. Work mostly. Nothing like what you've been doing with DEMA. I saw in the last newsletter that you were in the Caribbean during that tropical storm last month."

"You follow DEMA?"

"Um, sure. They do good work." She wasn't

going to admit that she was from time to time looking for news of him.

"You know, you used to talk about seeing the world, and your skills could be invaluable to DEMA. If you were interested—"

"No," she said, too quickly. She smiled to cover her nervousness. "I'm settled here in Alaska. My family is here."

"You're married?"

"Not anymore." At his questioning look, she added, "I'm a widow. How about you? Are you married?" she asked, trying to avoid that awkward conversation where people felt compelled to ask about the details of her husband's death.

He shook his head. "Never in one place long enough." He paused. "But that goes with the job."

At least he'd been honest about that. An insecure part of her had always wondered if his explanation of how he couldn't maintain a relationship with his job was just an excuse to brush her off. She'd met Scott when he was still a resident, working in a hospital in Hawaii. She was going to college then, studying kinesiology, with plans to become a physical therapist. They'd met, oddly enough, at the botanical gardens in downtown Honolulu. Oddly because neither of them was in the habit of taking off from their busy schedules for things like walking through gardens.

But Volta had hardly left her dorm room for three days, working on a research paper. She'd turned it in and decided to spend the afternoon outdoors among the tropical flowers. Scott was there, de-stressing after a rough day at the hospital. They'd fallen into conversation under a plumeria tree, which led to dinner, which led to more dates. They both knew it was only temporary. Volta was a sophomore, after all, and Scott would join DEMA as a traveling doctor once his residency was finished.

But Volta's heart failed to get the message. She fell hard for Scott Willingham, and from the tender way he treated her, she thought he loved her, too. Despite knowing his plans, Volta came to believe that love would triumph, that somehow they would find a way to be together. She was wrong.

Toward the end of the semester, he'd called it quits. He said it wasn't fair to lead her on, that he wasn't the kind of man who could balance work and marriage, especially in his sort of career. Devastated, she'd limped through her finals and then dropped out of college and gone home. To Alaska. Where she belonged.

Where she'd never expected to run into

Scott. "Is it everything you thought it would be? Working for DEMA, I mean?"

"Yes and no. I love being able to help the people who need me most, but sometimes it's a finger in the dike. And I never stay anywhere long enough to get to know my patients. It can be lonely. But I feel like we do a lot of good, not only in emergency situations but in setting up programs for ongoing improvements in health care."

"DEMA doesn't usually work within the US, does it?"

"Not to give medical care, but I'm here as a consultant. Have you heard of Leo Travert?"

"The billionaire aviation guy in Oregon who died last year?"

"Yes. He got his start in Alaska, as a bush pilot."

"I heard that somewhere. But what does that have to do with you?"

"Well, when Travert lived in rural Alaska, his wife died in childbirth, due to complications that might have been avoided if she'd had better access to prenatal care."

"How sad."

"Yes. But in his will, he left a great deal of money to start a foundation with a mission to improve prenatal care in rural Alaska."

"That's great news." Anything they could do

to make medical care more accessible was a step forward. In many of the villages, medical services consisted only of a volunteer health aide.

"A lot has changed in the years since Travert lost his wife, but the infant mortality rate in the bush is still twice that in the cities. The focus of my study is to learn about what care is available now, and how the Travert Foundation can help fill in the gaps. The chairman, Ransom Goodman, was a good friend of Travert's. He hired DEMA because of our experience in dealing with hard-to-reach populations."

"So you're in Sparks to see how a village clinic works."

"Yes. I've already learned a lot from Daniel and Libby about the setup here. I'll need to get a feel for the facilities around the state before I can make specific recommendations, but I have some ideas." He gave a sheepish smile. "I'm not sure how to incorporate volcano eruptions into my recommendations, though."

"Some things you can't anticipate. You just have to take them as they come." Like the realization that the attraction she'd felt when she met Scott at the botanical gardens was still there, tugging on her heartstrings. But she could ignore it.

Scott shrugged. "You're right. No use worrying about what can't be changed. Let's get this incubator going."

Together they carried the incubator into the exam room and set it up, further crowding the small area. "I need to examine my patients," Scott said. "Bridget, could you stay with me, please? The rest of you can wait in the other room."

Daniel nodded and slipped through the door. Paul handed his son to Bridget and watched her carefully tuck the baby inside the incubator. It was only after Bridget had taken the other baby from Lori's arms and snuggled her beside her brother that Paul kissed his wife and left, with Volta filing out behind him.

Paul crossed the waiting room to stand beside Daniel at the window. Volta followed. The landscape had transformed since she arrived. Outside, a fine gray powder had coated every surface, and more drifted from the sky in a parody of a snowstorm. Across the street, a woman with a bandanna tied around her face made her way home from the washateria, huddling over a basket of laundry in a futile attempt to keep the ashes out.

"It looks like another planet," Paul commented.

A few minutes later, Scott joined them. "Everyone is doing fine. Paul, your wife would like your company. Bridget has volunteered to stay here with you for the time being and suggested the rest of us get some lunch."

"In that case, I'll head home and have lunch with my wife," Daniel said. "Call me if you need me."

"Wear a mask," Volta suggested. "You don't want to breathe that stuff."

Daniel nodded and pulled on a surgical mask before he slipped outside and started up the street. Paul returned to his chair beside Lori's bed, and Volta could hear them murmuring to each other.

Scott turned to Volta. "Are you ready? Libby said something about a special treat. I can't remember what she called it."

Volta chuckled. "Akutaq?"

"Right. What is it?"

"People sometimes call it Eskimo ice cream. It's basically whipped fat—some use shortening but she uses caribou fat—sweetened and mixed with berries. She first got me to try it a couple of years ago."

Scott's eyes crinkled in amusement. "Did you like it?"

Volta waggled her hand in a so-so gesture. "It's not terrible. Very rich."

"Is this Libby's test to see if I'm open to new experiences?"

"Probably. She seems determined that any-one who spends time here needs to taste it. I think she figures if you won't try her food, why should she trust your judgment?"

"She has a point. Sharing food is a bonding experience."

"Yes." She and Scott used to love trying out the different cuisines of the Hawaiian Islands. Scott had given her her first taste of poke, a raw diced fish she still craved from time to time. And then there was their favorite res-taurant. "Remember that little noodle place over by the college?" As soon as she said it, she regretted bringing it up. The last thing she should do was talk about their history together.

But Scott smiled. "I've never found yakisoba as good anywhere else."

Volta's phone rang. She checked the screen. "It's my mom. Why don't you head on over and I'll be there in a few minutes?"

"I'll wait."

Volta nodded and answered the phone. "Hi. I was just about to call you. You heard about the volcano?"

"Yes, they put out a bulletin. Where are you?"

"I'm in Sparks, and it looks like we'll be here for the night at least, possibly more. Are you okay keeping Emma?"

"Of course. They're not sure if they'll have school tomorrow. It depends on how the ash falls over the next couple of hours. Anyway, Emma will be fine with us. We're going to paint birdhouses this afternoon."

"That sounds fun. Say, I ordered her birthday cake a month ago, but would you mind calling the bakery to verify?"

"All that sugar." Volta could almost hear her mother shaking her head. "Are you sure you want to serve cake?"

Volta laughed. "Mom, it's a birthday party. Absolutely, we want cake." Volta was in middle school when her mother had decided to cut sugar out of their diet. In mutual rebellion, Volta, her brother and her dad used to sneak to the bakery during Mom's tai chi class on Saturday mornings and indulge in the most sugar-laden treats they could find.

"I could make cookies for the party," Mom offered.

Volta rolled her eyes. What her mom called cookies were more like organic hockey pucks. She couldn't imagine any of the children at the party would eat them. On the other hand, the party was at a reindeer farm, and they might make a good substitute for alfalfa pellets. She'd have to ask her friend Marissa, who ran the farm, if Mom's cookies would upset the reindeer's digestion. "Sure, Mom, but we'll have birthday cake, too. And you'll be happy to know, we're also having fruit and vegetable trays."

"Well, that's something, I guess. Here, your daughter wants to talk to you."

"Mommy?"

"Hi, sweetie."

"Grandma says you probably can't come home tonight because of the volcano."

"I'm afraid she's right. We flew into a village, but we can't fly back out until the ash is out of the air."

"Why?" One of Emma's favorite questions. Sometimes, Volta felt as though she'd earned an advanced degree just from looking up the answers for Emma.

But this one she knew. "Because volcanic ash is made up of tiny, tiny little rocks, and if the rocks get into the engines on the plane, they could make the engines stop running and then the plane couldn't fly anymore."

"Oh. Will you be back for my birthday?"

"I should be. It's not until Saturday, and I imagine the volcano will have gone back to sleep by then, don't you think?"

"Maybe somebody should sing it a lullaby."

Volta laughed. "Or read it a bedtime story?"

"Yeah, like the one about the moon."

"That's a good one."

"Everybody's coming to my party. Madison wasn't sure she could because she had a piano lesson, but her mom says she can skip it just this once because she wants to see the reindeer at the farm."

"I'm glad she can make it."

"Ryan's so lucky he gets to live on the reindeer farm all the time. With horses."

"You're lucky, too. You get to live at our house, and sometimes at Grandma and Grandpa's, and sometimes with Leith."

"Oh, yeah, I forgot to tell you. Uncle Leith said Sabrina wants to take me to that new movie. With the princesses."

"That will be fun."

"The bake sale at school is tomorrow." A gust of wind rattled the window and sent ash swirling.

"I know," Volta whispered, "but don't tell Grandma because she'll want to make cookies."

"Grandma's cookies are awful," Emma whispered.

"Grandma says they might not have school tomorrow, so I'm not sure whether they'll have the bake sale. I'll call Sabrina and ask if she'll make a batch of cookies. If school is open, she can drop them off and if not, she can freeze them until they reschedule."

"Sabrina makes excellent cookies."

"She does." Volta looked over at Scott, still standing at the window. "I need to go. Be good for Grandma, okay?"

"Okay. I love you to infinity."

Volta smiled. "I love you to infinity plus one. Bye, Emma."

"Bye."

Volta put the phone in the pocket of her flight suit and pulled a mask from the supply cabinet. "Are you ready to brave the ash?"

Scott turned toward her. "Sure. Everything okay at home?"

Volta nodded. "It's all under control."

"Who's Emma?"

She felt an odd reluctance to share her personal life with Scott, although there was no reason for him not to know about Emma. Besides, Libby was sure to ask about her. "Emma is my daughter. She's seven."

"A daughter. Somehow I didn't imagine you with a child."

She wouldn't have thought he'd imagined her at all. She'd always assumed once he broke up with her, he'd gone on single-mindedly with his life plan. Volta stuck her head into the exam room. "Dr. Willingham and I are going to Libby's for lunch. Can we bring you something back?"

"A sandwich?" Paul requested.

"Sure. Lori, are you feeling up to eating yet? Maybe some soup?"

Lori dragged her eyes away from the baby snuggled up against her chest. "Okay."

"Bridget?"

"I'll wait until you get back and take a turn. Did I hear something about akutaq?"

"That's the rumor."

"Tell Libby to save me some."

Volta grinned. "Okay. See you in a little while."

She returned to the reception room, where Scott was staring out the window. "I've never seen anything like this." He turned toward her. "And I've seen a lot."

"I'll bet you have. You were in the Philippines after that earthquake. Was it as bad as it looked in the photos?"

"It was. Conditions made it difficult to get clean water and supplies to the people who needed them. I lost some patients there." He let out a breath. "I don't like losing patients."

"It never gets easier."

"No, it doesn't. But we didn't lose anyone today." He grinned. "Volcano or no, today is a good day."

"Absolutely. Let's go get some lunch."

They both pulled on masks, and Scott followed Volta next door. They slipped inside the store and quickly shut the door to seal out the swirling ash, jangling a strip of sleigh bells.

The usually bustling building appeared to be deserted. They were wiping their feet on the rug when Libby appeared from the door leading to the mailboxes.

"Where is everyone?" Volta asked her.

"I sent them all home before the ash got here. Did Lori deliver?"

"A boy and a girl," Volta reported. "Both healthy."

"That's wonderful. And how is Lori?" Libby looked at Scott.

He hesitated, probably weighing how much information he should be sharing, but he must have decided Libby counted as family. "Tired, but happy. She's going to be fine."

"That's good news. You know, Dr. Willingham, it's funny. You told me yesterday that you hadn't planned to visit Sparks until next week."

"That's right. I finished with personal business more quickly than I expected, so I decided to get a head start on this assignment."

"It's no accident you were here when Lori needed you. I'm convinced there is an unseen hand that guides us to the places we need to be." Libby included Volta in her smile. "And it brought you both here today. Even with the volcano."

Tiny goose bumps rose on Volta's arms. Unlike Libby, Volta was not the sort to go looking for signs and omens, but here she was, in a village in the Alaskan bush, in the same room as a man she used to love. Was it fate?

No. They'd burned their bridges long ago. Their lifestyles were never compatible, and now Volta was rooted here in Alaska, raising her daughter, which meant they were further apart than ever.

And yet being in the same room with Scott was dredging up memories. Memories of laughter and fun. Of swimming in the ocean and building castles on the beach. Of feeling his arms around her when he kissed her goodnight under swaying palm trees.

"Volta, aren't you hungry?" Libby was ladling something from the slow cooker she always had going beside the microwave.

Volta jumped. "I'm sorry, Libby. What's in the pot today?"

"Salmon chowder. And those little crackers you like."

No wonder everyone in Sparks loved Libby.

Two months ago, when Volta was in town to help with an immunization drive, she'd mentioned in passing she liked oyster crackers. Libby never seemed to forget anything. "Chowder sounds fabulous, thank you. But let me take something for Paul and Lori first. He said he wanted a sandwich." She crossed to the cold foods case.

Libby joined her and reached for a sandwich. "Paul will want ham and cheese, barbecue potato chips and baby carrots." She dropped her voice to a whisper. "The doctor seems to know what he's doing."

"Yeah, Scott's great."

"Scott?" Libby looked at her speculatively.

"Dr. Willingham," Volta amended quickly. "I'll take a bowl of chowder for Lori." Volta ladled the soup into a paper bowl and snapped on the lid. "Please put them on the tab with mine."

"Nobody's paying today. We're celebrating." Libby looked toward Scott, who was pouring a cup of coffee. "So, you and the doctor—"

"I'd better take this to Lori before it gets cold. I'll come back for mine in a little while. Thanks, Libby." Volta grabbed the food and headed toward the door.

"Don't forget your mask," Scott called.

"Right." Volta stopped to juggle the food items. Scott set down his coffee and came to hold them while she pulled up her mask. "Thanks."

"Hurry back. We have a lot of catching up to do."

That was exactly what Volta was afraid of.

CHAPTER THREE

SCOTT WATCHED VOLTA practically sprint out the door and across to the clinic. Something Libby said seemed to have spooked her. Or maybe it was him.

He wasn't sure where he stood with Volta. She'd looked stunned to see him in the delivery room, but who wouldn't given the same circumstances? Afterward, she hadn't hesitated to come into his arms for a hug. But then she'd drawn away, and an invisible curtain of awkwardness seemed to fall between them.

She looked good in her snug flight suit, her dark hair pulled back into a ponytail. Not much different than she'd looked when she was in college. A beautiful woman.

A beautiful woman with a daughter. Why was that such a surprise? Did he think nothing would have changed in Volta's life in the last eleven years?

"Doctor, come eat your chowder before it gets cold," Libby said. "I'm sure Volta will be back soon, and you can have a second bowl with her."

He sat down across the table from Libby and tried the chowder, made with sockeye salmon, savory vegetables and evaporated milk, of course. Over dinner last evening, Libby had explained that—because of transportation costs—fresh milk in the villages ran four times the price of milk in Anchorage. They'd discussed alternative ways for pregnant and nursing women to get calcium and vitamin D. Libby was a font of knowledge about the challenges of health care in remote villages. They really should have hired her for this study.

"Good soup," he told Libby.

"Wait until you taste my akutaq. I had to fight off my grandkids to save you some."

"I'll look forward to it."

Libby took a drink from her coffee. "I thought last night you said this was your first time in Alaska."

"It is."

"Then how do you know our Volta?"

He took his time with another spoonful of soup before answering. "I knew her in Hawaii."

"Volta was in Hawaii? I thought she grew up in Alaska."

"She did, but she was in college in Hawaii

while I was doing my residency at Royal Honolulu Hospital."

"Hmm." Libby was clearly not satisfied with that answer. "And you were friends, in Hawaii."

"Yes." Much more than friends, but that was between him and Volta.

"I never heard about that. You kept in touch?"

"No."

"But you came to Alaska to reconnect with her."

"I came to Alaska on the assignment we talked about yesterday." And maybe partially to find Volta. Maybe mostly to find Volta. But officially, he was here on assignment.

"Hmm." Libby clearly wasn't buying it.

Scott felt as if he'd already said too much, so he asked, "How long have you known Volta?"

"For about three years. Daniel does a health fair and a vaccination clinic every year, and Volta has helped with two of them. She stays overnight with me when she does. We've become friends."

It sounded like they'd only spent a handful of days together, but some people didn't take long to get to the heart of a person. Libby seemed like one of those people. "You know her daughter?"

"Emma?" Libby smiled. "We've never met,

but I've heard so many stories, I feel as if I know her. Volta has her hands full with that one."

"Oh?" Scott started to ask more, but Volta chose that moment to return from the clinic.

"Susie and Sadie have arrived, and they're giving Lori and Paul child-rearing advice."

Libby shook her head. "Those sisters of mine are so excited about another pair of twins in the village, Lori will never get rid of them."

"I suspect she'll be glad for the help over the next few weeks. She's breastfeeding, and preemies are notorious for not sleeping more than two hours at a time." Volta sat down at the table next to Scott. "Her BP is down another five points."

"Excellent. Here, let me get you a bowl of Libby's chowder." He was determined to keep Volta in place long enough for at least one conversation. He would have preferred a private conversation, but he'd take what he could get.

"We were just talking about Emma," Libby said. "Show him a picture."

"Nah, I don't want to be one of those parents always shoving photos in people's faces." Volta dipped her spoon in the chowder.

"I'd love to see a picture of your daughter," Scott insisted.

Volta ate another spoonful of chowder. Libby and Scott watched her and waited. She shrugged, pulled up something on her phone and passed it to Scott. "This is Emma."

He studied the photo of a dark-haired little girl hugging a German shepherd with one arm and holding a little terrier with the other. Her eyes were brown, not blue like her mother's, but her pointed chin and the arch of her eyebrows were all Volta. So was her gleeful smile. The same smile that used to make his heart feel lighter.

"She's cute. Are those your dogs?"

"No, Tal is my brother Leith's dog, and the little dog belongs to his girlfriend, Sabrina. If Emma had her way, our house would be overflowing with animals, but my job doesn't lend itself to taking proper care of pets."

"I sympathize with Emma," Scott said. "I'd love to have a dog, but I never know where I'm going to be from week to week."

Volta gave him a little smile. "You've never had a dog, have you?"

"No. The closest was my neighbor's dog when I was a kid. I spent a lot of time over at their house, playing with their animals."

Libby looked at the photo and chuckled. "I had a brother, three sisters and all sorts of cousins. When we played outside in the summer, our neighbor's dog used to climb over his fence to join us and our dogs. When the neighbor would discover him missing, he'd take him home, but the next day the dog would be back. Finally, he gave us the dog and got one of those wienie dogs that couldn't jump the fence."

Volta laughed. "Your parents didn't mind taking in an extra dog?"

"They hardly noticed," Libby replied. "Cousins and friends and dogs were always coming and going. At supper time, they counted heads and fed whoever was there."

"Don't tell Emma," Volta told her. "She's lobbying for a horse now, and if she heard your story she'd probably try to sneak one into our garage and hope I didn't notice."

The pilot who had flown Scott into the village yesterday stepped into the store and pulled a bandanna down from his face.

"Hi, Mike. What's the word?" Volta asked.

"It's looking better. The volcano has gone quiet. There's still ash in the air, but unless Spurr puts out another plume, it should settle overnight. If it does, we'll be clear to fly by tomorrow afternoon."

"Good news," Volta said, her voice relieved. Was it Scott's imagination that at least some of that relief was to be able to get away from him?

"Do you need a bed tonight?" Libby asked Mike.

"Nah, I'll camp out with Zeke. You've got a full house with Volta, Bridget and the doc."

Mike pulled the bandanna up and sauntered outside.

"Now for the akutaq." Libby scurried off to the cold foods case and returned with a bowl of purplish froth. She spooned a generous portion into a paper bowl and set it in front of Scott. "Volta?"

"Just a taste. Save some for Bridget."

She gave Volta a small portion and turned inquisitive eyes toward Scott.

He dipped in his spoon and tasted the concoction. "Mmm. Blueberries and raspberries?"

"And a few salmonberries." Libby smiled her approval at his culinary taste. "I use caribou fat."

Scott took another bite. "It's good. It reminds me a little of kaymak with honey."

"What's kaymak?"

"It's kind of a soft cheese made from water buffalo milk. Very rich, but not as rich as this."

"Water buffalo milk?" Libby blinked. "How unusual."

Volta looked down, but not before Scott caught a glimpse at her amused grin. "I'll check on Lori and let Bridget have a lunch break," she said, getting up from the table. "And maybe run the aunties out. Lori's probably ready for a nap."

Scott spent the afternoon at the clinic. The

twins were doing fine, nursing well and sleeping, and Lori's blood pressure was slowly improving. The clinic didn't have much lab testing, but Scott was used to working in less than optimal conditions and was confident Lori was on the mend. He and Daniel spent the afternoon brainstorming ways to improve prenatal care.

Sadie and Susie had each claimed a baby to hold in the waiting room while their mother rested. Scott approved. Such tiny babies had little fat stored, and while the incubator would keep them warm, Scott preferred body heat and human contact when possible. The aunties took turns crooning to the babies. Paul and Lori were going to have a fight on their hands to claim them back.

Bridget had volunteered to spend tonight in the clinic, and so Volta had taken over Lori's care for the afternoon. He could hear her in the exam room talking and laughing with Lori and Paul. Once or twice she darted in and out of the clinic, fetching items for her patients, but she never seemed to have time to stop and talk with him.

By late afternoon the wind had died down, and while ash still blanketed every surface, it was no longer floating in the air. That seemed to be the signal for everyone in the village to stop by the clinic to bring gifts and admire the babies. Daniel moved the babies into the incubator partly to keep the crowds from breathing on them, but that didn't slow down the party in the reception area.

About five thirty, Libby came into the clinic. The crowd parted like the Red Sea to let her through. She took Scott's elbow and said, "Show me these babies you delivered." It was a royal command.

Scott led her to the exam room, where Lori was nursing one of the babies. Volta was rearranging pillows to support her back and arms. Volta greeted Libby before stepping out into the lobby to make room. Libby laid her hand on Lori's shoulder as she smiled down at the tiny baby in her arms. "Is this the girl?"

"Yes."

"Look at those beautiful eyelashes. Let me see her brother."

Scott opened the portable incubator so that Libby could see the baby's face. Libby ran a finger over his cheek. "He looks like his father."

"You think so?" Paul asked.

"Oh, yes. He'll play center on the basketball team one day."

Paul grinned. Libby passed her hand over the soft patch of hair on the other twin's head.

"This one will be a fine player, as well. A point guard, I think. Have you named them?"

"Not yet, but we have some ideas."

Libby smiled and turned to Paul. "You'll find stew and casseroles in your refrigerator when you're ready to go home. I'll have a talk with Susie and Sadie about boundaries. Is there anything else you need?"

"Um, no. Thank you."

Libby smiled again and gestured for Scott to follow her out. On the way through the lobby, she summoned Volta, as well. Once they were outside away from the others, she whispered, "Are they really all right? They're so tiny."

"Yes," Scott assured her. "They'll grow fast."

Libby closed her eyes and whispered something before smiling up at Scott. "All right, then. I'm going home now. Dinner will be ready in about an hour."

"I'll help cook. Just let me get Daniel or Bridget to cover," Volta said.

"No, my kitchen's too small for two cooks. Bridget is having a nap at my house. We'll let her sleep. I'll see you both in an hour."

At six, Daniel ran all the guests out of the clinic, including Sadie and Susie. After another quick exam, Scott left Daniel in charge until Bridget came to take a shift. Volta hugged

Lori. They waved goodbye to Daniel and made their way to Libby's cabin. Volta opened the door and walked in, calling out, "Something smells scrumptious."

"Caribou goulash." Libby stuck her head out of the kitchen at the back of the cabin. "Could you set the table, please?"

"Yes, ma'am." Volta went to a rustic corner cupboard and pulled out plates and silverware.

Scott crossed to the kitchen. "Anything I can do to help?"

Libby thrusted a bowl of rice into his hands. "Put this on the table." She followed behind with a platter of meat with vegetables and a red sauce.

Bridget climbed down the ladder leading to the loft and greeted them. "Everything all right at the clinic?"

Scott gave her a medical update. They all sat down at the round table. Libby reached for each of their hands. "We have so much to be grateful for today. Let's say our thank-yous." They bowed their heads. "We give thanks for this food, for the birth of two beautiful babies and for bringing Scott, Bridget and Volta here today. Amen."

Scott opened his eyes. Volta sat across the table from him, looking even lovelier since she'd let her shiny dark hair down to fall in waves over her shoulders. It all felt so familiar. How many meals had he and Volta eaten together, talking, sharing and laughing?

Tonight might well be their last meal together. So he would enjoy it, would linger and tell funny stories to make her smile. And then, he would ask to be alone with her because he had some things to say to Volta before they parted again. Maybe forever.

After dinner, Bridget excused herself and headed for the clinic to relieve Daniel. Volta insisted on washing the dishes, so Scott insisted on drying, but Libby stayed to put the dishes away. Then the two women fussed over getting sheets and blankets for one of the cots in Libby's loft and loaning Volta some sweats to sleep in. Scott noticed that of the three cots left in the room, Volta chose the one furthest from his. He was starting to wonder if fate was playing with him, dangling Volta in front of him without ever giving them a minute alone.

He reached into his pocket for his cell phone to check his email. When he pulled out his phone, something else came out of his pocket and skidded across the wooden floor.

Volta picked it up. A grin tugged at the corners of her mouth. "You're still carrying this around." She examined the tiny silver horseshoe.

"A little extra luck never hurts." The charm

was the only thing he owned that had belonged to his mother. He'd told Volta the story of discovering it wedged in a crack in a drawer. It must have fallen off his mother's charm bracelet. One of his few memories of his mother was of that bracelet jingling when she would dance around the house. Volta knew all about that, too.

She handed him the charm, but then she withdrew to her side of the room, still in conversation with Libby. Eventually, Libby climbed down the ladder and disappeared into her bedroom, and Volta couldn't avoid him any longer.

Not that she didn't give it a valiant effort. It was only eight thirty, but she gave a big yawn. "Wow, long day. You're probably exhausted."

"In fact, I'm feeling a bit restless. Now that the ash has settled, it's nice outside. Why don't we take a walk?"

"I don't really feel like walking."

He blew out a breath. "Then just sit down with me for a few minutes. Talk to me. Please."

"I—" Volta's phone rang, and she snatched it from her pocket. "I need to take this."

"Of course."

"Hi, Emma. What's up?" Volta listened for a little while. "Uh-huh. So school isn't canceled tomorrow? Sabrina said she'd do cookies."

There was a pause. "That sounds fun. Is she picking you up after school? Because if she is, I'll need to call in and put her on the approved pickup list." Volta got up and paced around the room. "Yes, I can do that. It looks like we'll be able to fly tomorrow so unless something changes, I'll be back in town. Tell Grandma I said it's fine for you to go with Sabrina." After another long pause, Volta laughed. "All right. You should get to bed, sweetie. I love you to infinity." She listened for a moment and smiled. "Okay. See you tomorrow. Good night."

She dictated a reminder to call the school tomorrow and pocketed the phone. "My daughter."

"I guessed. Big plans?"

"Tomorrow is a half day at school, and my brother's girlfriend wants to take her to a movie afterward. She's excited."

"She sounds like a busy kid." Good; they were talking. Maybe if he eased Volta into a conversation, she wouldn't run away. "You mentioned she was asking for a horse before."

"Yeah. We went to visit friends on a farm. They have two horses and let Emma and their son, Ryan, ride them around in a corral. She loved it. I've registered her for a two-week session of horse camp this summer. It was expensive, but she'll love it. It will be her birthday present."

"Horseback riding made a world of difference to me."

"How old were you when you started riding?"

"Nine. That was when my father married Gayle. She had horses, so we moved to a property where we could keep them, and she taught me to ride competitively. It was great. Of course, when their marriage broke up, she took her horses with her."

"That's a shame."

"Thankfully, one of our neighbors let me ride his horses in exchange for stable chores. He was good to me. In fact, in high school he got me an after-school job as a riding instructor."

"Once horse camp is over, I'm not sure horses are in the cards for Emma. I did some checking and it costs a fortune to keep a horse in Alaska. We'd be better off with sled dogs, which I'd better not say out loud or Emma will want them, too."

"Do they rent riding horses in Anchorage? Maybe we could all ride together."

"Thanks, but no." Volta answered quickly.

Well, chitchat wasn't working. Maybe the

direct route was better. "Can we talk about Hawaii?"

Volta's eyes darted around the room as though she were getting ready to make another excuse, but finally she sighed. "Let's go out on the porch."

They climbed down the ladder from the loft and tiptoed outside. Scott sat on a rustic bench. Volta perched on the other end. The landscape didn't seem so weird at night, the moonlight washing out the ash and displaying only the undulations of the land.

Volta broke the silence first. "What did you want to talk about?"

He decided to cut to the chase. "I never got the chance to say I'm sorry."

"For what?"

"For the way I ended our relationship."

Her eyes narrowed. "What do you mean, the way you ended it? Didn't you want it to end?"

"No. I mean, yes, it had to end. But I'm sorry I broke it off so abruptly."

"Oh, so, I had to go, but you should have, what? Dropped a few hints first? Let me fall even deeper in love with you before you said goodbye?"

This was going from bad to worse. "When I asked you out, I never thought it would get serious."

"Well, it didn't for you, did it?"

"That's just the thing. It did. That's why—"

"Don't." She stood up and paced to the corner of the porch, then turned to face him. "Don't give me that stupid line about how you broke up with me because you loved me. It didn't work then, and it doesn't work now."

But he did love her. How could he make her understand? "I was a few months away from starting my career with DEMA. You still had five more years of college and grad school to go. I couldn't ask you to—"

"You didn't ask me anything. You informed me of your decision."

"I watched a marriage go down the tubes because my father devoted all his time and energy to his career. And he lives in Houston, whereas most of the time, I don't know where I'll be next. That's no basis for a marriage."

"So when you said you didn't want to see me anymore, you were just looking out for me. Protecting me. Is that what you're saying?"

"Yes. Exactly."

"It's so good you were there to make that decision for me. After all, you were a doctor. I was only a college student. I guess my opinion was irrelevant."

"Volta, no. I never..." He shook his head. "It wasn't that I thought I was smarter than you. Just that I'd lived with my father. And I'm enough like him to know I can get caught up in work to the exclusion of everything else."

"And you didn't want to have to feel guilty about that. It sounds like you broke up with me for your own convenience, not for mine."

"Volta…" He'd made a hash out of this one. He'd only wanted to apologize, make her see why he'd had to hurt her. "I'm sorry."

"Yes, you've said that. It doesn't really matter, though, does it? We broke up and I went home. I got married. I have a daughter. I have a career. Congratulations. You saved me from whatever terrible fate awaited me if I'd stayed with you."

For someone saying she'd moved on, exactly as he'd hoped she would, she was surprisingly sarcastic. He wanted to ask if her marriage had been happy. If she would have preferred her original career choice of physical therapist. But it really wasn't any of his business.

"You're right. I made my choice. What I have to say now doesn't matter."

"Well, then. Let's get some sleep. With any luck, tomorrow we can fly home."

Home. She spoke with such certainty of where her home was. Scott didn't have a home. Certainly not in Houston, where he'd grown up. After a couple of days there with his father last week, he'd been itching for an excuse to leave.

He loved working all over the world, but once in a while, it might be nice to have a place to come home to. But as Volta had pointed out, he'd made his choice.

THE NEXT MORNING after breakfast, Libby handed Scott a handmade baby afghan and sent him and Volta to deliver it to the clinic. "Good morning," Bridget greeted them at the door. "Daniel's here."

"Good morning yourself. How did it go last night?" Volta asked.

"Good. No problems to speak of. Lori's feeding one of the twins now." She yawned. "I think I'll get a nap in until Mike says we're ready to go."

"Good idea," Volta said.

Daniel was in the lobby, working on his laptop. He greeted them and waved them through to the exam room. Scott knocked on the door frame and entered at Lori's invitation. Volta followed. Lori was sitting up in bed, smiling down at a sleeping infant. "He passed out halfway through breakfast."

"That means he'll be demanding the other half in an hour or so," Scott predicted.

"Libby sent this for you." Volta took the blue blanket from Scott and handed it to Lori. "She says she's working on a pink one."

"Aw." Lori pressed the blanket to her cheek. "Everyone has been so good to us."

"You've been good to them, taking care of everyone at the school and helping Daniel. And look at these beautiful babies. Have you come up with names yet?"

Lori looked at Paul. He grinned. "We have. We're both so grateful to all of you from yesterday." He took the sleeping baby from Lori. "We've named this one Daniel Scott Vaughan."

"Daniel Scott. I love it!" Volta said.

"I'm honored." Scott ran his hand over the baby's head. "And I'm sure Daniel is, too." He turned toward the other baby, sleeping in a bassinet beside the bed. "And what are you calling her?"

Paul and Lori exchanged glances. "Well, Volta was holding my hand—"

"Oh, no, no, no." Volta cut in. "I'm flattered, but please don't do that to another innocent little baby. I've never forgiven my father."

Lori laughed. "We were thinking Morgan Bridget Vaughan. We'd call her Morgan."

Scott vaguely remembered Daniel introducing her as Volta Morgan. Her married name. It would take some getting used to. She was still Volta Jordan in his mind.

"Morgan." Volta crossed to the incubator and looked down at the baby. Color rose in her cheeks. "She looks like a Morgan Bridget. I'm sure Bridget was over the moon."

"She was."

The baby girl woke up and yawned. Volta picked her up and cuddled her. "Hi, little Morgan. You're a sweetheart, aren't you?" She brought the baby to Lori. Lori rearranged a shawl over her shoulder and brought her daughter to her breast. The baby made happy little noises as she nursed.

Volta laughed. "What an appetite. By the time you bring them to the tournament in December, the babies will be so big I won't even recognize them."

"What tournament?" Scott asked.

"The high school teams play in the state tournament in Anchorage every year after Christmas," Paul explained. "For the last three years, Volta has been letting the whole team from Sparks camp out in her living room."

"It's fun," Volta said. "Besides basketball, we take the kids to a movie and the mall. They have a blast."

"Sounds like a good tradition." Traditions were something missing from Scott's life. He loved his job, but he didn't have connections like this. Even his coworkers were constantly changing. "Well, Daniel promised to go over some statistics with me this morning, so I need to head in that direction, but I'll do one more health check before we all get on the plane."

Volta sat in with Scott and Daniel, going over infant mortality and complication rates in rural Alaska and discussing how to mitigate some of the dangers. It was obvious Volta and Daniel had discussed the subject before and they both had suggestions Scott intended to include in his report.

Bridget stopped in at the clinic a little before two. "Mike says they're lifting the flight ban. He's checking all the equipment, so let's load up."

"Okay." Scott gathered up his notes and shook Daniel's hand. "Thanks for all your help. It was invaluable."

"Anytime."

Scott and Bridget went to do a final check of Lori and the babies and get them ready for transport. Mike stepped into the clinic. "They've cleared us, and the plane is good. Let's boogie before they change their minds."

Everyone worked together to transport the incubator holding the two babies into Libby's SUV. Lori followed along behind, supported by Volta and Paul. Libby drove them all to the plane and waved her goodbyes.

They got the babies' incubator loaded onto the plane and Lori settled comfortably on the patient bed. Paul kissed his wife and strapped himself into a seat, near Volta and Bridget. Scott found himself sitting in the front beside Mike. Once they were in the air, the pilot turned chatty.

"Did you get what you needed from Daniel?"

"Yes, Daniel is very knowledgeable. He tells me I'd be better off taking someone local with me on the rest of my visits to help smooth the waters and show me the ropes. Do you know anyone in your company who could do that?"

Mike glanced over his shoulder. "Volta would be good. She's always volunteering to help with events in the villages, so they all know her."

"I'm not available next week," Volta said into her headset. "I'm doing that transport to Boston on Monday."

"Jaci would take it, I'll bet," Bridget said. "She's got a boyfriend in Boston now. You should ask if you can switch."

Volta was silent. When he looked back, Volta had muted her mic and was whispering something to Bridget. Scott decided to table the subject for the moment. "What river is that?" he asked Mike. The rest of the trip, Mike pointed out the sights. They hardly heard a sound from the back of the plane.

They landed at the airport and taxied to their headquarters. Ash covered the ground here as well, but only a dusting compared to what had fallen in Sparks, and the runways had been cleared. An ambulance was waiting, and the team efficiently handed off to the paramedics. Volta gave Lori a hug. "Take care of yourself and those two precious babies." The crew jumped in, closed the doors to the ambulance and drove away.

Bridget and Volta walked toward the door to the Puffin facility adjoining the hangar. Scott followed them into the offices. The two women disappeared upstairs and returned a few minutes later in street clothes.

Bridget stretched. "I could go for some coffee. Anyone want to join me at Kaladi's?"

Volta checked her watch. "Thanks, but I need to get home. Next time." She started for the parking lot.

Scott grabbed his bag, made his excuses to Bridget and hurried to keep pace with Volta. "Will I see you again?" He couldn't let their relationship end on that conversation they'd had last night.

She shrugged. "If you're using Puffin, we might cross paths."

Might cross paths? "Why don't you want to fly with me to the villages?"

"It's just—I don't know—awkward."

"Why? We're both professionals. Clearly, you've established relationships around the state. I don't see why we can't work together on this project."

She walked several more steps before answering. "I don't know, Scott. I'd have to think about it."

"Fair enough. We'll talk Monday?"

"If you want to see me before I fly out to Boston, I'll be at the 7 a.m. meeting at Puffin." She reached into her pocket. "Oh, no."

"What?"

"I just realized I left my car keys lying on the top of Libby's dresser."

"Oops. Do you have another set at home?"

"Yes."

"I'll drive you to get them."

She shook her head. "I'll take a cab."

"I have a rental car right here. By the time you catch a cab, I can probably get you there and back."

"Well—"

He laughed. "Hey. I'm a very good driver, according to the driving examiner who tested me last week in Houston."

"You had to take a driving test?"

"I'd let my license expire more than a year ago, so yes."

"Don't get home much, huh?"

"Not much." He stopped at a white compact and pressed the fob to unlock the doors. "Are you going to let me take you to get the keys, or are you going to hike back across the parking lot and catch a taxi to prove—what—that you're self-sufficient? I already know that."

She gave a wry smile. "I'd appreciate a ride. Thank you." Volta slid into the passenger seat and gave him directions.

It wasn't long before he pulled into her driveway. If someone had turned him lose on the street and asked him to find Volta's house, this one with creamy yellow siding, crisp black shutters and a teal blue door would have been his first guess. Gray ash lightly coated the grass out front, but someone had hosed off the steps, sidewalk and driveway. Short pink tulips lined the walkway between the driveway and the front steps. On the porch, blue-and-white pillows with pictures of dragonflies rested against the back of a wooden bench. It looked like the definition of home.

"I'll grab the keys and be right back." Volta punched a code into a box, and her garage door rose. She disappeared into the garage and the door closed behind her. Scott got out of the car to enjoy the sunshine while he waited.

An old Land Cruiser pulled up to the curb

in front of the house and a girl slipped out the back door. Scott easily recognized her from the photo Volta had shown him, although now her hair was twisted up in an elaborate braid. She started toward him, but a man got out of the driver's side and called for her to wait.

He shut the door and walked toward Scott. A German shepherd jumped down from the car and moved close to Emma. This must be Volta's brother with the dog.

"Can I help you?" he asked, clearly suspicious about a stranger in his sister's driveway. His eyes were the same bright blue as Volta's.

"Hi. I'm Scott Willingham." Scott paused for a second to see if the name registered, but it was clear Volta's brother didn't recognize it. "I flew back from Sparks with Volta."

"Oh. I'm Volta's brother, Leith Jordan." He offered a hand, and Scott shook it.

The little girl popped up, with the dog beside her. "Hi, I'm Emma." She had wide brown eyes and her mother's bright smile. Those eyes, combined with the braided crown of hair and how she danced across the grass, made Scott think of an elf. A very cute elf.

He smiled. "Hello, Emma. I'm Scott. I gave your mom a ride from the airport."

"I'm almost eight," Emma told him.

"Eight? Wow."

"My birthday is tomorrow. We're having a party at the reindeer farm."

"No kidding. I've never seen a reindeer."

"You haven't? Reindeer are cool. You should come to my party. Lots of grown-ups will be there. It's at two at the reindeer farm."

"Emma," Volta called from the porch.

"Mommy!" The girl flew toward the house while her mother ran down the steps. Volta dropped to her knees and wrapped her daughter in a hug. The smile on her face was pure joy.

After a moment, the girl stepped back and twirled around. "Mommy, look. Sabrina braided my hair."

"It's beautiful. How was the movie?"

"Funny. And we had popcorn."

"Sounds like you had a good time." Volta looked past her daughter toward Scott, and her smile lost some of its wattage. She stood. "Scott, I really appreciate the ride, but my brother is here now, so he can take me back to the airport to pick up my car."

"I don't mind," Scott said. "My hotel is near the airport, so I'm heading in that direction anyway."

"Thanks, but Leith can take me. Right, Leith?"

"Uh, sure." Her brother seemed as mystified as Scott about why Volta seemed so flustered.

Scott had been counting on the ride back to the airport to press his case about working with her. "So, we'll talk Monday about those village visits?"

"Yes. Sure. That's fine." She took a step forward, past her daughter. "Goodbye, Scott."

"Goodbye." Scott nodded at Volta's brother. "It was nice to meet y'all." He got in the car and backed out of the driveway. When he looked up, Emma had walked down the steps and was watching him. She waved, and he waved back before driving off.

Clearly Volta adored her daughter and her job, but he sensed something missing. He needed to spend more time with her, to earn her trust so she would be honest with him. Until he was sure she was happy, he wasn't ready to let her go.

CHAPTER FOUR

"AND WE PAINTED BIRDHOUSES. Grandma painted hers green with little flowers on it, but mine has people." On the drive back from the airport to fetch Volta's car, Emma filled her mom in on everything she'd missed while she'd been grounded at Sparks. "And we read a story about a girl and a horse. It was really good."

"I'll bet." Any book or movie that included a horse was a hit with Emma. Ever since she'd taken Emma to the reindeer farm and she got to ride with Ryan, she couldn't get enough of horses. Fortunately, the miniature plastic herd she'd collected didn't eat, because Volta's paycheck didn't run to stable fees and feed bills. "Are you excited about your party at the reindeer farm?"

"Yeah! Livy got me a present. She won't tell me what it is, but I think it's a horse. Rafe might come, too."

"Who's Rafe?"

"He's in my class. He's new. He looked sad yesterday, so I invited him."

"That's sweet, but you need to ask me before you invite more people."

"Why? It's my birthday."

"Because when people are planning parties, they need to know in advance how many people are coming to know how much food to make and everything. I already told Marissa at the reindeer farm how many to set up for." Not to mention the cake she'd ordered and the goody bags she and Emma had assembled last week. Shoot, did they have enough goody bags? She should probably pack a couple of spares. "You didn't invite more kids besides Rafe, did you?"

"No." Emma sighed, as though refraining from inviting everyone she'd come in contact with in the past two weeks had taken a terrible toll. It probably had. "Will Marissa be mad if there's an extra person?"

"No, I'm sure it will be fine." Leith's car pulled into the driveway behind her. "Let's go get your stuff from Uncle Leith and carry it inside." Leith handed over Emma's purple duffel bag and her stuffed dog. Poor Rufus was starting to look a little worse for the wear, but Emma wouldn't go to sleep without him.

"Thank Sabrina for taking Emma to the movie," Volta said to Leith.

"Sabrina had a blast. I would have gone, too, but you know, princesses."

Volta laughed. "Well, thanks for helping me pick up my car. And thanks for driving Emma home. Emma, what do you say to Leith?"

"Thank you, Uncle Leith," Emma sang out and ran to give him a hug. "Tell Sabrina I had fun."

Volta and Emma waved goodbye. Volta grabbed the duffel and carried it into the garage, pressing the button that closed the door on the way. "What do you want for dinner?"

"Macaroni and cheese," Emma said immediately.

Volta laughed. "You always say that. I'll bet you had Grandma make you mac and cheese already."

"Yes," Emma said. "Grandma likes to make macaroni and cheese with me. I helped grate the cheese, and I stirred the milk, and I mashed the bread crumbs with a rolling pin. Grandma says I'm going to be a good cook when I grow up."

"I don't doubt it, but let's try something else tonight. We have chicken in the freezer. Let's make a chicken stir-fry."

"Can we use sesame seeds?"

"Yes, and we have broccoli, too."

"Broccoli?" Emma asked, her voice heavy with suspicion. "Do I like broccoli?"

"Sure you do. Broccoli looks like little green trees. Remember?"

"Oh, yeah. I like little trees."

Volta set Emma's duffel at the bottom of the stairs. She put supper together while Emma set the table. Once they'd eaten and loaded the dishwasher, Volta announced it was time for a bath. "When you're in your pajamas, we can read some stories."

"Can we read about a horse?"

"We can read anything you want," Volta promised.

Emma opened her bag and pulled out her pajamas. "Oh, my birdhouse. I forgot to show you." Emma held up the wooden birdhouse she'd painted a cheery pink with three human figures and an animal along the side.

Volta pointed at the smallest figure. "Is this you?"

"Yes."

"And this one with the blue dress is me?"

"Yes, because you like blue."

"So this one must be Uncle Leith."

"No, a girl and her mommy and her daddy and her horse."

"Her horse?"

"Yeah, she had a mommy and a daddy and a horse. They're a real family."

That nagging sense of inadequacy pricked at Volta. "Real families come in all shapes and sizes, Emma. Just because your daddy died doesn't mean we're not a real family."

"Well." Emma peeked up from beneath her eyelashes. "If I can't have a daddy, I should at least get a horse."

"Oh?"

"Yes." Emma tried the puppy-dog eyes.

Volta chuckled. "Nice try, but we've talked about this. Horses are very expensive."

"Ryan has a horse."

"Ryan lives on a farm. We live in Anchorage."

"We could keep the horse in the backyard."

"Our backyard isn't big enough for a horse to live."

"We could move to a farm."

"No, we couldn't, Emma, because I'm not a farmer. I'm a paramedic."

Emma shrugged. "Maybe Grandma and Granddaddy will get a horse for my birthday."

Volta shook her head. "No, sweetie, they're not going to get you a horse. We have no place to keep one. I'm sorry, but that's how it is."

Emma frowned. "When I grow up, I'm going to live on a farm and have lots and lots of horses. And my friends can come and ride with me, and I'll ride the prettiest horse of all."

"Sounds like a plan. But right now, it's bath time. Do you want to take some of your horses swimming with you?"

"I'll take the Arabian and the Clydesdale." Emma started down the hall, but she stopped after two steps to send back a parting shot. "But someday, I'm going to get a real horse."

SCOTT WOKE UP restless on Saturday morning. He'd already written up his notes from his visit to Sparks and had nothing else scheduled until Monday. His plan had been to use this weekend to locate Volta and decide how to approach her, but their accidental meeting in Sparks had taken care of that. In theory, he could check it off the list, but it didn't feel finished. In fact, it felt distinctly unresolved. He needed to convince her to accept that position as liaison. But he couldn't do anything else about it for two more days.

Spare time was a luxury and he hated to waste it. He looked out the window. A heavy rain last night had washed the volcanic ash away. Scott decided he needed a nice, long run. Ordinarily, his exercise routine involved a few push-ups and crunches plus whatever running or hiking he could fit in wherever he happened to be.

On the recommendation of the front desk clerk, Scott headed down the coastal trail. Plenty of locals seemed to have the same idea. As he ran, he passed dog walkers, bikers and skaters. Across the inlet, snow clung to the top of a long mountain range. The air smelled of damp earth and sunshine.

Eventually his stomach reminded him it was getting close to lunchtime. He'd passed a soup and sandwich place that looked promising. After he'd changed and eaten, he would decide what to do with the rest of the day.

Scott returned to his hotel, showered and pulled on a pair of jeans. He was digging through his suitcase looking for a clean shirt, when he came across a carved wooden elephant. It had been a gift from the husband of a grateful patient after a breech birth.

He ran a finger over the intricate pattern of the blanket on the elephant's back carved into the kadam wood. The elephant almost appeared to be smiling. It would be a good toy for a child. And he happened to know a child who was having a birthday today. And she *had* invited him to her party.

No, he couldn't do that. He set the elephant on the desk, pulled on a Henley shirt and headed out for lunch. The soup and sandwich place was packed, so he got his to go and sat on a bench in the town square while he ate it. Empty flower beds lining all the walkways suggested this would be a colorful showcase during the summer. On his way back to the hotel, he passed a gift shop. On impulse, he went inside and bought tissue paper and a gift bag.

Back at the hotel, the front desk clerk waved when Scott walked in. "Enjoy your run this morning?"

"I did. Great trail." Scott paused. "Do you happen to know anything about a reindeer farm?"

"Oh, sure. It's one of the big tourist attractions in the area." He came out from behind the desk, selected a card from a nearby display rack and handed it to Scott. "It's not far. Just take the highway past Eagle River and then exit and take the road north for a couple of miles."

"Is it the only one?"

"Only one I know of. I took my nephew there once. It was fun."

"Thanks." Scott looked over the brochure. Why not?

Thirty minutes later, he spotted the welcome sign with a picture of reindeer and a sleigh, made the turn onto a gravel drive and followed it until he reached a parking area near a white farmhouse. He parked, but he didn't get out. He probably shouldn't be here. A verbal invitation from an overexcited almost-eight-year-old was hardly a binding contract.

But he'd been jumpy all morning, thinking about Monday, wondering if Volta would agree to work with him. He had his suspicions she was just humoring him, and that when Monday arrived, she'd tell him no and take off to Boston.

She was excellent at her job and seemed to enjoy it, and to be on good terms with the people she worked with. She obviously adored her daughter. He sensed a sadness there, too. An emptiness that echoed the empty places in his own life. But she'd been married and then her husband died. Of course, a part of her would be sad.

And what if she was sad? What did he think he could do about it? It wasn't as though he was going to recruit her to join him at DEMA. Not when she had a child in elementary school. Still, he would appreciate her help on this study.

A small SUV pulled up beside him and two little girls hopped out, carrying wrapped packages. They jumped up and down, urging the woman with them to hurry. "Come on. We're late. We might miss the reindeer." The woman followed them across the parking area toward a red barn. Beside the barn, a group of reindeer hung their heads over the fence, watching the people arriving.

Should he or shouldn't he? Why not? He was here. The worst that could happen is someone would ask him to leave. And the best? He wasn't even sure.

He grabbed the gift and headed toward the barn. A chalkboard outside read Happy Birthday, Emma, so he was in the right place. He stepped up to one of the reindeer near the barn. The deer nudged his hand, and so he scratched her forehead, which seemed to please her.

Scott hadn't lied when he told Emma he'd never seen a reindeer. He had seen gazelles and wildebeests and oryx in Africa, and barking deer in Indonesia, and pudus, the tiny Peruvian deer, but never reindeer. He had to admit, their antlers were impressive. And they were surprisingly gentle. No wonder Santa Claus chose reindeer as his favorite transportation.

A bearded man in a red polo stepped out of the barn and greeted Scott as he walked toward the gate. He picked up a couple of halters from a rack nearby and slipped inside the reindeer pen. The reindeer Scott had been petting immediately left him and went to nudge the man, who offered her a treat and slipped the halter over her head, buckling it behind her antlers.

Scott stepped inside the barn into a whirlwind of activity. A group of children were gathered around one blindfolded child who was attempting to hit a star-shaped piñata with a stick. Someone was raising and lowering the piñata, and the other children were shouting encouragement. "Go, Rafe!"

After three misses, another boy stepped up for a turn. He settled into a classic batter's stance and swung wildly at the piñata, his momentum carrying him in a complete circle that sent the other children scattering and almost took out a nearby table. A corgi gave a sharp bark. A man with a weathered face caught the boy by the shoulders and pointed him in the right direction for another try.

Past the piñata, a group of adults stood watching and laughing. Volta was at the center of the group, snapping pictures of the children. She wore a simple blue shirt over jeans, her hair tucked back from her face. Scott stopped where he was and watched her expression change, so familiar, especially when she laughed. Beautiful.

"Hi, it's Scott, right?" Volta's brother had come up beside him. "Did you need to see Volta for something about work?"

"Hi. No. Nothing in particular. I hope it's okay that I came."

"Sure, it's fine. Emma invited you. Help yourself to sodas or water on the table over there." Beside the drinks table, a grinning boy shook a can of soda. "Oops, excuse me." Leith hurried over to intervene.

Scott edged his way toward the group of adults. Volta was tying the blindfold onto Emma now. She handed her the stick and spun her around a couple of times. Another woman in a red polo herded the rest of the children a safe distance away before calling, "Okay, go."

Emma took a swing with the pole. Whoever was manipulating the piñata jerked it upward. Emma completely missed but made an impressive whizzing noise as the stick cut through the air. The piñata lowered again in preparation for her next swing, but instead of winding up, Emma immediately swung back in the same arc and knocked a limb off the star, and a few pieces of candy tumbled to the ground.

The kids squealed and three of them dived on the candy. Someone grabbed the stick from Emma's hand before she could take another swing and take out a crowd of children while she was at it. She jerked off the blindfold, but the other kids had already grabbed all the candy. She turned to her mother.

Volta pointed at the piñata. "There's a lot more stuff inside. Christy, I believe it's your turn."

"Go, Christy," Emma chanted. "Knock out the candy."

Volta blindfolded the girl, spun her around and gave her a little nudge in the direction of the piñata. One good whack and the bottom fell out, sending the rest of the candy flying. This time all the kids made a mad dash for the candy, scooping up handfuls.

Volta handed out paper bags. "You can put your goodies in here to take home later." She pointed at a table that held markers and stickers. "Go write your name on the bag and decorate it."

Once the kids were convinced they'd found every last piece of candy, they drifted toward the table. An older woman standing in front of Scott chuckled. "I've seen bears at Katmai that weren't that competitive. You'd think they were starving."

Volta laughed and turned toward her to comment, but her laugh died in midstream when she spotted Scott. The older woman turned to him. "Hello. I don't believe we've met. I'm Dawn Jordan, Emma's grandmother."

"Scott Wi—"

"Scott and I know each other from work."

Volta came striding to them. "Scott, what are you doing here?"

"You came!" Emma rushed over to him. "You really did want to see the reindeer."

"They're spectacular. Thank you for inviting me."

"Pretty soon, we're going to pet the baby ones and then we're going for reindeer rides. You can pet the reindeer, too. Right, Mommy?"

"Um, sure."

Emma leaned closer and whispered, loud enough for her mother and grandmother to hear, "They have horses, too, but we can't ride them because there's only two, and that's not enough for the whole party."

"Oh," Scott said. "That's too bad. But the reindeer are awesome."

"Hey, kids. We're going to do pin the tail on the reindeer now," the woman in the red polo called. Scott realized it had a sleigh embroidered on it.

"Go on over with Marissa," Volta told Emma. "I'll be right there."

Emma skipped away. Her grandmother looked at Scott and then at Volta. When neither of them answered her unspoken question, she said, "Well, it's nice to meet you, Scott. I'm going to go watch Emma and give you and

Volta a minute to talk about…whatever it is you're here to talk about. Excuse me, please."

"Nice to meet you, too, Mrs. Jordan," Scott said quickly.

As soon as she'd stepped away, Volta grabbed Scott's elbow and dragged him to the far corner of the barn, away from everyone. "Once again. Why are you here?"

"Emma invited me."

"That's not what I asked."

Scott shrugged. "I wanted to see you again."

"Why?"

"I want you to work with me as liaison."

"You came to my daughter's birthday party to talk me into working with you?"

He tried for a disarming smile. "And to see the reindeer."

"Really?" She tilted her head. "You wanted to see reindeer? You've been everywhere."

"Nowhere with reindeer. Not until now. By the way, why didn't you let me introduce myself to your mother?"

"Why? Because my dad and my brother are here, and I'd rather not have any bloodshed at Emma's party."

"Bloodshed?"

"They never met you, but my mother knew your name, and my parents were none too pleased with my emotional state when I came home from Hawaii."

"Oh." Scott hadn't considered that. Of course they would be protective of Volta and predisposed to dislike the man who broke her heart. Not that he blamed them.

The man with the weathered face Scott had noticed earlier walked over to them, a wrinkle in the center of his brow. "Is everything all right here?"

"It's fine, Dad," Volta said. "Scott, my father, Russ Jordan. Dad, Scott's a doctor with DEMA."

The man's face relaxed. "Oh, DEMA. I've heard good things. Nice to meet you, Doctor."

"Scott, please." Scott offered his hand and Russ shook it.

"What brings you to Alaska, Scott?"

"I'm working on a study. In fact, I was just asking your daughter if she would act as my liaison. I understand she's well connected in the villages."

"That's a great idea." Russ wrapped an arm around Volta's shoulders.

Volta gave a tight smile. "Thanks, Dad. I'll keep it in mind. But for now, we'd better get back to the party. Chris and Marissa are rounding everyone up to visit the reindeer calves."

"I'd better get my video camera," Russ said as he hurried away.

Volta frowned at Scott. "Can we talk about this later? My daughter is celebrating her birthday and I don't want to miss any magic moments arguing with you about work."

She was right. He shouldn't be using her daughter's birthday party to push his own agenda. "I'm sorry. I shouldn't have come. We can talk Monday." He gave a little bow and left the gift bag on the table with the others. "I'll go now."

Suddenly Volta laughed. "Aw, you're as bad as Emma with the sad eyes. Stay. Pet a reindeer. After all, how often are you going to be in Alaska? You might never get another opportunity."

He returned the smile. "Truer words were never spoken."

CHAPTER FIVE

A SMALLISH REINDEER whose velvet-covered antlers didn't quite match nudged Emma's hand. She giggled and reached into her cup for more alfalfa pellets. Emma and the other kids were having a ball feeding the baby reindeer.

So was Scott. Volta looked over to see him in the corner, talking softly to one of the shyer calves. Slowly the calf approached his outstretched hand and took the alfalfa pellets. A few minutes later, Scott was stroking the calf's neck and the deer was rubbing his face against Scott's leg.

Volta smiled. Scott had always had a way with children and animals. Strange dogs would wag their tails at him. All the children who lived in his apartment building in Honolulu had known him, and Volta was often drafted to participate in elaborate games of capture the flag with a gaggle of kids in the nearby park.

And yet he'd never wanted children of his own. Over time, as they'd gotten to know one another, Scott had confided in her about his childhood. Losing his mother when he was very young had affected him deeply, and his father was seldom home and never emotionally available. And Scott had somehow decided he wasn't meant to be part of a family. Her heart ached over his lonely childhood.

But that was all in the past. They'd gone their separate ways, built separate lives. So Scott wanted her to work with him on this study. Honestly, if it were anyone else, she'd have jumped at the chance. She did have good relationships with most of the village health aides, and prenatal health was an issue that concerned her. Surely, after eleven years, she and Scott could work together. Couldn't they?

She went back to snapping photos of all the kids and reindeer. Her friends Chris and Marissa, who ran the reindeer farm, had everything under control.

Outside in the open area between the barn and the house, Marissa's uncle Oliver was hitching reindeer to little carts, getting ready for the reindeer rides. Oliver's white beard, red polo shirt and hint of a potbelly made him a dead ringer for Santa Claus. Already a couple of the kids were whispering and pointing in his direction.

After another ten minutes with the baby reindeer, Chris herded the children out the gate and toward the carts. The parents followed, although a couple would obviously have preferred to stay in the pen with the reindeer. Chris delivered half the kids to Marissa for cart riding and promised the other half a trip to the big barn to see the goats and rabbits. Emma was in the reindeer ride line, but Scott followed the children to the barn.

Ryan, Chris and Marissa's son, led one of the reindeer over, and Marissa helped two children climb into the cart. Ryan led them away for a ride around the farm, and Oliver brought his reindeer cart up to the front of the line. Emma climbed in, but her friend Christy leaned over to whisper something to Oliver. He answered with a gentle, "Ho, ho, ho," leaving Christy wide-eyed as she joined Emma in the cart for a ride.

They timed the events very well, with the children in carts returning from their lap around the farm just as the other kids came back from the barn, talking about goats, chickens and rabbits. They switched activities.

Once all the children had their turns with the reindeer, they headed back to the barn to watch Emma blow out the candles on her pink cake with strawberries. Marissa's aunt Becky cut the cake, while everyone trooped through the food line where the vegetable trays slowly diminished, mostly due to conscientious parents urging their kids to take a carrot. Mom's cookie tray remained largely untouched.

Having settled the kids at a table, the parents gathered their food and sat down at another table nearby. Volta chose the chair next to her mom, who was nibbling on a stalk of celery. "Having fun?"

"It's a lovely party. Emma can't seem to smile enough."

"Yeah, she's having a blast. I think the other kids are, too."

Mom looked askance at the frosting-heavy slice of cake on Volta's plate. "Once they finish all that sugar, they're going to be bouncing off the walls."

"They'll be fine. Besides, the only thing we have left is opening presents."

"Oh, good. I can't wait to see how Emma likes our present."

Something in her mother's voice struck Volta as ominous. "What did you get her?"

Mom gave a Mona Lisa smile. "You'll see."

Scott took the chair across the table from them. His plate held only a pile of vegetables and several of Mom's cookies. Mom nudged Volta. "There. I told you some people wouldn't want all that sugar. Good thing I made cookies."

Scott had never been one to shun dessert.

Then Volta remembered. "You're allergic to strawberries."

"Yes," he admitted. "But these cookies look delicious, especially now that I know your mom made them." Scott popped one of the small disks into his mouth and chewed. And chewed some more, trying to smile pleasantly with his mouth closed while his teeth ground their way through the woody roughage. Finally he swallowed. "Very unusual. Is that banana I taste?"

"Yes," Dawn chirped. "And flaxseed and quinoa and oat flour. I created the recipe myself based on a recipe for teething biscuits."

"Very inventive." Scott nudged another cookie out of the way and picked up a carrot.

Mom beamed at him, until someone further down the table called her name to ask about yoga class. While she was turned away, Scott smuggled the rest of Mom's cookies off his plate and under the table. Volta snorted and then coughed to cover it up. Scott winked at her.

Once everyone had finished eating, Volta went to the kids' table. "Now we're ready to open gifts, okay, Emma?"

"Yay." Emma jumped up.

As she crossed the barn, Volta whispered in

Emma's ear, "Remember how we talked about manners and saying thank you to everyone?"

"I remember," Emma assured her. "I want to open the one from Uncle Leith and Sabrina first." She chose a box with blue marbled wrapping paper, tied with a giant bow of tulle. Sabrina's work, obviously. Leith would have struggled to tape a bow on the store bag.

Emma untied the bow, draped the sheer fabric around her shoulders and then ripped off the paper and opened the box. She pulled out a pair of cowboy boots with pink stitching. "Oh, thank you!"

Volta had told them about horse camp, but she hadn't expected them to help outfit Emma. Very thoughtful. The next few packages held toys and games, and Emma happily thanked the givers. She reached for a gift bag with a cartoon bear on the outside, tugged the tissue paper aside and pulled out a wooden elephant with elaborate patterns carved into it. "Ooooh, look, Mommy. It's an elephant. I love it. I'm going to name him Peanut," Emma declared. "Thank you…" She looked for a tag but couldn't locate one.

"That one was probably from Scott," Volta told her. "I suspect he brought it from overseas."

"India," Scott admitted.

"Wow. Thank you," Emma said, wide-eyed.

THE GRAND FINALE was the box from Volta holding a certificate stating Emma was enrolled in horse camp in June. Emma squealed. "Horses!"

After she'd hugged Volta and thanked her profusely, her grandfather cleared his throat. "Oh, look here." He pulled an envelope from his shirt pocket. "I found one more thing for Emma."

He handed her the envelope. Emma ripped it open and sounded out the words on the paper. "Oh, my gosh. Oh, my gosh. Riding lessons!" She looked up. "Mommy, they gave me riding lessons. More horses!"

Wonderful. Volta had scrimped and saved to afford horse camp, but her perfect present was overshadowed by the private lessons from her parents. She forced a smile, knowing it wasn't deliberate. They loved seeing Emma happy, just like she did. "That's great."

Emma ran to her grandparents and hugged them. "This is the best birthday ever."

Volta reached under the table for the box of party favor bags. She helped Emma pass them out to the kids, thanking everyone for coming. "Don't forget your candy bags from the piñata." The party guests started to drift away, but many stopped to talk on their way out.

Once the party favor box was empty, Volta

gathered up the gifts. Emma carried the boots over so Sabrina could help her try them on. Volta picked up the wooden elephant, which looked to be hand-carved. It was lovely. She raised her head to see Scott's brown eyes watching her. She flashed him a smile.

He crossed the barn to the table and helped her stack the gifts into a box. "Thank you for letting me stay for the party. I had fun."

"I'm glad."

He set the last gift into the box. "Want me to carry this somewhere?"

"No, I've got it."

He met her eyes. Her heart jumped in remembered anticipation. Once upon a time, this would have been the moment when he kissed her goodbye. Funny how her heart still remembered these things.

"Okay, then. See you at Puffin headquarters."

"Scott."

"Yes?"

"I'll text my supervisor. If he approves, I'll work with you on this study."

He smiled. "Fantastic. Monday, then."

"All right. Goodbye, Scott."

"Bye." He stopped to wish Emma a happy birthday and admire her new boots on his way out. Sabrina and Leith were with her, as were her grandparents. Scott chatted with them for a few minutes. Emma grinned at something he said, and everyone else laughed.

Best birthday ever, indeed.

MONDAY MORNING, SCOTT entered the Puffin Medical Transport office fifteen minutes before the scheduled meeting. He wanted a chance to talk with the supervisor before Volta arrived to smooth over any issues. But when he walked into the conference room, Volta and Bernie Bench, her supervisor, were already there.

"Good morning, Doctor." Bernie dumped a packet of sweetener into his coffee and stirred. "Volta tells me you want her along on your junkets."

"Yes. When I was in Sparks, Libby suggested having a local liaison would help make the introductions to the caregivers a lot smoother for me, so folks wouldn't feel as if they're talking to a complete stranger."

"That's sound advice, and Volta is a good choice." He turned to Volta. "I can cover your shifts over the next couple of weeks."

Volta nodded. "Sounds good."

Bernie sipped his coffee. "You and the doc will be in the old turboprop. Mike's piloting.

And Jaci can take the transport to Boston this morning."

"Thanks, Bernie." Volta poured a cup of coffee from the carafe and handed it to Scott. "Still take it black?"

"Sure do." She remembered. He accepted the mug from her and tasted the brew. Two more employees came into the conference room and headed for the coffee machine. Scott moved aside and took a chair at the table.

Volta poured a cup and made her way over, but instead of sitting beside him, she chose a chair on the other side of the table. "Where are we going today?"

Scott checked the note on his phone. "A village called Talpukna."

"Good thing we're in the smallest plane. Talpukna's landing strip isn't any longer than the one at Sparks. Does Ruby know you're coming?"

Scott's note listed his contact as Ruby Byrd. Impressive that Volta knew the name of the health aide in a random village without any prompting. "Yes. The plan is to spend the first part of the day with her, and then fly to Black Bear to meet with Benny Hunter."

"Be prepared. Benny has opinions. Numerous and strongly held."

"That's good. I can find out a lot by talking to these people."

Volta tilted her head and addressed one of her colleagues at the coffee machine. "Jim, wasn't it Talpukna where you evacuated the pregnant woman in a diabetic coma a few months ago?"

"Yeah. February. It was touch and go, but she made it." He shook his head. "The baby didn't."

Scott nodded. No matter how hard they tried, they couldn't save them all, but most times, against all odds, they saved a life. And that was why they did what they did.

"Back here after Black Bear?" Volta asked Scott.

"Yes. We have a lot to cover, though. It may be a late evening."

"No problem. I'm on a twenty-four-hour shift anyway. Emma's spending the night with my folks."

Bernie sat down at the table and outlined what they had scheduled for the day and what level of care they'd need to provide for the long-haul transport to Boston. There was some general discussion before Bernie looked at his watch. "All right, then. The ambulance from the base hospital should be here in about thirty minutes. The jet is fueled. Let's get her loaded." He turned to Scott. "Once they're on their way, you're up."

"Understood."

The teams secured the necessary equipment in the jet for transport. Scott helped. "Take good care of this guy," one of the men mentioned to Jaci, the assigned paramedic. "He's a vet. His mom lives down the street from me. Good man."

"What can he get in Boston that he can't get here?" Scott asked.

"He's an amputee. Lost both hands. They're evaluating him for a possible transplant."

"That's fantastic."

The crew rolled the plane from the hangar. Shortly afterward, the ambulance arrived, and they transported the patient on board. The young man had a joke and smile for everyone. A few minutes later, the jet taxied out toward the runway.

"We should be ready to go in twenty," Mike told Scott and Volta.

"Okay." Volta motioned to Scott. "Did they assign you a flight suit?"

"No, but—"

"Company policy," Bernie told him. "Last time you were hitchhiking back, but if you're flying with us, you need a flame-retardant suit. Volta, can you take care of that?"

"Sure." Volta gestured for Scott to follow her. "I'm sure we have something that will work." They left the hangar, and Volta led him through the adjoining office space and upstairs to a large room with a couple of couches, a television and a compact kitchen.

She took a hallway to the right, which led to an area with computers, phones, a fax machine and filing cabinets. She opened a door and stepped into a large walk-in closet. Scott followed behind her. A row of blue flight suits hung on the rails. She swept her eyes over him and selected one, holding it up beside him. "I think this will fit you."

"How about you?"

"I've got mine in my bag. I'll change in the other room, so you can get dressed in here. I'll meet you in the middle in five minutes."

Scott stripped down, stepped into the jumpsuit and zipped it up. Not the scrubs he was used to wearing when he worked, but comfortable enough. In the living area, he found Volta already dressed. He waved a hand toward the other hallway. "What's back there?"

"Sleeping quarters."

"You sleep here?"

"Sometimes. Especially when I'm in the first team up on call. But my house is within ten minutes, so I mostly sleep in my own bed."

"How many days a week are you on duty?"

"It varies. I work eight twenty-four-hour days a month. Sometimes they're packed in together, and sometimes spread out. Come on. Let's see if Mike is ready to fly."

Scott followed her down the stairs. "I was wondering how you manage such an unpredictable job along with being a single mom, but I can see it has its advantages."

"Yes. I volunteer in Emma's classroom twice a month, and if they have a field trip or something planned, I try to schedule it so I'm free to chaperone. On the days I'm on duty, Emma stays over with my mom and dad. They only live a couple of blocks from me, so Emma rides the same school bus. It works out well."

She walked over to a row of shelves and lifted a box labeled Black Bear. She rifled through the items inside and then closed the box and carried it with her to the plane.

"What's that?" Scott asked.

"Sometimes the villages have people drop off items they need transported, and we bring them along when we come. Benny must have had a relative send a few things he can't get in the village."

At the plane, Mike completed his checklist, and soon they were soaring far above Anchorage. Scott gazed out the window, watching the snowcapped mountains in the distance. Train tracks snaked across a valley and crossed a winding river, only to cross again in another few miles. They followed the valley for a while before flying over a mountain pass to a second, more heavily wooded watershed.

After almost an hour of flying, Scott spotted a landing strip carved out from the forest. The town was clustered between the landing strip and a bluff overlooking a wide blue river. Mike set the plane down and they climbed out. Volta led the way.

Mike walked on past. "I'll head over to the diner," Mike said. "Call me when you're ready to go."

"Okay." Volta opened the door and called, "Ruby, are you here?" as she stepped inside.

A middle-aged woman with black hair swept up in a loose bun stepped in from another room and exchanged greetings with Volta and Mike.

"Ruby Byrd, this is Dr. Scott Willingham," Volta said. "Ruby is the community health aide here in Talpukna."

"Hello, Doctor." Ruby was tall, only a few inches shorter than Scott. She wore a blue calico dress with a deep front pocket and a ruffled hem over faded jeans. As she shook his hand, she studied his face as though she was trying to size him up.

"Call me Scott."

Ruby nodded. "I got your email, but I'm not sure exactly what you want from me. Do you want to see the clinic records?"

"No, nothing like that. I only want to know about the challenges you face in a remote village like this."

She shrugged. "It's mostly blood pressure and temps. Bandages and braces. If it's more than I can handle, I send them to Anchorage. I just do the best I can."

Volta stepped closer and smiled. "Scott isn't here to evaluate you. Somebody donated a bunch of money to help bring better pre-natal care in the villages, and they decided the first step would be sending someone to talk to people and find out the best strategies to support you. So they don't have the prom scenario again."

Ruby laughed. Scott shot a quizzical look at Volta.

"One of the high school girls won some dream prom contest," Volta explained to him. "The package was for a five-hundred-dollar dress, tux rental, flowers, hairstyling and a limo for twelve friends."

"But we only have about a hundred and twenty students in school," Ruby said. "Only eight graduated that year, and the closest thing we have to a prom is a village potlatch in the gym."

"It was supposed to be a big surprise," Volta said. "The dress company sent a representative and film crew to ambush the girl. They were really excited about filming in a small town in Alaska until they figured out there were no paved roads, no limos and no prom."

"What did they do?" Scott asked. "I assume there was some clause in the rules?"

Ruby smiled. "Technically she was disqualified, but they'd already come all the way here to film her getting the prize."

"And Markie was particularly photogenic," Volta pointed out. "Everyone huddled and they came up with an alternate prize."

"She got the dress," Ruby explained. "And they allowed her to use her limo allowance for an air taxi to Anchorage for the Alaska Teen pageant."

"She came in second and won a scholarship," Volta said. "She's a senior at UAF now, studying nursing. She's also done some modeling work for the dress company."

"Sounds like it all worked out, then," Scott said. "But yes, that's what we're trying to avoid. Wasting money on something you can't use. I chose Talpukna as a place to visit because I saw you had several births in the last three years."

Ruby chuckled. "My nieces and nephews were responsible for five of those births."

"Can you walk me through the usual prenatal process?" Scott asked.

"Yes." Once she relaxed, Ruby was an excellent source of information on the sort of care she could and could not offer pregnant women in the village, and how things had changed over the years she'd worked as a health aide. She explained that taking an air taxi to see the doctor throughout pregnancy wasn't in the budget for most of her patients. "A midwife comes in every month to check them."

"Tell me about the midwife program," Scott urged.

"It's connected with the hospital in Kotzebue. They handle the prenatal, and then two weeks before they're due to deliver, the women travel to the hospital in the city."

"Where do they stay?"

"There's a residence adjacent to the hospital for them," Volta said.

"How do the women feel about it?"

Ruby shrugged. "My niece Cassie had her baby about two months ago. Do you want to talk to her?"

"That would be great."

Ruby led them along the narrow street. A few four-wheelers were parked in front of buildings, but Scott didn't see any cars. They reached a small house, and Ruby opened the door. The sound of television and children's voices filtered out. "Cassie?" Ruby called.

"Auntie Ruby!" Two preschoolers ran to Ruby and wrapped their arms around her knees.

A young woman stepped from the kitchen. "Hush. Don't wake the baby. I just got him to sleep." She looked toward the door, her eyes widened in surprise. "Oh, hello."

Ruby introduced them to her niece and the children. "The doctor wants to know about the home by the hospital when the youngest was born."

"Come in." Ruby's niece led them to a small kitchen, where they all sat at a square table. The kids followed them in. The middle daughter climbed onto Ruby's lap, while the older girl leaned against her mother and peered at Scott. On the floor in the corner, a baby slept in a homemade cradle. "What about it?"

"How long were you there?"

"Almost three weeks this time. It was four with this one," Cassie put her hand on her older daughter's head. "She always keeps us waiting."

The girl giggled.

"The care is good," Cassie continued. "But it's boring. You know, waiting. That last month is hard anyway, and to be away from home, especially when you have other kids... I felt like I was going to be pregnant forever. My husband flew up one weekend, but he couldn't be there when the baby came."

"That's a shame."

"If I could, I'd stay home until it's time to have the baby, but the doctors say it takes too long to get to a hospital."

"We try not to deliver a baby on a plane," Volta said. "Lower oxygen and air pressure differences put stress on the baby and the mother. And we can't fly in bad weather."

Cassie nodded. "Some of the first-timers really like being there. They get a break and meet women from other villages who are going through the same things they are."

"I imagine being around experienced moms like you helps the first-timers."

Cassie laughed. "Some of them don't even know how to change a diaper. So I guess that part is good."

Cassie answered more questions candidly. The baby let out a cry. Cassie reached into the boat-shaped cradle and picked him up. "This is Sammy."

"Hi, Sammy." Scott smiled at the tiny baby. "May I hold him?"

"Sure." Cassie seemed surprised but pleased. She passed the baby into Scott's arms.

Reflexively, Scott examined the baby. Good color, bright eyes. A little cradle cap, but nothing to worry about. "He's a handsome boy."

"He looks like his father."

Scott passed the baby back to Cassie. "You have a beautiful family. Thank you for talking with me today."

After they stepped outside, Scott checked his watch. "I guess we'd better round up our pilot and head out."

"Or we could take Ruby to lunch first," Volta whispered. "Mike said he'd be at the diner," she said louder.

"Great idea." Scott turned to Ruby. "May I buy you lunch before we head out, as a small thank-you for all your help?"

"I… Yes that would be nice." Ruby smiled. "Although I don't know that I was much help."

"Believe me, you were. The information you've given me was invaluable."

After lunch, Mike flew them to Black Bear. Once they'd climbed out of the plane, Volta stopped and pulled out her cell phone. "Good. Three bars. I didn't have any in Talpukna. Can you give me a minute? I want to check in with Emma."

"Sure."

Volta walked a few steps away, but Scott could hear snippets of the conversation. "This afternoon? Yes, that's fine. Can't wait to hear all about it when I get home tonight. Love you to infinity. Bye."

She caught up with Scott, a smile on her face. "Emma has her first riding lesson this afternoon. She's so excited, she's about to ignite."

"That's great. I'm sure she'll enjoy it."

"Come on." Volta led the way. "I'll introduce you to Benny."

Just as Volta had predicted, Benny Hunter, the community health aide at Black Bear, had opinions on everything from the model of plane they flew in on to the best brand of dental floss. In fact, when he opened the box Volta delivered, it contained a twelve-pack of his favorite floss, along with some first aid supplies.

They followed him into the clinic, where he put away the supplies. "So, what's this study for?" Benny asked suspiciously. "To get some sort of grant or something?"

"It's kind of the opposite," Scott explained. "They have the grant, but they want to figure out how to use it to do the most good."

"Scott is with Doctors, Education and Medicine for All," Volta said. "They hired them for the study."

"You work for DEMA?" Benny's expression told Scott he'd just stepped up a notch in Benny's estimation. "Okay, what do you need to know?"

Three hours later, Scott had collected a massive amount of information, some of it pertaining to the subject at hand. It was going to take some work to organize everything he'd gathered.

They each shook Benny's hand, found Mike at the diner where he was watching a baseball game with a group of locals, and headed for the plane. Before they reached it, Scott's phone rang. He checked the screen and frowned. His dad was calling.

"Go ahead and take it," Mike said. "I need to run through my checklist."

Might as well. Scott answered the phone. "Hi, Dad."

"I can hardly hear you. Are you still in Alaska?"

Scott walked a few steps closer to the plane, where Volta had her phone out and was texting. "How's that?"

"Better."

"Yes, I'm in Alaska doing that study I mentioned."

"When will you be done?"

"Not sure. Why?"

"Because it's time. We didn't finish our talk while you were here, but you've been saving the world for ten years now. When are you going to join my practice and make some money?"

Scott shook his head. "You've been making money for a lot longer than that. When are you going to shut down your practice and save the world?"

His dad scoffed. "Seriously. I can barely meet the demand. I'm going to have to bring on another surgeon. It should be you."

"Thanks, but no thanks. That's not the kind of surgery I do."

"No reason it shouldn't be. You can always learn."

"I could. But I don't want to take up sports surgery."

"Think about it. I'm not kidding about expanding the practice. I need you here."

"You'll be fine without me. Got to go, Dad. A plane is waiting. Talk with you later." He ended the call.

Volta looked up. "Sorry, but I couldn't help overhearing. Your dad?"

"Yep."

"He's still trying to get you to join his sports medicine practice?"

Scott nodded. "He says I've spent enough time saving the world."

"Like he would know." Volta rolled her eyes. "Is he still promising to name it Willingham and Son?"

"I don't know. We didn't get that far."

Volta pocketed her phone. "Ready to board?"

He nodded and followed her to the door. "Good day. Lots of useful information, and I doubt they'd have been as open if you weren't there to vouch for me." He smiled at her. "I'm glad you decided to come along."

She returned the smile. "Me, too."

CHAPTER SIX

THE MINUTE VOLTA stepped into the doorway at her parents' house, a missile flew across the living room to hug her. "Mommy!"

Volta wrapped her arms around her daughter. "Hi, sweetie. How was the riding lesson?"

"Awesome! Granddaddy got video. Come look."

Volta allowed her daughter to drag her into the living room and sat down on the couch beside her mom and dad. "Hi."

"How was the trip?" Dad asked as he manipulated the television remote.

"Good. Scott got the information he needed. We're scheduled for another one on Wednesday. Does that still work for you?"

"Sure," Mom said. "We had meat loaf for dinner. Can I fix you a plate?"

"I'd love that, but first I want to see this riding video."

While her dad got the video queued up, Emma explained all about the lesson. "My horse is named Butternut. She's seven years old and she has black legs and a white star on her forehead, and really long eyelashes."

"She sounds great. Will you always be on the same horse?"

"Yes. Cait says—Cait is my teacher—she says it's better 'cause Butternut and me get to know each other that way."

"And is she gentle? The horse, I mean."

"She's really nice, and she likes carrots. She took the carrot right off my hand and didn't bite or anything. Cait's nice, too, and she says they're going to have a horse show in four weeks and that I can be in the beginner class if I work hard."

"Four weeks? That doesn't seem long."

"Cait was very complimentary," Mom told Volta. "She said Emma has good natural abilities."

"Here, I've got it ready to go." Dad pushed the remote button, and Volta watched Emma buckle on a helmet and approach a horse whose coat was the yellow-brown color of a baby moose. Emma gathered up the reins in her hand, slid her foot into a stirrup and swung onto the horse's back as if she'd been riding for years.

"Wow, look at you," Volta said. Emma beamed with pride.

A young woman with a red ponytail came

into the picture, and a moment later the horse walked forward with Emma riding. In the background, other horses and riders seemed to be practicing in the same arena. One of them jumped over a bar. Volta wasn't too sure she wanted Emma jumping any fences, but maybe these were advanced riders.

They continued to watch for another ten minutes until the video ended. "That's when my battery died. I forgot to charge it," Dad said sheepishly.

"That's amazing, though. When is your next lesson?"

"They said they have an opening tomorrow," Mom said.

"Good, then I'll get to take you." Volta hugged Emma. "Did you thank your grandmother and granddad for the lessons?"

"Oh, several times," Mom assured her. "Now, how about some supper?"

"I'd love some." Volta followed her mother into the kitchen. Emma and Dad stayed in the living room to watch the video once again.

Mom pulled a plate piled with meat loaf and roasted vegetables from the refrigerator and set it in the microwave. Volta knew what her mom called meat loaf was a token amount of ground turkey mixed with mushrooms and lentils, but she was hungry enough to eat it and enjoy it.

Volta wrapped her arms around her mom and hugged her. "Thank you."

"For what?" Mom returned the hug but looked mystified.

"For giving Emma the riding lessons. That was an incredibly thoughtful gift. Especially since you'll probably end up taking her for many of her lessons."

Mom smiled. "We were happy to do it. She was so excited about riding horses with Ryan a few weeks ago, and your dad and I thought this would be good for her."

"I confess, I had my doubts about the whole business, but seeing her on that horse…" Volta smiled. "She didn't look scared at all. Just happy, like a cowgirl who grew up on a ranch, instead of in Anchorage."

Mom started a kettle of water heating. "Your doctor friend sounds like he might have grown up on a ranch."

"Scott? Oh, you mean because of the Texas accent?" Volta shook her head. "No, he grew up in one of the suburbs near Houston. He did ride horses, but not on a ranch. His father is a surgeon."

"Ah, so he followed in his father's footsteps." Mom selected a package of herbal tea, removed a tea bag and set it in a cup.

"Not really. His father specializes in sports

injuries. He's well-known in the field, and quite wealthy, I gather. Scott works for DEMA and travels all over the world, taking care of people who can't pay."

"You seem to know a lot about him. How long have you known this doctor?" The microwave dinged. Mom pulled out the plate and set it on the table.

"Oh, awhile." Volta grabbed a fork from the drawer and sat down at the table. "It looks like Emma was falling in love with that horse. I hope you made it clear we were not going to be taking Butternut home to live in the garage."

"Yes, that was part of the lesson." Mom poured hot water into a teacup and settled into a chair across from Volta. "Cait took her into the stable and showed her how they take proper care of the horses. Tomorrow, Emma is supposed to saddle the horse herself, and brush her after the lesson."

"Sounds like they teach responsibility. Did it seem safe? I saw the helmet, but some of the horses were jumping over things in the background."

"It seemed safe to me. I don't know much about horses, but everyone was wearing helmets, and nobody fell off that I saw. Why, are you worried? You never fuss when Leith takes Emma camping and fishing."

"I'm a little nervous. I guess it's because I know about camping and fishing, and I trust Leith to take good care of her. I've never even been on a horse. I don't know what the dangers are with that."

"She'll be fine." Mom took a sip of her tea. "Has Scott worked in Alaska before?"

"No." Volta gave a little laugh. "Why are you so interested?"

Her mother shrugged. "I was watching you when you talked at the birthday party, and you didn't look like two people who barely knew each other. If you've known him awhile, and he's never been in Alaska before, where did you meet him?"

Volta stuffed her mouth full of meat loaf to avoid having to answer that question right away, but her mother watched her until she swallowed. "This is really good. Do I taste rosemary?"

"You know you do, because you asked that last time. Why don't you want to tell me where you met this doctor?"

Volta shrugged. "I knew him in Hawaii."

"Really? Was he in some of your classes?" Her mother's eyes suddenly widened. "Wait a minute. Scott? Oh, Volta, was this the man who caused you to drop out of school?"

"No one caused me to drop out. That was all on me."

"But you were so sad when you came home. He broke your heart." She stared at Volta's face as though she could read her thoughts. "It was him, wasn't it?"

"Okay, yes. Scott and I were dating in Hawaii. And I thought it was getting serious. But he already had plans to join DEMA once he finished his residency. He broke up with me. It's not that big of a deal."

"You were devastated."

"I got over it. I married Wade, and I had Emma. It all worked out for the best."

"But now you have to spend a lot of time with this man."

"So?"

"I don't want you to get hurt again."

"Yes, well, I don't particularly want that, either. That's why I'm keeping this relationship on a professional level."

"But he was at Emma's birthday party."

"That was Emma's doing, not mine. You know how excited she was about the reindeer farm. She ran into him when he was dropping me off and invited him."

"Why was he dropping you off?"

"I left my keys— It doesn't matter. The point is, I'm eleven years older now, and I hope wiser. Scott is doing important work with this study and I can contribute. He doesn't know Alaska, and I do. After I introduced Scott, the people we interviewed yesterday opened up and gave him valuable information."

"Are you sure this is a good idea?"

"I think I'm mature enough to work alongside a man without falling in love with him. Besides, it's only for a couple of weeks." Volta laughed. "What could go wrong?"

WEDNESDAY, SCOTT STEPPED onto the rickety porch outside the general store on the edge of the village of Apun. He paused to stretch and look around. They were on the tundra here, with not a tree in sight.

The sun was still high overhead even though it was almost six in the evening. He and Volta had put in a full day visiting three different village clinics. One of the health aides, Molly, happened to be pregnant herself, and she'd been able to give them information from both the health provider's and patient's point of view.

They'd just finished a productive interview with Mick, another health aide in Apun. Volta was inside the store now, fetching Mike for their flight home. Just like before, Volta had been a huge help in introducing Scott and vouching for him. Even the aide she hadn't met before had heard of her and welcomed them. Volta also seemed to have a sixth sense about guiding conversations to relevant topics he wouldn't have thought to ask about.

Volta stepped out onto the porch, looking at her phone. She smiled at something, returned her phone to her pocket and looked up at Scott. "Mike will be out in just a minute. He's about to lose a round of checkers."

Scott laughed. "No hurry. Everything okay at home?"

"Yes. In fact, Emma just got home from her latest lesson." Volta's smile broadened. "She's had three now. I got to take her to the last one. I was amazed. She's already guiding that horse all over the arena as if she's been doing it forever. She loves it."

"I thought she would."

"They were telling me there's a horse show coming up that she can enter. I couldn't imagine she'd be ready for a show in a month, but her instructor says there's a special beginner's class. Emma's psyched."

"I'll bet."

"Scott." Volta shifted her weight to the other foot. "You don't think Emma's too young for competitive riding like this?"

She was asking his opinion about her daughter? Up until now, Volta had been all business. Scott felt honored. "I wouldn't worry. I'm not sure about the setup, but if they have classes for all levels, including beginners, I'd suspect it's more a place to showcase what they've learned than cutthroat competition."

"That makes sense. My brother took her to her lesson today, and she's excited because she's having dinner with him and his girl-friend, and Sabrina made tacos."

"Mmm. Love a good taco."

"Who doesn't?"

"I'll beat you next time," Mike said over his shoulder as he stepped outside. "You two ready to go?"

"All set," Scott said.

A cell phone rang. Not the usual ringtone he'd heard from Volta's phone but a loud, in-sistent ring. Volta pulled a large phone in a heavy-duty case from the cargo pocket on her pants. Her work phone. "Volta Morgan."

Another loud ring, and Mike pulled out an identical phone and stepped away to answer. They were both hurrying toward the plane while they talked. Scott followed.

Volta pocketed the phone. "Severe burns. Three patients."

"Yellowrock is about ten miles from here,"

Mike told him. "No landing strip. They're bringing them to us on ATVs."

Mike and Volta went to work getting their equipment ready for when the patients arrived. Scott lent a hand where he could. Volta's phone buzzed again, and she checked the message. "Harold Emory is our contact."

Mick came from the clinic carrying another equipment pack. "They're on their way."

It seemed to take forever, but eventually they heard the rumble of motors in the distance. A four-wheeler came into view on the faint trail leading toward the horizon. A couple of minutes later, a second one appeared.

A woman huddled behind the driver of the first ATV, a toddler strapped to her chest. Scott ran to her. "Where are you hurt?"

She turned toward him, her face blank. Clearly in shock. The driver dismounted and stepped out of the way. Volta gently lifted the baby, who coughed. A quick check revealed only a minor burn on the baby's arm, the infant seemed fine otherwise.

Scott examined the woman still sitting on the ATV. He didn't see any immediate injuries until he'd moved to her other side and realized the hand she hadn't been using to hold the baby was badly burned. "Sterile water?" he called to Volta.

"Yes." She pulled a bottle from her pack and passed it to him.

Good. He poured it over the woman's injured hand. Meanwhile, Volta passed the baby to Mick and came to take the woman's vitals and give her oxygen.

"Are you Harold?" She asked the ATV driver.

"No, he's bringing Lenny." He pointed toward the other vehicle still approaching which held two men. As it got closer, Scott realized the passenger appeared to be unconscious. The ATV stopped. The man's chest and arms were covered with second- and third-degree burns. His unconscious state was probably a reaction to the severe pain. A small mercy.

Volta had hooked up monitors and was giving the vitals over her phone. "Roger. Starting IV." She looked at Scott. "Oxygen?"

"I'll do it." He administered oxygen while Volta expertly started an IV on the man's ankle.

The driver of the second ATV stepped over to Mick. "I'm not sure what caused it, but there was an explosion in their cabin. Fuel can, maybe. Hazel carried the baby out, but we had to go in for Lenny. I know you're not supposed to move hurt people, but we had to drag him out of there."

"You did good," Mick assured him. "He's real lucky these people happened to have a plane here."

"Scott?" Volta passed him the phone. "Dr. Smyth in Anchorage wants to talk to you."

Scott took it. "Dr. Willingham here."

"Glad to have a doctor on-site. Fairbanks is forty minutes closer, but we have better burn facilities in Anchorage. What's your opinion?" the ER doctor asked.

"Hang on." He asked Volta, "What are their vitals?"

Volta checked both patients and quoted the stats. "They seem stable. I'd go with Anchorage."

"Agreed." Scott confirmed with Dr. Smyth that he'd be riding along and returned the phone to Volta. Working together quickly yet efficiently, the four of them loaded up the two adults and the infant. Minutes later, they were airborne, racing toward Anchorage.

CHAPTER SEVEN

THE FLIGHT WENT SMOOTHLY. With three patients to care for, Volta was glad Scott was there with his calming presence and expertise. She adjusted the oxygen and pressure as needed to compensate for altitude.

The baby cried out and tried to push the oxygen mask away. His mother reached with her good hand, but she was strapped in on the bed. Scott unbuckled the baby and picked him up.

"Shh. I know you're scared," he whispered. He held the baby against his shoulder and rubbed his back. "I know." Amazingly, the baby quieted and leaned into him.

Scott held the baby for the entire ride until Mike instructed them to buckle up. They received priority landing and taxied to the waiting ambulance. "I'll ride along," Scott told Volta.

"I'll pick you up at the hospital," she promised.

The EMTs shut the door and the ambulance

headed off. Volta cleaned and restocked the packs before she left for the hospital.

She found Scott in the waiting room outside the ER. "How did it go?"

"Fine. They're admitting them now. Dr. Smyth says they may transfer them to a burn center in Seattle in a couple of days."

"And the baby?"

"They want to observe him overnight, to make sure there's no delayed response to the smoke."

"Good."

Scott looked at her with a proud smile. "So this is what you do for a living?"

"Awesome, isn't it?"

He chuckled. "It is indeed. I believe we're overdue for refueling. Care to join me for dinner before you drop me off?"

Volta hesitated. She'd promised her mother, and herself, that she would keep this relationship with Scott strictly professional. On the other hand, if anyone else she worked with had suggested dinner, she wouldn't give it another thought. It was only dinner.

"What did you have in mind?" she asked, to gain time.

He grinned. "Tacos."

"All right." How dangerous could it be to share some tacos? "I know just the place."

She drove him to her favorite Mexican restaurant in the center of a downtown neighborhood. Small but popular, with an extensive Tex-Mex menu, El Gato Amarillo was a family favorite. But tonight, it seemed to be everyone's favorite. The parking lot was packed, with cars lining the street.

She slowed and shook her head. "We'll never get in. They only have about a dozen tables. I know another place near the airport. It's a little more expensive, but it's good."

"Fine with me. Are there a lot of Mexican food places in Anchorage?" Scott asked.

"You can find almost any kind of food in Anchorage." She thought about it. "Well, maybe not water buffalo cheese."

"That's okay. Just get me some tacos and I'll be happy."

But when they arrived at the second restaurant, it was just as busy. Volta pulled into a lot next door to find out what was going on. They got out of the car, but a woman passing them warned, "They told me it's a forty-five-minute wait for a table."

"Thanks for letting us know," Scott told her. He looked at Volta and raised his eyebrows.

She shook her head. "I'm too hungry to wait that long. I can't imagine why the restaurants are so full today. It's Friday, but we're not into the main tourist season yet." Then it dawned on her. She slapped her forehead. "Oh, of course. Today is Cinco de Mayo."

"Oh, yeah. I'd forgotten about that."

"There are several more Mexican restaurants but they're probably just as crowded. Besides, I'm still technically on call and can't be more than fifteen minutes away from the airport. But I have another option, if you trust me."

"You know I do."

"Then I will get us tacos." She steered toward home. At one point, the two-way road divided into two one-ways, leaving an awkward triangle-shaped lot between them with a tiny flamingo-colored building in the middle.

Volta pulled up in front of the drive-through menu. "I'll have combo number three," she enunciated into the speaker, "with a side of guacamole and chips." She turned. "Scott?"

He was scanning the sign. "Taco Cheapo? Really?"

"You said you'd trust me."

"All right then. I'll have the number seven, extra salsa."

Volta repeated his order into the speaker and the disembodied voice crackled, asking them to pull forward to pay and then park in spot number two. Five minutes later, a teenage boy delivered the bag to their car, and Volta resumed driving.

"It smells good," Scott admitted. "Too bad I can't get a take-out bottle of Mexican beer to go with it."

"I've got you covered." Volta pulled up into her own driveway. "Leith left some in my fridge last week."

Scott smiled. "It's all coming together."

He followed her into the house and set the take-out bag on the kitchen counter. She opened the refrigerator and took out a beer. "Oh, look. I even have a lime." She sliced the lime, perched it on the mouth of his beer and handed him the bottle.

"A dream come true," Scott said. "Aren't you joining me?"

"No, I'm still officially on call, remember?"

"Oh, right. Tough to be you."

"Just enjoy your beer." She set the kitchen table with plates and forks. Then she swiped the tiny cactus growing on the window ledge and set it in the center of the table. "There. Ambience."

He looked at the table and then across at her face. He smiled. "Beautiful."

She poured herself a glass of water and distributed the contents of the take-out bag. They sat down to eat. Scott tried his first bite of taco.

"This isn't bad." He chewed for a moment. "In fact, that's a darn good taco."

"I know."

He ate another bite. "So why do they call themselves Taco Cheapo?"

She shook her head. "Taco Cheapo has been there for, I don't know, thirty years? Their tacos used to taste pretty much the way you'd think they would. I don't know how they stayed in business for so long, unless it's that they're literally on the drive home for so many people."

"Teenagers, maybe, when cheap and filling is the biggest draw?"

"I ate at Taco Cheapo once as a teenager and I said I'd never go back. But about six months ago, someone told me what good tacos they had. I didn't believe it at first, but after someone else mentioned it, I tried them again. It seems they have a new owner. He raised the prices, but it's still cheap by Anchorage standards. I asked if he was going to change the name, but he said he doesn't want to shell out for a new sign."

"So, it's your secret source."

"Not exactly secret. I've been telling everybody I know. I want this guy to stay in business, so I can keep getting his food."

Scott finished his first taco. "I agree. Remember that little hole-in-the-wall Chinese restaurant a couple of blocks off Kapiolani?"

"Do I! Their mu shu pork melted in my mouth."

"And their spring rolls."

"Oh, yeah. I would kill for their spring rolls."

"We ate there, what, three times? And then they just disappeared."

"I remember. And not like there was a closed sign on the door. We couldn't even find the door."

"I never was absolutely sure if we were on the wrong block, or if someone had remodeled the facade of the building."

"Or maybe the restaurant got sucked into another dimension."

Scott nodded. "The dimension of impossibly delicious spring rolls."

"I wanna go there."

"If I find a portal, I'll bring you with me."

"You'd better." And suddenly the silliness struck her. Volta snorted and coughed and then discovered she couldn't stop.

Scott grinned at her. "What?"

"I don't know," she gasped. "I'm just... picturing a wormhole—" she took a breath "—like the ones with clocks they used to have on cartoons when they went back in time, but with flying egg rolls and chopsticks and plates of lo mein." She gulped some water.

"I can see it." Scott chuckled. "Oh, and flying prawns and those little white dishes of sweet-and-sour sauce twirling around."

Volta burst out laughing before she'd managed to swallow her water. Fortunately, most of it went back into the glass and not out her nose. She jumped up from the table and blotted up the spill. "Okay." She held up her hands in surrender. "Stop." After a moment she was able to continue. "I need to eat my tacos before they get cold. Don't be funny anymore."

"I'll try to control myself," Scott promised, but he couldn't stop grinning.

After pacing around the kitchen for a minute or two, Volta was back in control. She sat down and finished her first taco. Scott smiled and took a bite of refried beans. As Volta spooned hot sauce onto her second taco, she shook her head.

Scott chuckled. "It's been a long time since anything I said provoked a spit take." He shrugged. "It never gets old."

"I can't say I agree with you there. I think spitting water all over my kitchen would get old in a hurry."

"It's a comedy classic."

Volta finished her second taco. Scott leaned

forward. "You have some hot sauce right here." He pointed to the corner of his mouth.

She picked up a napkin and dabbed. "Did I get it?"

"No, to the left."

She tried again, but he shook his head. He leaned close, bringing his face to within inches of hers, and wiped with his napkin. And then, before he drew away, his lips brushed across hers, so lightly she almost thought she'd imagined it.

It all felt so familiar. He'd done the same thing so many times when they were dating. He was always teasing her about her messy eating habits and then using the opportunity of wiping away a dribble to steal a kiss. She suspected there hadn't always been anything to wipe away.

They both froze for a second. Then Scott returned to his chair and unwrapped another taco, staring at the wrapper with the sort of concentration he might have used to make a surgical incision. Volta fiddled with her plastic fork. This was nothing, really. Not even a real kiss, just the lightest touch. It might even have been an accident.

She decided the best course was to rewind to earlier in the evening, before things got awkward. "I can't believe I got the giggles like I did. I haven't had one of those uncontrollable laughing fits in years."

"How many years?"

"I don't know," Volta said. But she did. "Eleven, maybe?"

"Why would you say that?" Volta picked up a chip and dipped it in the bowl of guacamole between them, concentrating on creating the perfect chip to dip ratio. It was safer than looking into those warm brown eyes.

"Because that's how long it's been since anyone found me funny enough for a spit take."

"Maybe you should work on your material."

"Or maybe I should be more selective of my audience."

Volta crunched the chip to avoid having to answer. After a moment, she replied, "We shouldn't be doing this, you know."

"Eating tacos?"

"Remembering old times."

"What's wrong with remembering? Those were some of the happiest days of my life."

"*Were* being the operative word."

"The past can't hurt you."

She looked up at him in shock. "You don't really believe that, do you?"

He stole a chip off her plate and dipped it in the guacamole. "I believe that while the past may have shaped us, every day we have the opportunity to start over. We make choices."

"And then we live with them. So our choices in the past can very much hurt us today."

He set the chip on his plate before looking up at her. "You mean like your choice to have dinner with me that day at the gardens?"

"Yes. And a whole series of choices I made after that."

"I'm sorry I hurt you."

"You say that, but you wouldn't have changed anything. You aren't sorry you broke up with me because it gave you the freedom to pursue the career you wanted, without being weighed down with the burden of someone who loved you."

"You make me sound so cold."

"I never thought so. Not until the day you told me I was less important than your plans."

"There are a lot of people in the world who need medical care and aren't getting it."

"Yes, there are."

"They need people like me."

"No argument there."

"Besides, it worked out for you. You fell in love and got married to someone who could be there with you, not traveling all over the world, occasionally calling you at three in the morning because he's lost track of time zones."

"Yes." Volta straightened her shoulders. "Yes, I was married. Wade loved me very much." Probably more than she deserved. He was thoughtful and sweet. But he'd never induced a fit of giggles she couldn't control. Still, he had married her and given her everything he had to give, including an amazing daughter. "Maybe you're right. Maybe it was all for the best."

Scott crunched the chip between his teeth. "I could say I'm sorry I started dating you, but that would be a lie. I'm glad you were in my life, even if it wasn't meant to be forever."

"Well, that makes one of us."

"So you wish, that first day when I spotted you among the hibiscus blossoms, looking as pretty as any flower there, that I would have kept walking?"

Did she? It would have saved her a truckload of pain. Not to mention guilt. Because if she'd never been in love with Scott, she never would have known her love for Wade was lacking. She never would have felt like a terrible wife, because even though she loved her husband, she didn't feel the sort of finish-your-sentences connection she'd had with Scott. She hoped

Wade had never known that she was capable of a deeper love than they'd shared.

Was ignorance bliss? Volta didn't know. "It doesn't really matter, does it? What happened, happened. You told me about your plans with DEMA that very first night. I knew what I was doing, and I could have bailed at any time. But I didn't. You had to be the one strong enough to end it."

"Why didn't you finish your degree?"

"Because I couldn't stay in Hawaii, not after what happened. And then I met Wade, and he loved me. We'd only been dating two months when he asked me to marry him. And it felt so good to have someone who wanted me in his life that much that I said yes. I decided to stay in Alaska with the man who loved me. Is that so hard to understand?"

"No. No, it's not hard to understand at all."

"I had a happy marriage. And now I have Emma, and she is the light of my life. So, yes, you did me a favor. Because if you hadn't broken my heart way back then, I wouldn't have my life now. Thank you, Scott. You made the right choice."

SCOTT TYPED A comment from Molly, the pregnant health aide, into his notes. He thought back to what she'd said about traveling for health care while pregnant and wishing air taxis had bathrooms. Volta had joked about her pregnancy at that point, saying she wouldn't have fit inside an airplane bathroom anyway. And they'd laughed together.

He could imagine Volta pregnant. Her skin and hair even more radiant than usual, her blue eyes soft, her belly swollen with promise. Singing to the baby. Making plans. Volta had always faced each day with gratitude, like a gift to be cherished. She was never cocky, but confident in her abilities. He remembered how she'd struggled in her physical chemistry class, but she'd never doubted she would pass if she put in the effort. And assuming she'd passed her final after they broke up, she had.

Yet her life had taken a different path than what she'd planned. Would she tell him if he was the reason she hadn't gone into physical therapy? She'd said it wasn't, but then, she'd always been kind.

It was clear that her family meant the world to her. But he hadn't been able to answer his biggest question: Was she happy?

She'd looked happy last night. She'd smiled and laughed the same way she had when they used to be together. Sitting at the table with her, it was almost as though they'd gone back in time. It was that illusion of living in the past that had led to that kiss. A kiss they were both pretending never happened.

Why had he done it? It wasn't as though she'd encouraged him. She hadn't flirted, hadn't done anything to attract him except be herself. That was all it had ever taken.

He'd felt that way the first day he ever met her. He'd convinced himself it wouldn't hurt to date for a while. After all, he wasn't in the market for a lifetime commitment. He'd already made one of those to DEMA. He was up-front about it. And yet, the more time he'd spent with Volta, the more he wanted. She had this undefinable quality. A warm glow that drew him like a fire on a chilly day.

But he hadn't realized how dangerous that pull was until the day he'd walked past a real estate office and saw a picture of a little island cottage on Kauai, known as Hawaii's Garden Isle. He could still see the place in his mind. White, with a brilliant pink bougainvillea climbing over the porch and a sago palm in the yard. A fenced yard, good for dogs and kids. There were two wicker chairs on the porch, and he'd pictured himself in one of them and Volta in the other, sipping lemonade and laughing. And that was when he knew he had to break up with her before he went and did something stupid.

Last night in Volta's kitchen, he'd felt that pull again.

He wouldn't be surprised if she refused to work with him anymore. She would be well within her rights to file a complaint against him, although he doubted she would. Volta had never been one to go through channels if she had the choice of dealing with a problem directly. He should have apologized. He only hoped she gave him another chance. Otherwise, he might never see her again, and Scott didn't want to think about that possibility.

"Emma, are you ready?" Volta called up the stairs.

"I can't find my boots. I thought I left them in the bathroom."

"I put them in your closet, where they belong." Always the last place Emma looked. But why would she? She never put anything there.

While she waited, Volta unloaded the dishwasher. In the top rack, she found the salsa bowl from her dinner with Scott. She rubbed her forehead. What had she been thinking, bringing him into her home? Her memories of Scott were all tied up with sand, palm trees and the scent of plumeria. This was the home she'd bought together with Wade. Scott didn't belong there.

And yet he fit. It felt so right, even the way he'd wiped the hot sauce off her mouth. He was always doing that. It was a running joke. As was the stolen kiss.

That simple brush of his lips across hers was more devastating than a long, seductive kiss would have been. This was a kiss between lovers who knew each other, who felt comfortable in a relationship. A quick reminder that there would be time later for long, deep kisses. A secret joke.

Volta blew out a long breath. Maybe that was all it was. A joke. Nothing to get excited about. No reason to tell her supervisor to find someone else to accompany Scott on his village visits. She cared about this study, and she wanted to stick with it until he was finished. She just needed to draw a clear line between their past personal relationship and their current professional one.

She put the salsa bowl in the cabinet. A minute later, a stampede sounded as Emma galloped down the stairs in her cowboy boots and burst into the kitchen. "I'm ready," she announced, holding out her arms in a diva-worthy declaration.

"Then let's go. You don't want to lose any riding time."

Emma climbed into the car and buckled in. "Do you think Cait will let me trot today?"

Volta backed out of the driveway. "I don't see why not. She did on your last lesson."

"Do you think she'll let me jump?"

"I'm not sure about that. Jumping looks fairly advanced to me."

"Cait said I need to learn to check my horse's hooves. Why do horses have hooves instead of feet like dogs?"

"Um." Volta remembered something about this from an exhibit in the children's science museum when Emma's class took a field trip. "As I recall, prehistoric horses had toes, but over a long, long, long time, their middle toenail grew bigger and stronger until it developed into a hoof."

"A horse's hoof is a toenail?"

"Yes." At least, Volta thought so, and if she sounded positive, Emma was less likely to bombard her with more questions.

"Mooses have hooves, too."

"Yes."

"But their hooves have a line in the middle. Uncle Leith showed me moose tracks and they don't look like horse tracks."

"I guess moose evolved to have two toes, but horses only have one toe on each foot."

"Why?"

"I don't know. I guess we'll have to look it up." They pulled in at the riding stable. As they crossed the parking lot, Volta's phone rang. She wasn't on call today, but she checked the caller ID just in case. She smiled. "Oh, it's your grammy Hannah."

"Are they here?" Emma jumped over a big rock at the edge of the parking lot. "Can they watch me ride?"

"I'll find out." Volta answered the phone while escorting Emma to check in at the stable. "Hi, Hannah. Where are you today?"

"We're on the Seward Highway. We should be in Anchorage in another two hours."

"Oh, good. Plan to eat dinner with us." Emma's paternal grandparents lived in Homer but traveled all over the state in their motor home. They loved seeing their only grand- daughter and always came by when they were in Anchorage.

At least this time they'd given her two hours' notice. They used to just drop in. Wade said his parents always kept a strict schedule when they were running their business in Anchorage, but once they retired and moved to Homer, they swore off making plans in advance. After all, they never knew when they'd hit a hot fishing run or a stretch of particularly nice weather and decide to stay a few extra days on one of their RV excursions.

It used to drive Volta crazy during her marriage when her in-laws would drop in when the house was at its messiest but eventually, she realized Hannah and Jim truly didn't mind a few dishes stacked in the kitchen sink. They'd welcomed her into the family and they loved her, and she loved them in return. "Emma will want to tell you all about her horseback riding lessons."

"We can't wait to hear about that and see the pictures from Emma's birthday party. We're on our way to the airport to pick up Stacy."

"Stacy is coming to visit?" Volta had mixed feelings about her sister-in-law.

Hannah's answer was drowned out by Emma's happy squeal. "Aunt Stacy is coming? When?"

"Excuse me, Hannah." Volta turned to Emma. "Today. She's coming to dinner with your grandparents. Look, there's Cait. Better scoot." Emma scurried over to her instructor. Volta waved and returned to the phone. "Sorry. Emma's excited. What time does Stacy's plane get in?"

"Seven fifteen. So with luggage and all, we probably can't get to your house before eight. Is that too late?"

"No, that's fine. See you soon." Volta hung

up the phone and went through a mental check-list of the contents of her pantry. She had fro-zen chicken breasts, basic vegetables, and she'd picked up a chunk of parmesan last time she shopped. If she had a jar of sun-dried toma-toes, she could make that chicken linguine her father-in-law had liked so much the last time they were in town.

She and Emma could pick up a jar on the way home, along with a bagged salad. And maybe a six-pack of purple and yellow pansies. She could tuck them into a basket to use as a centerpiece and plant them in the yard later. Volta always felt the need to be a little more impressive when Stacy was around.

Volta followed Emma and Cait to the barn and watched Cait teach Emma how to saddle a horse.

It was Stacy who had introduced Volta to Wade. They'd all lived in Anchorage then. Volta and Stacy had gone to different high schools, but they had friends in common. That summer after the big breakup in Hawaii, most of Volta's friends had been busy or out of town, but she'd run into Stacy at the coffee shop, and they'd started hanging out.

One day Stacy needed a ride home from the auto repair shop, and when Volta had dropped her off at her parents' house, her brother was there, visiting. He was tall and lean, with coffee-colored eyes so dark Volta couldn't tell the pupils from the irises. And those eyes were completely focused on her. It had taken him about five minutes to ask Volta for a date, which was exactly the balm her bruised ego had needed.

Stacy had been happy about Volta dating her brother at first. But as Volta's relationship with Wade grew stronger, Stacy seemed less pleased. And when they'd announced their engagement, Stacy had been downright argumentative. She'd insisted they were rushing into marriage. Even though Wade had never told her so, Volta knew that his sister was working on him at every opportunity, trying to talk him out of the wedding. Stacy should have realized that telling her brother not to do something was the surest way of making it happen.

The disconcerting thing was, Volta knew Stacy was right, that they were rushing into marriage, but she didn't want to slow down, afraid if they lost the momentum, it would never happen. Wade loved her, and he wanted to marry her. She loved him, too. Maybe it wasn't with the same intensity she'd felt with Scott, but every relationship was different, right? Besides, after the pain of the breakup, she wasn't sure she ever wanted to love that way again. She wasn't sure it was even possible.

But she did know that just like Wade, she wanted marriage and a family. And so, she'd accepted his proposal, and she'd married him. He did everything he could to make her happy, and she'd done the same for him.

She'd been a good wife, loving, caring, supportive. They never fought about things like him forgetting to put his clothes in the hamper or her squeezing the toothpaste wrong. She'd never clogged his weekends with chores or demanded he give up his friends or his hobbies. Which was another thing Stacy held against her.

Wade and two of his lifelong buddies had plans to use their snow machines one weekend. It had been a weird weather week of mixed rain and snow, then subzero temperatures, followed the next day by a heavy snow. The forecasters had warned that conditions were dangerous, but Wade had insisted he and his friends were experienced enough to know which slopes to avoid, and Volta believed him. After all, he'd been riding for years and won several races.

But this time, he was wrong. They'd been high marking, cutting across the top of the slope to gain speed on the downhill, when the snowpack broke loose.

Wade's two friends were lucky. One was completely out of the path of the avalanche, and the other was on the very edge. He lost his snow machine but managed to "swim" to the edge and avoid getting swept away. But Wade was in the very middle of the slide. Even with his emergency beacon, it had taken search and rescue a full day to recover his body.

It was while the family was gathered together, awaiting news, that Stacy had accused Volta of wanting him to die. "Everyone knew conditions were unstable. If you'd loved him, you would have made him stay home. He would have, if you'd asked."

Hannah had tried to smooth it over. "Now, Stacy. You know how hard it is to talk your brother out of anything he wants to do."

"She could have." Stacy had raised her chin and glared at Volta. "He'd do anything for her. But she didn't care enough to stop him." She'd run from the room, in tears.

Hannah had hugged Volta. "She doesn't mean it. She's just upset."

She did, though. When they received the news that they'd recovered Wade's body, Stacy had collapsed, sobbing. Meanwhile, Volta just felt numb. Cold. As though she was drifting in a fog, with no idea which way to go to find the shore, or even if there was a shoreline.

Wade was never coming back. Volta had known that, and yet she couldn't really grasp the reality. She'd realized only two days before that her period was late, but she'd decided not to say anything yet. After she'd dropped him off at his friend's house on Saturday morning, she'd stopped by the drugstore for a pregnancy test, and stashed it in the hall closet. When Wade got home Sunday night, she'd take it while they were together.

So he never knew he was going to have a daughter. He would have been so excited. He should have been there to listen to the heartbeat, and assemble the crib, and dither over names. But he wasn't. And according to Stacy, it was all Volta's fault.

They'd gotten through the funeral as a family. Volta had decided to wait until the end of her first trimester to share the news of her pregnancy, not wanting to risk putting Wade's family through another loss. Hannah and Jim were thrilled at the idea of a grandchild. Stacy had demanded to know the due date, but after she did the math, she accepted that this was Wade's child. And once she'd seen how much Emma looked like Wade, she'd been a devoted aunt. Even after she moved out of state two years later, Stacy always sent cards and birthday presents.

But Volta had never been able to get past Stacy's accusation. Maybe it was her fault that Wade died. She had asked about the weather report, but when Wade said it was okay, she'd trusted his judgment. He had all the right safety equipment, and he was riding with friends he trusted, but he had to know it was dangerous. If she'd told him then that she might be pregnant, would he have stayed home instead?

Volta gave herself a mental head shake. Wondering about what might have been was a waste of time. Right now, she had a daughter who was having the time of her life. Cait had mounted another horse, and they were trotting side by side, with Cait instructing Emma on her posture and positioning.

Volta didn't know enough to be sure, but it looked like Emma was doing a good job. They circled the arena, and when they passed, Emma flashed her a huge smile. Volta smiled back, glad that she could be there to share the moment. And if Wade was there somewhere on the other side, watching, maybe he was sharing the moment, too.

DINNER WAS NICE. Hannah and Jim listened to Emma's stories of horsemanship with pride.

"You'll have to show me the pictures from your birthday party after dinner," Hannah told her. "I'm sorry we couldn't be there. Grandpa had a bad cold and we didn't think we should share it."

"My teacher says you should always cover your mouth when you cough and wash your hands a lot," Emma advised her.

"Your teacher's right."

"Emma loved the shirt with the picture of a sea lion you sent," Volta said, as a nudge.

"I wore it to school and everybody wanted to know where I got it so they could get one," Emma said.

"I came across a woman who paints them by hand," Hannah explained, "and she doesn't ever do any two alike, so nobody will ever have one exactly like yours."

Stacy had been unusually quiet throughout dinner, but maybe that was because Emma hadn't stopped talking long enough for her to get a word in. Volta racked her brain, trying to remember what gift she had sent for Emma's birthday. Oh, yes. "Did you tell Aunt Stacy thank you for the doll?"

"Thank you," Emma sang out, obediently. "I like her dress. Sabrina said she'd show me how to make her other dresses."

Volta smiled at her. Emma wasn't big on

dolls in general, so she was pleased that Emma had managed to find something to like about Stacy's gift. And something nice to say.

But Stacy frowned. "Who's Sabrina?"

"My brother's girlfriend. She designs clothes for Orson Outfitters."

Stacy sniffed. "Whatever happened to his wife?"

Stacy knew very well what happened. Why rub it in? "They divorced years ago. How are things in Salt Lake?"

"Fine."

"Are you still working for the insurance company?"

Stacy exchanged looks with her mother. "I'm looking for something better."

"Oh." What did that mean?

Stacy shrugged. "I got caught up in a staff reduction. I'm sure it was my old supervisor—she always bore a grudge that I left her department. They had to give me a nice severance package, at least, and so I decided to take some time and visit my family. I wasn't that happy there anyway."

Volta nodded. She'd learned long ago that whether it was where to meet for lunch or what color her bridesmaid dress should be, it was easier to give Stacy her own way than to deal with her unhappiness. Of course, that was a long time ago. Stacy had matured since then. Presumably.

"Anything else exciting going on in your life?" she asked Stacy.

"Well, let's see. I painted my kitchen yellow. Oh, and there's a guy I've been dating."

"What shade of yellow?" her father asked in an innocent voice.

Hannah elbowed him. "Tell us about this boyfriend. What's his name?"

"George Carsten. He's a school principal."

"How long have you been going out?"

"Oh, about a month now. He's divorced, has a daughter who lives in California. He's there visiting now."

Hannah continued to quiz Stacy while Volta brought in dessert: strawberries and angel food cake she'd spotted when she ran in for the sun-dried tomatoes. She handed a can of whipped cream to Emma, who jumped up to help with her favorite kitchen task.

"Do you want cream on yours, Grammy?" Emma interrupted.

"Shh," Volta whispered. "Grammy's talking to Aunt Stacy. Wait until she's done."

"You can put some on yours and mine," Jim told Emma. "We'll eat our cake, and if they aren't through yakking by the time we finish, we'll eat theirs, too. What do you say?"

Emma giggled and squirted a generous pile of whipped cream over her grandpa's dessert. After a moment, Hannah put her hand on Emma's shoulder. "I'd like about half that much, please."

"What are your plans from here?" Volta asked Jim. "Are you heading out right away?"

"We're staying in Anchorage for a few days," he told her. "Stacy wants to catch up with some of her old friends. We've got a spot reserved at that RV place over by Earthquake Park. We're thinking of catching a baseball game tomorrow evening. Are you and Emma interested in joining us?"

"Corn dogs?" Emma asked hopefully.

"I suspect they'll have corn dogs at the concession stand."

"Goody."

"Sure. Sounds great," Volta said.

"You're not working?"

"Not tomorrow. The day after, I'm flying to Unak and Alder."

"They're scheduling emergencies in advance now?" Jim asked.

"Wouldn't that be nice? No, I'm working with a doctor looking at how we could improve prenatal care in the bush."

"One of the local doctors?"

"No, he's from DEMA."

"Dr. Scott came to my birthday party," Emma volunteered.

"Did he?" Hannah raised her eyebrows at Volta, who pretended not to see.

"Speaking of birthday parties." Volta handed her phone to Emma. "Why don't you show Stacy and your grandparents the pictures from the reindeer farm?"

Volta started collecting dessert plates, but when she reached for Stacy's, her sister-in-law refused to relinquish it. "Why was a doctor at Emma's party?" she whispered.

Volta shrugged, trying to keep it casual. "He's from out of town and had never seen a reindeer, and you know how enthusiastic Emma can be."

"Emma invited him? What was he doing around Emma?"

Shoot, she was just digging herself in deeper. "Dropping me off after a flight. You should look at Emma's pictures. There's a great one of her unwrapping your doll." Volta managed to wrestle the plate away from her. Stacy didn't immediately ask more questions, but if she were a hunting dog, she'd be pointing.

Volta retreated to the kitchen with the plates. Stacy had been the recipient of several tearful conversations about her and Scott the summer after the breakup. Volta needed to keep Scott's name out of any future conversations with her. Because if there was one thing she didn't need, it was Stacy butting into her life.

CHAPTER EIGHT

SCOTT TOOK HIS place at the conference table for the morning meeting at Puffin Medical Transport. Volta was already seated, flipping through some papers. She looked up and gave him a little smile. He breathed a sigh of relief. If she planned to pull the plug on their working relationship, she wouldn't be smiling at him.

Bernie started the meeting, bringing everyone up-to-date and laying out the agenda for the day. "The Learjet will be out first this morning, to the burn center in Seattle, and then you're up next," Bernie advised Scott.

"Is this the man from Apun?" Scott asked.

"Yes. He's stable enough for transport now, and the burn center in Seattle is better equipped for his long-term care."

"Good." Scott had stopped by the hospital the day after they'd transported the burn victims. The child had been discharged to an aunt. Both parents were under heavy medication, but the woman had recognized him and insisted on thanking him. Her hand would be heavily scarred, but the prognosis was good.

While he was there, he'd talked with a few of the local ob-gyn specialists, asking for their input on his study. They all seemed pleased to hear about the possibility of extra funding to help with prenatal care. Dr. Bart Thomas was especially enthusiastic. "You've seen it, I'm sure, working with DEMA. Problems that could have been avoided if we'd caught them early in the pregnancy. Things like that happen when patients are a flight away from health care."

"Yes, I've seen it. DEMA has had success with several programs involving traveling prenatal clinics. That's why we were hired to do this study."

"Excellent. I'll look forward to hearing more once your report is complete." Dr. Thomas handed him a card. "Give me a call if I can be of help in the meantime."

Scott had kept the card. It was always good to have local support when trying new ideas, and it was clear that Dr. Thomas was a leader in the community.

"I'll help you load up," Volta offered to the team that was flying to Seattle.

"Thanks."

The meeting broke up, and Volta took off

with the other flight team into the hangar. Scott headed upstairs to change into his borrowed flight suit. He sat down in one of the desk chairs and checked his email. Nothing urgent. His supervisor asked how the project was progressing. He'd send an update tomorrow.

Scott got up and crossed the room to pour a cup of coffee from the pot in the kitchen area. Something crinkled when he walked. He moved over to the mirror mounted on a door and looked over his shoulder into the mirror to see a scrap of paper attached to the back of his leg.

"Getting ready for a photo shoot?" Volta appeared at the top of the stairs, grinning.

He peeled off the label. "Something was stuck to me."

"Sure. Not preening or anything." She chuckled as she poured a cup of coffee for herself and turned off the machine.

Scott laughed. "Okay, since you're here…" He glanced back toward the mirror. "Do you think this suit makes my butt look big?"

Volta snorted. She opened her mouth, and judging by the little lines around her eyes, she was ready with a zinger. But then she gave a little head shake and deliberately adopted a neutral expression. "No comment. The crew for Seattle is cleared for takeoff. Mike says he'll be ready in ten. I'll get changed."

"Someone left a sticker on the desk chair," Scott insisted.

"I'm not judging." She opened the mirrored door and disappeared inside. A few minutes later, she returned, dressed in her own flight suit. Which, Scott was obliged to notice, fit her quite nicely.

Her cell rang. She checked the ID and frowned. "Can you give me a sec?"

"Sure. I'll…" He gestured that he'd leave the room if she wanted, but Volta shook her head and answered.

"Yes, hello." She listened for a minute. "Oh, I'm sorry to hear that." There was a long pause. "Okay, but when…will someone else…but can't…?" Her expression was growing increasingly frustrated. "No, I understand. Thank you for calling me. Good luck." She hung up.

"What's wrong? Is it about Emma?"

"Yes. Oh, Emma's fine," Volta hastened to add, "but her horseback lesson is canceled. That was Cait, her riding instructor. It seems she's also a college student and she's apparently been spending too much time at the stable and not enough with her books. She's taking time off to complete a semester project and study for finals."

"She told you all this?"

"And more. Like what classes she's taking and the name of her 'super-picky' instructor. As well as her parents' policy on not paying her tuition if her grade point drops any lower."

"Ah. And no one can fill in for her?"

"Apparently all the other instructors are completely booked, and they're not doing group lessons right now." She checked her watch. "Emma should be getting ready for school now. I'll text my mom to tell her about the canceled lesson, but I'll have her wait until after school to tell Emma. Otherwise, Emma will call to demand an explanation, and we'll both be late."

"It's a shame that Emma will miss her lessons. She was so excited at the party."

"I know. But Cait says she'll make the lessons up this summer, so Emma will have to wait." Volta grabbed a shoulder bag and headed down the stairs. Scott followed her to the plane.

Mike greeted them when they climbed inside. "We might hit a little bit of turbulence on the way, but weather should be fine for landing."

Darn. Scott realized he'd forgotten to bring any seasick patches. Ordinarily he never went anywhere without them, but he'd used his last one on a ferry crossing a couple of weeks ago and forgot to get his prescription refilled.

Volta opened her bag, pulled out a plastic tube and handed it to Scott along with a bottle of water.

"What's this?"

"Motion sickness pills."

"Oh. Thanks." They'd spent a weekend on Maui once, and decided to drive to Hana. The curving road had left him a little green around the gills. Funny that she would still remember. "Why do you carry these? You don't get motion sickness."

"No, but Emma does sometimes. Better to be prepared."

"I see." Scott capped the water and fastened his seat belt. He shouldn't be surprised. Volta's magic purse had always contained everything from aspirin to folding pliers, which had come in quite handy once when he'd stepped on a fishhook. She'd even produced an antiseptic wipe and a Band-Aid. Becoming a mother would only have increased her tendency to prepare for emergencies.

The little bit of turbulence turned out to be a twenty-minute roller-coaster ride, which Scott didn't enjoy, but did manage to weather with his stomach contents intact, thanks to Volta's foresight. Volta hardly seemed to notice the bumps. Eventually they pulled out of it and the rest of the flight was smooth.

They went over their last mountain pass and started to descend. Scott and Volta looked out the windows at the landscape below. The budding birches cast a yellow-green haze across the forests, contrasting with the dark spruce. Soon a village came into view. It seemed tiny, but perhaps it was mostly hidden in the trees. The plane dropped toward the airstrip beside it.

Volta's voice suddenly crackled over the headphones. "Mike, moose at two o'clock."

"Roger."

The engine gunned and the plane buzzed low over the airstrip before rising into the air on the other side. Startled, the gawky animal galloped across the airstrip and into the woods. Scott followed his progress as best he could until he was assured the moose wasn't planning on making another pass.

Mike circled, and this time set the plane down and coasted to a stop. Scott let out the breath he hadn't realized he was holding. "Does that happen a lot?"

"Just enough to keep us honest. More often it's an ATV with an oblivious driver."

Scott nodded. He'd had similar experiences in Africa, except there it was usually a herd of antelope. Or a jeep. Drivers were much the same everywhere.

They fell into the routine they'd established of meeting up with the community health aide and touring the clinic. Only this particular aide didn't seem to have much to contribute to the conversation. "Not sure what you want from me. I just patch 'em up."

Even Volta couldn't seem to charm him. By noon, he was mostly answering in grunts, and Scott admitted defeat. They headed to the village store, where they found the owner, a man with an untidy mop of gray hair, playing cribbage with Mike.

The man laid down a card and looked at them. "You're the doctor doing the study about pregnant women, right?"

"That's me," Scott said.

"So what are you doing here? Ted's wife took off to Juneau last Christmas. The lady schoolteacher up and left, and they replaced her with a man. Jill over at the post office already has five boys and she says she's fixed it so she's not having no more. That's all the women we got."

"There are no women of childbearing age in this village?" Scott pulled out his notes.

"Nope."

Scott frowned. "The last census showed

approximately fifty women between eighteen and forty-five in Unak."

Volta peered at the printout. "That's Munak. The M is smudged."

"Munak is on the other side of the state," the storekeeper commented helpfully.

Scott closed his eyes. "Great." He'd wasted the whole morning on a wild-goose chase. "Okay, then. That explains Ted's attitude."

The old guy laughed. "No. Ted's wife running off with a bush pilot explains his attitude. You just made a mistake."

They returned to the plane to head to the next village, but before they boarded, Volta's work phone rang. She listened for a minute. "Okay. I'll let you talk to him. Hang on."

She handed Scott the phone. "They've canceled the meeting in Alder."

Scott put the phone to his ear. The dispatcher at Puffin explained, "Connie sends her apologies. Her kids got into poison sumac and she's got her hands full. She says if you'll call tomorrow or the day after, she'll fill you in."

"Understood. Thanks." He handed the phone back to Volta. "Well, today was a bust. I guess this means we're returning to Anchorage."

"You could still go see the clinic in Alder if you want, but it's pretty much the same setup as most of the others."

"No, let's head on back. Sorry to waste the day for both of you. I should have been more careful with my notes."

Mike shook his head. "No skin off my nose. Any day I get paid to fly is a good day."

"Where and when are we going next?" Volta asked.

Scott listed the villages he still wanted to visit. "I'll double-check that I have the correct name from the census data and make sure I don't mess it up again."

"Anyone would have read that as Unak if you didn't notice the columns don't line up. When did you plan to go?"

"I'll have to contact the community health aides, but I was thinking of scheduling the first batch Wednesday."

Volta studied the map. "You know, Porcupine is big enough that they probably have a hotel. We could hit these two villages the first day, spend the night in Porcupine, and the next day visit the clinic there and these two villages within easy flying distance."

Mike looked over the map. "That would work."

"In fact, Mike could drop us in Fairbanks the second night. Then we could rent a car and drive to the places you've flagged on the road system on the way to Anchorage."

"That sounds great, but can you be away for three days at a stretch?"

"It's not that much different than when I'm on duty for three days in a row at home. It would all be done in one fell swoop so I'd have time off when Emma gets out of school." She turned to the pilot. "Would it work with your schedule?"

Mike nodded. "It works."

"All right," Scott said. "I'll contact the various people and if they agree, we'll plan on it."

Mike made a note on his phone. "Ready to head out?"

Volta checked her messages. "Oh, Emma texted me. Mike, can you give me a minute to call while we still have cell service?"

"Sure. Got to kick the tires anyway." He headed toward the plane.

Volta dialed without moving away from Scott, so he had no qualms about eavesdropping. "Hi, Emma… I know, I heard. But Cait has other responsibilities she has to take care of." There was a long pause, with Volta occasionally making "mmm-hmm" noises. Finally, "I don't know, but I'd assume you might have to skip this first show. I know, sweetie, but Cait said you need certain skills, even in the beginner class, and…" Another long pause. "Didn't

Grammy Hannah mention taking you shopping? Maybe…oh, tomorrow."

After another minute or so of soothing, Volta said, "Listen, I have to go now. I'll be home in a couple of hours. Love you to infinity… Bye." She ended the call and pocketed the phone. "She's not happy."

"I can tell." They walked toward the plane.

"She was all revved up about this show they're having in three weeks, and now it looks like she's not going to be able to participate."

"I could teach her," Scott found himself saying.

A little line formed between Volta's eyebrows. "You?"

He nodded. "I rode, you know. I've even worked as an instructor at summer horse camps when I was in high school. If the stable will give me access to horses, I could be her trainer."

Volta climbed into the plane and waited while he followed her. She shut the door and latched it. "But you have this study to complete."

"Yes, but even DEMA doesn't expect me to spend every waking moment working. I'm allowed a few hours of leisure time. And I happen to enjoy riding. In fact, I rode one day when I was in Houston. I still remember how."

"I don't know."

"Think about it."

Volta nodded as she pulled her headset over her ears and buckled into her seat. Scott followed suit.

The turbulence they'd hit on the way must have dissipated, because the plane only rocked two or three times on the flight back to Anchorage. Good thing, since Scott had forgotten to take another dose of motion sickness medicine.

Back at the airport, Scott changed into street clothes. When he came out of the changing room, Volta was already there, standing at the window, looking toward the mountains. She splayed her fingers wide and then folded them, one at a time. He recognized it as a tension-releasing exercise she'd once taught him. He often used it before surgery.

He shut the door behind him, and she turned. "Were you serious about teaching Emma to ride?"

"Of course." It was the least he could do. And besides, he would enjoy it.

"When?"

He looked at his watch. They still had a good six hours of daylight left. He wasn't sure about the stable's hours, but if they were doing after-school lessons, they probably stayed open.

"Now would be good. Why don't I call the stable and see what kind of arrangements we can make?"

"You're sure you have time for this?"

"I'm sure."

In fact, when Volta gave him a grateful smile, he realized he'd never been more sure of anything in his life.

VOLTA WATCHED SCOTT make a slight correction in the way Emma held the reins. She said something, and he chuckled. They seemed to be getting along quite well. Volta wasn't sure if that was a good thing or not.

Her relationship with Scott was supposed to be strictly professional. It was too dangerous to let Scott into her personal life, especially after that almost kiss the other night. But Emma had been so disappointed about missing her riding lessons, and when Scott offered to fix everything, Volta couldn't resist. Of course, resisting Scott had always been difficult.

Trouble was, this time she wasn't the only one who could get hurt. When he left to pursue his true love, work, he'd be leaving Emma behind, as well. But Emma understood that Scott was simply a visitor, filling in until Cait returned. Volta understood it, as well. At least, intellectually she did. Her heart still fluttered like a rabble of butterflies whenever Scott smiled at her.

But she could handle it. That flutter was just a habitual response, like looking at your wrist when you weren't wearing a watch. The occasional heart flutter didn't prove anything.

It had all come together easily. He'd called the stable and mentioned a couple of names of people he'd worked with in the past. A few minutes later, presumably after checking his credentials with someone, they called back, eager to let him work with Emma. Volta got the idea the stable manager wasn't too happy with Cait's sudden absence, but she couldn't fault the girl for her priorities.

"There's our beautiful girl. Just look at her on that horse." Hannah and Jim had come up behind Volta without a sound.

Or maybe they'd been stomping and shouting, and she was just too wrapped up in watching Scott and Emma to notice. Volta gave them each a hug. "She's doing well, I think. How was your lunch with friends?"

"We had a great time, as you can see since it's almost five and we're only now getting back," Hannah said.

"They're all getting so old, though," Jim commented with a twinkle in his eye. "Funny how everyone around us ages and we stay the same."

Volta laughed. "You must have stumbled across the fountain of youth somewhere in your travels."

Hannah waved at Emma, who flashed her a big grin before reining her horse in a circle according to Scott's instruction. Jim took a picture. "I thought Emma said her instructor was named Cait."

"She was, but Cait can't teach for a little while, so Scott is filling in."

"Scott?" Hannah frowned in concentration. "Where have I heard that name mentioned recently?"

Volta shrugged. Hannah would no doubt figure it out for herself. "Where's Stacy?"

"She's getting together with some friends from high school who are in town visiting. Is it still okay if she and I take Emma shopping tomorrow after school while you go to the dentist?"

"Sure."

"Day after tomorrow, we thought we'd take a run down to Soldotna. I've heard rumors of an early sockeye run starting to trickle in." Jim mimicked casting a line.

"Nice," Volta said. "Can I count on some smoked sockeye in my Christmas stocking?"

"We'll see. Never count your salmon before you've landed them." Jim smiled.

"Is Stacy going with you?" Volta asked.

"As far as I know. She's always liked to fish," Jim said.

Hannah looked a little more doubtful. "Although it might depend on how long her friends are staying in town. We'll see. Would Emma want to go with us? You know how much she enjoys camping in the RV, and we'd love to spend some time with her."

"She's got another week of school yet."

"Maybe we could run back up on Friday and take her down for the weekend."

"Are you sure? What if the fish are biting?"

Jim grinned. "Then I'll have Hannah drive to Anchorage while I fish."

"What if I decide to run off with some good-looking man in Anchorage instead of coming back for you?" Hannah challenged.

"Then I suppose I'll just have to keep fishing until you get tired of him and return to your true love," Jim declared.

Hannah beamed.

"Okay, we'll ask Emma, but I'm sure she'll want to come. She's getting to be a good caster. She still wants nothing to do with fish guts, though. Not that she's ready to handle a fillet knife anyway."

"Wish I could get someone to take care of my fish guts." Stacy stepped up to the fence. "Hi, Emma," she called, causing Emma to look over and wave instead of concentrating on whatever she was supposed to be doing. Scott didn't seem to mind, though. He said something, and Emma urged her horse into a trot around the perimeter of the arena.

Stacy leaned against the fence. "Who's the hottie?"

"Volta said the instructor quit or something so this guy took over," Hannah said.

"She didn't quit," Volta corrected her. "She just needed off a couple of weeks."

"Nice." Stacy ran her eyes over Scott, from the thick brown hair, to the plaid shirt and well-washed jeans, to the soft leather of his favorite cowboy boots. "Wonder if he's married."

"Aren't you dating someone in Salt Lake?" Volta asked, a little more sharply than she'd intended.

Stacy shrugged. "Nobody's made any commitments. I wouldn't mind spending an evening or two with a cowboy."

"I doubt he'd have time. He's only in town for a little while and he has a job to do," Volta said.

"The riding instructor isn't from here?" Hannah asked.

"He's not a professional riding instructor," Volta admitted. "He's a doctor with DEMA. I've been assisting him on a study he's doing, and when he heard Emma's riding lessons had been canceled, he volunteered to fill in until her regular instructor gets back."

Stacy raised her eyebrows. "Oh, so this is the doctor Emma mentioned. The one who came to her birthday party."

"Uh-huh." Volta pulled out her phone. "I'll try to get some video of Emma riding." She walked farther along the fence line.

Unfortunately, Stacy followed her. "Are you sure you're not dating this guy?"

"I think I'd know." Volta turned her back and pointed her phone toward Emma.

"But would you tell?" Volta could hear the smirk in her voice.

Volta ignored her and started the video. The horse was so tall and Emma so small, but she seemed to be completely in control of the big animal. As Volta watched, Emma gave some signal and the horse switched to a different gait, less bouncy and more like a slow run. Emma's grin almost reached her ears. Wow, look at her.

"I can see why you'd keep it a secret," Stacy went on. "Especially from your mother-in-law.

She might not be so thrilled with the idea of Emma's mom having a boyfriend."

What Stacy meant was that she didn't like the idea of anyone taking her brother's place. And even though Scott was not her boyfriend, Volta couldn't help feeling annoyed. Wade had been dead for almost nine years. If Volta did decide she wanted to date, what business was it of Stacy's?

"If I were dating someone, I'm sure Hannah and Jim wouldn't object," Volta said. "In fact, they tried to fix me up once with the new school superintendent down in Homer."

"When?" Stacy demanded. "And why?"

Volta shrugged. "They got to know him when they rented him their RV for a month until he could find a permanent place to live. I took Emma down to visit last summer, and they invited him to dinner."

"That doesn't mean they were setting you up. Maybe they had extra food."

"Maybe." Volta wasn't going to waste a lot of energy trying to convince her. Stacy believed whatever she wanted to believe anyway. But it was definitely a setup. Hannah and Jim had even volunteered to babysit Emma if Volta and—what was his name?—Garrett wanted to go out after dinner for a drink. Which she didn't.

Volta had figured the last thing she needed in her life was a guy who lived a five-hour drive away. Besides, while he seemed like a perfectly nice person, there was no spark. No little flutter of attraction. Volta had made some excuse, and the four of them had spent the evening playing Chinese checkers instead.

Volta turned her attention to Emma, who was riding along and then, at Scott's instruction, pulling back on the reins and bringing the horse to a quick stop without losing her balance in the least. Scott beamed proudly at her. Speaking of a flutter of attraction.

Whoa. Volta reined in her heart as firmly as Emma had reined in the horse. So Scott was attractive. Volta could acknowledge that fact without acting on it.

"I visited them in Homer last summer," Stacy complained. "Why didn't they invite the school superintendent over to meet me?"

Volta laughed. "You do live in Salt Lake."

"For now. But if I found the right guy…"

"Why don't you ask them to introduce you?"

"Maybe I will." Stacy paused. "Or maybe not. What's wrong with him?"

"Nothing. What do you mean?"

"You said they *tried* to fix you up. But you didn't take the bait. So what's wrong with him?" she repeated.

"He's fine. I just wasn't interested."

"Mmm-hmm. Like you're not interested in this Dr. Scott."

"Right," Volta lied smoothly.

"So you wouldn't mind if I offer to show him around a little?"

"Who?" Volta sincerely hoped she meant the school superintendent in Homer.

"The hot doctor, of course."

"I told you, he's only here temporarily."

"No problem. So am I."

Volta tried to come up with a valid reason Stacy shouldn't go out with Scott. Or an invalid reason. Any excuse, really. Because she didn't want Stacy anywhere near Scott. For any number of reasons.

Emma was climbing down from the horse now, and she and Scott headed toward the barn. Volta watched them walking side by side, the man she'd once loved, and the girl she loved more than anyone else in the world. It was like a colliding of worlds, and yet they seemed so natural together beside that horse.

Judging by the "mmm-mmm" noise she was making, Stacy appreciated the view as well, although probably not for the same reasons. Volta knew it would take about ten minutes for Emma to unsaddle and brush her horse.

She pocketed her phone and walked over to Jim and Hannah. Stacy followed.

"So that's it for the lesson," Volta told them, hoping they'd take the hint and head out. "Emma still has to take care of her horse, so she'll be a little while. Do you want to meet up for dinner? I could order pizza."

"Why don't we wait for Emma and we can all go out for pizza together?" Hannah suggested. "We could go to that place with the games she likes so much."

"Good idea," Jim said. "Emma owes me a rematch on Skee-Ball."

Okay, that didn't work. But maybe she could still save the situation. "Emma will love that. But you should go on ahead and save us a table," Volta said.

"That's not necessary. We shouldn't have any trouble getting a table on a Wednesday," Jim said. "Besides, I want to meet this doctor and thank him for working with Emma. He's obviously a good teacher."

Looked like they weren't going anywhere. Volta glanced at Stacy, trying to think of how to lure her away, but Stacy's feet were planted solidly on the ground, her eyes glued to the barn door. No doubt planning her strategy on how to charm Scott.

Hannah nudged Jim. "Look at that girl on

the black horse. Do you suppose our Emma will be jumping over fences like that one day?"

"I'd bet on it," Jim declared. "Knowing our granddaughter, it will be sooner rather than later."

Volta wasn't too sure she wanted Emma flying over obstacles from astride large animals, but Jim was right. Once Emma set her mind to something, it wasn't easy to stop her. Emma didn't seem to know the meaning of fear. She was like her dad in that way. It fell to Volta to encourage her to try new things while keeping her safe, a constant balancing act. Volta tried hard not to use what happened to Wade as an excuse to swaddle Emma in bubble wrap, but it wasn't always easy.

Soon Emma darted out the barn door and over to her grandparents. "Did you see me ride?"

"We did!" Hannah and Jim piled on the praise. Stacy joined in as well, but she kept one eye toward the barn, and as soon as Scott appeared, she smoothed her shirt and pushed back her shoulders.

He walked over to their group. "Hello. You must be Grammy Hannah and Grandpa Jim. Emma pointed you out to me." Scott smiled. "She's doing amazingly well for only four lessons. If she continues to practice, she'll easily be ready for the show at the end of the month."

"That's great," Jim said. "Volta told us how you'd offered to help Emma after her instructor canceled. That's very generous of you."

"Not at all. I enjoy being around horses and riders, especially when they're as enthusiastic as Emma."

Stacy apparently got tired of waiting for Scott to notice her. She circled her parents and leaned against the fence. "Hi, I'm Emma's aunt."

Scott nodded. "Hello."

"Is that a Texas accent I hear?"

"Yes."

Stacy's gaze fell to the worn leather boots on his feet. "Emma's lucky to get a real Texas cowboy for a riding instructor. I'll bet you grew up punching cattle or whatever."

Scott chuckled. "Afraid not. I grew up in a suburb of Houston. I learned to ride by taking lessons, just like Emma."

"Oh." Stacy blinked, but wasn't discouraged. "Well, anyway, Volta tells me you're only in Anchorage for a short while. I'd be happy to show you around. I lived here most of my life. I could take you to my favorite restaurant this evening. I'm Stacy Morgan, by the way."

His eyes sought Volta's for a moment before they returned to Stacy. "Scott Willingham.

Thanks, but I have a lot of notes to transcribe and organize while they're still fresh in my mind."

"Scott Willingham." His name oozed out of Stacy's mouth. "That name sounds familiar."

Volta decided to take control of the situation before Stacy connected the dots. "Emma, what a day you're having. First a riding lesson and now your grandparents want to take you for pizza and games. Do you have homework?"

"Only spelling, and I already did it on the bus," Emma said. "Grandpa, can we play Skee-Ball?"

"We sure can," Jim assured her. "But today, I'm going to beat you."

"No way." Emma grinned.

While they were distracted, Volta stepped closer to Scott. "Thanks so much for giving her a lesson. This means a lot to Emma."

"Anytime. I'll try to line up those interviews. If I can swing it, we'll fly out Wednesday. I'll make the hotel reservations." He smiled at her, murmured nice-to-meet-yous to everyone, and without a second glance toward Stacy, walked toward the parking lot.

"Hotel reservations?" Stacy asked Volta, her eyebrows almost at her hairline.

"For work. We're doing a three-day sweep visiting several villages." *And sleeping in sep-*

arate hotel rooms, she almost added, but that would only make Stacy more convinced there was something going on.

Stacy smirked. "Nice work if you can get it."

Volta resisted the urge to answer.

Surprisingly, Stacy didn't say much during dinner. Of course, Emma hardly gave her an opportunity, chattering on about horses and then challenging her aunt to a game of Whac-A-Mole. It was while Emma was playing Skee-Ball against both her grandparents that Stacy asked, "What did you say Scott's last name was?"

"Willingham." Volta tried to say it as though it didn't matter.

Hannah plopped down in the seat beside them. "Ha ha. Beat them both. They wanted a rematch, but I figure I'll quit while I'm ahead." She looked from Stacy to Volta. "What were you girls talking about?"

"Nothing important," Volta said. "It's getting late for a school night. How many tokens does Emma have left?"

"This is their last game." Hannah turned to Stacy. "Are you going shopping with Emma and me tomorrow after school? Volta has a dentist appointment, so we can spoil her as much as we like."

"Sure. I could use some new shoes."

Emma skipped back to the table, with her grandfather following at a more reasonable speed. "I won! Now we get to trade in our tickets."

"You can have mine." Her grandmother handed over the row of tickets she'd earned by winning Skee-Ball. She scooted farther into the booth to make room for her husband. "By the way, we're heading down to Soldotna this weekend for salmon fishing. Do you want to come and stay with us in the motor home?"

"Yes I—" Emma's face suddenly fell. "I can't. Dr. Scott says he'll give me riding lessons on Saturday and Sunday."

"I'm sure he could reschedule so you can spend time with your grandparents," Volta said.

Emma shook her head. "But I need more lessons before I can ride in the show. And Dr. Scott says he'll be gone for three days, so we need to do it this weekend."

"Are you sure?" Jim asked. "I'm taking the drift boat. I know how much you like fishing from the boat."

Emma bared her teeth as though the decision was physically painful, but she shook her head again. "No, I need to ride. But thank you," she added and looked to her mother.

Volta smiled her approval, proud that Emma

had remembered her manners. "I'm sure once school is out, you'll get more chances to fish with Grammy and Grandpa."

"In that case, if the fish are running, we'll probably stay a few more days down at Soldotna," Jim said. "There's a low tide on Friday morning, so maybe we'll stop off at Clam Beach and gather some nice razor clams for the freezer."

"You know, I think I'll stay with Volta while you fish," Stacy announced suddenly. "That way Emma and I can spend more time together. You still have a guest room available, don't you, Volta?"

"I'm not sure that's going to work," Volta said. "I'm working out of town Wednesday through Friday and Emma will be staying with her other grandparents then."

"See, that's perfect. I can babysit Emma while you're out of town."

"I'm not a baby," Emma protested.

"Of course not. I'll supervise, not babysit."

"That would be fun! We can eat popcorn and paint our toenails and watch movies."

"They're school nights, not slumber parties," Volta said. "My parents know Emma's routine."

"Hey, I'm responsible," Stacy said. "I'll make sure she does her homework and gets to bed on time. And take her to her riding lessons. Oh, wait, there won't be any lessons while you're gone because the good doctor will be traveling with you."

"Are you sure you wouldn't rather fish?" Volta asked. "Emma will be in school all day."

"That's fine. It gives me more time to see my friends while they're in town."

Unable to come up with another excuse, Volta managed a weak smile. "In that case, *mi casa es su casa.*"

"I'll bring my stuff when I take Emma home from shopping tomorrow night. This will be great. Emma and I have so many things to talk about."

Volta had to wonder exactly what those things were.

CHAPTER NINE

EARLY WEDNESDAY MORNING, Volta tiptoed into her daughter's room. Emma looked like an angel, her eyelashes brushing her pink cheeks, her lips pursed in a sweet little O. She lay diagonally across her bed, her arm tangled in the ears of Rufus, the stuffed basset hound Leith had given her Christmas before last. Rufus was beginning to look a little threadbare from too much loving.

Volta brushed her daughter's hair away from her face. "Emma. Wake up, sweetheart."

"Ung?" Emma ask, inelegantly.

"It's morning. I have to go to work now, and you need to get up soon and get ready for school."

Emma blinked. "Is Aunt Stacy here?"

"Yes, she's here. She said something about making pancakes for breakfast."

Emma grunted, and Volta smiled. Her daughter was never at her most communicative first thing in the morning. She leaned forward and planted a kiss on Emma's forehead. "I've got to go. You're awake? You're not going to fall back asleep, are you?"

With a groan, Emma sat up. "I'm awake." She reached out her arms, and Volta gave her a big hug.

"I'll call you this afternoon, after school. You have fun with Stacy. I should be back on Friday by bedtime."

"Okay." Emma yawned. Then her eyes brightened. "Chocolate chip pancakes?"

"I don't know. You'll have to ask Stacy. Bye, sweetie. I love you to infinity."

"I love you to infinity plus one."

Volta smiled and shut the door. She grabbed her bag from her room, pausing to squirt some scented lotion onto her hands. She'd received a tropical spa set at the company gift exchange last year but hadn't opened it until last night, when she'd run out of her regular shampoo. One whiff of plumeria-scented shampoo and she was back in Hawaii. As she'd massaged the lather through her hair, the memories flowed. Good memories. She'd packed the bottle for the trip.

She carried her suitcase down the stairs and stuck her head into the kitchen, where Stacy was pouring herself a cup of coffee. "Emma's up. My mom's and dad's phone numbers are on the bulletin board. They're only two blocks away, so if you decide to go out or anything, you can drop Emma with them."

Stacy nodded as she yawned, looking remarkably like her niece with her hair hanging in her eyes.

Volta smiled. "Okay, then. My taxi's here, so you can use the car while I'm gone. Is there anything you need before I go?"

"No, I'm good. Don't work too hard."

Stacy had put an odd emphasis on the word *work*, almost as though she thought Volta was using work as an excuse to—what—sneak away to be with Scott? Whatever. Volta answered with a vague smile and headed out the door.

"You'll need the splint for four to six weeks, and you'll be good as new," Scott told the teenager in the clinic at Munak. The real Munak this time. "Ice and ibuprofen for pain," he told her mother.

"Can I still play basketball?" the girl asked.

"As long as you're wearing the splint. If you have any problems, come back and see Delores." Scott escorted them from the exam room and looked at his watch. Twelve thirty. The clinic was only supposed to be open until noon and the plan was for Delores, the physician's assistant who ran the clinic, to meet with them for the afternoon.

When he and Volta had arrived at around eleven, though, the waiting room was full. It turned out the receptionist had called in sick, and Delores was trying to run the place single-handedly. Volta had immediately offered to fill in. She was wrangling the patients and paperwork while Delores and Scott treated the patients. Luckily he'd secured his locum tenens license before coming to Alaska.

Delores popped out of the second exam room and checked in with Volta. "Where are we?"

"Three patients left—a strep test, possible ear infection and a nasty cut from a fillet knife. It looks like it's going to need stitches."

"I can handle that one, if you like," Scott offered.

"Fine." Delores appeared less frazzled than when they'd arrived. "Volta, please put the stitches in room two. I assume that wailing noise is the ear infection?"

Volta nodded. "Six months old. Tugging at her earlobe."

"Okay, put her in room three."

"All right. Do you want me to clean up room one and put the strep patient in there?"

"That would help immensely, thank you."

Since Scott traveled so often, finding his way around Delores's clinic didn't faze him. It took him a bit of time to locate all the supplies he'd need for the sutures, and he had to wait for Delores to access the anesthetic, but cleaning out the cut and stitching it together was straightforward.

The patient seemed more embarrassed than distressed. "For Christmas, the wife gave me one of those Kevlar gloves to protect my hand when I fillet fish, but I can't remember where I put it." He sighed. "I go forty years without cutting myself. Then the wife buys me the glove, I don't use it, and this happens. All the way over, she's talking. 'Why do you suppose I got you the glove, because you dance like Michael Jackson?'"

"Do you?" Scott tied off a second stitch.

The man guffawed. "Not hardly. Worst part is, she's right. I should have found the glove first. Are you married, Doc?"

"No."

"Well, let me clue you in. When a smart woman gives advice, you should always listen."

"I'll remember that. Did you at least get the fish filleted?"

"Yep, I was on the last fish. Rainbow trout. At least we'll have a good meal." He chuckled and looked at his hand. "Tonight, with the fish, my wife will make me those big onion rings—you know, the ones where you get eggs and flour and grease all over and spend half your life cleaning up the kitchen."

"Oh, yeah?"

"And she doesn't even like onions. She'll make them because she knows I like them, and she wants me to feel better." He grinned. "Nothing in the world guarantees happiness more than marrying a good woman."

Scott threaded through another stitch. "You're a lucky man, Tom Jefford."

"You bet I am."

Scott finished tying off the last stitch. "There you go. Keep it clean. If it turns red or infected, come see Delores right away. Though I doubt it'll give you any trouble."

Tom chuckled. "Now don't be telling my wife that. I need to milk it for a day or two. Maybe she'll bake a cake."

"My lips are sealed. Come back in two weeks to get the stitches out."

"Thanks, Doc." The man offered his good hand, and Scott shook it.

Delores was passing in the hallway when they stepped out. "Hi, Tom." She lifted his hand. "What happened?"

"Fillet knife."

"Ouch. You know, you should get one of those Kevlar gloves."

Tom nodded solemnly. "I think I'll do that." He looked past her shoulder and winked at Scott.

Scott opened the door to the waiting room. The woman there rose when she saw Tom. "I've already checked us out, so we're ready to go."

"Doc, I'd like you to meet the finest woman in Alaska, my wife, Marianne."

Sweet.

The woman's face turned red, but she offered her hand to Scott. "Nice to meet you."

"You, too. You take good care of Tom here. All right?"

"I will." She smiled at Scott before turning to examine the stitches in her husband's hand, shake her head and lead him out without another word.

Scott turned to find Volta coming out of exam room one. "The waiting room is empty. Everything okay?"

"It's all good. I put up the closed sign."

Delores came striding out of her office. "I called in the prescription for the ear infection. I think we're done. Volta, thank you." To Scott, she said, "You're lucky to have her working with you."

They were almost the same words he'd said to Tom, and he gave the same answer Tom had. "You bet I am." Scott was lucky. Lucky to be working with Volta on this study. Lucky she hadn't bolted the first time she saw him alone at the clinic in Sparks. Lucky she'd ever come into his life in the first place.

Delores grabbed a jacket from a hook on the wall. "Now we can go to lunch and talk about this study of yours." She gave Scott a teasing smile. "I have lots of suggestions."

"I want to hear them all."

THAT EVENING, SCOTT ambled along the concrete balcony that ran the length of the motel, reluctant to return to his stuffy room. Volta had retreated to hers immediately after dinner, saying she wanted to call home. They'd left Mike back in the bar and grill, playing darts with the locals.

The back of the Porcupine Inn overlooked what appeared to be a graveyard for dead machinery. Scott stopped at the end of the balcony to examine the rusty heap in the corner with a sapling growing through it. He was almost certain it had once been an AMC Gremlin, although how it got here, miles off the road system, was something of a mystery. It was the same in remote places the world over; people hung on to their old and broken things because one never knew when a forty-year-old hubcap might come in handy.

At least in Alaska, the trees quickly grew up around it, devouring the rotting junk and replacing it with vegetation. There was something comforting about the idea. He'd told Volta once that the past couldn't hurt you, but it wasn't true. His childhood scars had shaped the man he was today, for better or worse. But maybe new growth could crowd out old and useless emotions. It was something to think about. Volta stepped out of her room and slumped against the railing, her eyes on something far away. All day long, she'd been running at full speed, but her energy seemed to have deserted her. He stepped forward and Volta whirled toward him. "Oh, I didn't see you there."

"Are you okay?"

"Of course. Why wouldn't I be?"

"You just seemed…tired."

"Not especially." Her gaze went out over the junkyard to the horizon. "I talked to Emma."

"Is she okay?"

"She's fine. Busy. My sister-in-law, Stacy, is staying with her while we're traveling."

"That's nice." At her frown he asked, "Isn't it?"

Volta shrugged. "Stacy is not my biggest fan."

"Oh?" He had a hard time believing anyone could dislike Volta.

"She, uh, didn't want me to marry Wade."

"Why not?"

"She said we were rushing it. Accused me of trapping her brother."

"You mean—"

"No, I wasn't pregnant. She thought I was pressuring Wade to marry me quickly before he had the chance to change his mind. Really, though, Wade was the one who was in a hurry. He said he knew the first day he met me that I would be his wife, and there was no reason to wait." Volta took a few steps away before turning to face Scott. "He never put things off. Sometimes I wonder if he'd had a premonition that he would die young." She shrugged. "Once we were making dinner and I mentioned a new Turkish restaurant we should try sometime. He insisted we put the half-cooked chili in the refrigerator and go out for dinner that night."

He chuckled. "Was it good?"

"Delicious."

He thought about his conversation with Tom Jefford. "Your husband was a lucky man."

"You think so?" She seemed unconvinced.

"I do. He went after what he wanted and lived life to the fullest. And he had you."

She smiled. Almost to herself she whispered, "But was that a blessing or a curse?"

"What do you mean?" Scott asked.

"I… Never mind. It's not important." She moved to the edge of the balcony and stood stiffly.

"It sounds important." He followed her and put his hands on her shoulders. She didn't pull away. "You can talk to me, you know. I'm on your side."

She shook her head. After a few moments, she spoke. "Wade was always so good to me. The first year we were married when we lived in an apartment, he used to start my car in the winter so it would be nice and warm for me to drive to work. Every morning, even when I worked on weekends, and he could have slept in."

"I'm sure he wanted to do that, to see you smile." Scott knew how her smile could brighten anyone's day.

"Yes," Volta agreed. "He always wanted me happy. And I did my best to make him happy, too."

"He sounds lucky to me."

"But was he happy?" She stepped away from his touch before she turned and met Scott's eyes. "I loved him. I did. But did I love him enough? I did all the right things, went through all the right motions. He said he was happy, but he would have said that anyway because he never wanted to upset me. I was never sure how he was feeling because I never felt the same connection I felt..." She looked down, but not before Scott saw the truth in her eyes.

"The connection you felt with me."

She raised her chin as though she intended to deny it, but then she whispered, "Wade was my husband. Shouldn't I have felt closer to him than anyone else in the world?" Her eyes glistened. "Didn't I owe him that?"

Scott spoke softly. "I don't know. I don't have much of a frame of reference for what constitutes a successful marriage. But I know what a bad one looks like, and it isn't even close to what you've described."

A single tear ran down her cheek. She brushed it away with the back of her hand as if denying her tears. Denying her right to be sad.

Scott hated to see her hurting. He took her into his arms and held her until the trembling stopped.

He smoothed a lock of hair away from her face. Did she really think any man lucky enough to spend every day with her could be anything but happy? If only... But Scott had made his choices. "I stand by my statement. He was a lucky man."

"I was the lucky one." Volta sniffed. "He was there for me, every single day. He would have been such a good dad. I hate that Emma never got to know him."

Every single day. That was what counted, wasn't it? Not attraction. Not some vague connection. She'd married a man who was there for her. Every. Single. Day. She'd married the right man. The right father for her child. It wasn't fair that Volta had lost him, that Emma was growing up without her dad. But then, Scott had seen enough to know that life wasn't always fair. If Wade had suffered any regrets before he died, Scott felt certain that marrying Volta wasn't one of them.

CHAPTER TEN

THE REST OF the trip was a great success. Delores indeed had lots of suggestions. Good suggestions. The other people they visited filled in the blanks about the sort of support they needed. Scott felt like he had a handle on the holes in the system that the Travert Foundation might be able to help plug.

In fact, everything had gone so smoothly that Mike dropped them off in Fairbanks almost three hours earlier than they'd expected. While they waited in line at the rental car desk, Scott looked at his notes. "If I'd realized we'd be done this fast, I'd have scheduled the other two doctors I need to talk to in Fairbanks for today instead of tomorrow morning."

"Why not give them a call?" Volta suggested. "They might be available to meet with you."

"Good idea." The person in front of them finished, and they stepped up to the counter. Volta showed their driver's licenses and collected the keys while Scott made the calls. She was right; both doctors agreed that if he could get there within twenty minutes, they'd meet with him.

The doctors could only give him an hour, but Scott was able to get the information he was hoping for, as well as a sense of how supportive they might be of new services and ideas. Once they'd finished the interview, he and Volta left the hospital, but stopped outside. "I can't believe we're this far ahead of schedule. Do you want to check into the hotel now?"

"You know, it's not quite four o'clock. It's less than five hours to Talkeetna. Why don't we cancel our reservations here and drive down this evening?" she suggested.

"Will we find a place to stay at the last minute?"

"Maybe. Let me call." She found a number in her contacts and dialed. "Hi, Nate, it's Volta." She listened for a moment. "Yes, tomorrow afternoon was the plan, but we've finished up early and were thinking of driving down from Fairbanks tonight. Is Minnie up from Arizona yet?" She smiled and gave Scott a thumbs-up. "Yes, if you don't mind, that would work out great for us. The window box?" She laughed. "Sounds perfect. We'll see you in the morning, then. Thanks, Nate."

She ended the call. "We're in. Minnie Macon

is a doctor in Arizona who comes up to help staff the clinic during the summer, but she's not due until next week. Nate says we can stay in her apartment over the clinic. He's going to leave us a key."

"In the window box, I gather?"

"Yes." She smiled. "He says not to worry, that he's a better doctor than he is a gardener. Whatever that means."

"And he'll have time to meet with us in the morning?"

"Yes, before he opens the clinic. I've always loved Talkeetna. My whole family comes up for the Bluegrass Festival every summer. In fact, my brother named his dog after the town. Why don't we plan to eat a late dinner there? I've got snacks in my purse to tide us over."

"Suits me." They walked toward the rental car. "What kinds of snacks?"

"Peanut butter crackers, trail mix—" she dug around in her magic handbag "—and M&Ms."

"That should do it."

Volta held out her hand for the keys. "Let me drive. We'll be going right by Denali National Park, and with the clear weather this evening, there will be some spectacular views. You might as well enjoy them."

She was right. The hours went by quickly

as they traveled the Parks Highway. Most of the time, the silver-leafed birches that lined the road cut off any view, but every so often they would hit a rise and see mountains in the distance, rugged peaks glistening with snow.

"This would be a beautiful place to ride horses," Scott said. "I wonder if they have horse trekking in Denali National Park?"

"I think someone mentioned taking a riding tour out of Healy." Volta looked over at a trail-head beside the Nenana River. "Emma would love that. Maybe I'll bring her up sometime this summer."

"She'd be thrilled." After Emma's riding lesson, Scott was certain of that. Emma's natural balance and agility served her well in riding, but it was her confidence and love of animals that were going to make her into an exceptional horsewoman one day.

They passed a scenic pullout sign on the highway, and Volta stopped. "Sorry to make us later, but I need to call Emma before she goes to bed."

"No problem. I've been wanting to take some pictures."

While she dialed, he enjoyed the view. The sun had traveled to the northwest, and the rugged ridges of the towering mountains cast purple shadows across the snowy blanket. He snapped a few photos, admiring the majesty of the mountains. He took a pouch of Volta's trail mix from his pocket, shook a few pieces into his palm and ate them.

"Hi, sweetie. How was your day?" Volta listened for a long time, smiling as she did and making little noises of encouragement. "That's really good. Yes, I'll be there for field day. It should be fun."

Volta listened a little longer before telling Emma a few things about the trip. "I saw some of the sled dogs that ran in the Iditarod last year. Yes, they seemed very nice. And guess what? I found you a kuspuk. One of the women at Porcupine makes them for sale, and she had one just your size." She laughed. "Of course it's pretty. It's blue and light purple and it has purple rickrack. No fur. It's a summer kuspuk."

Volta pointed to a dark-headed blue jay watching from a nearby tree. Scott tossed his last peanut onto the ground. The bird swooped down to grab it.

"I'll be home tomorrow. We're spending the night in Talkeetna. Of course we'll visit the mayor. Day after tomorrow? I don't know, sweetie. He might be busy. He has a whole lot of writing to do."

After a long pause, Volta asked Emma to hang on. "She wants to know if she can fit in a lesson day after tomorrow. I told her you might be busy, but…" Volta shrugged.

Scott grinned. "Let me talk to her." He took the phone from Volta. "Hi, Emma. It's Scott."

"Hi. Mommy says you're coming home to-morrow, so can we ride the next day?"

"That's fine with me. I'll have to call the stables and make sure your horse is available, though."

"When can you do that?"

Scott checked his watch. "They won't close for another twenty minutes. I'll call now and see if I can reserve the time. Here, talk with your mom while I make the call." He handed off the phone and pulled his out. The stables had a two-hour spot available on Saturday af-ternoon, so Scott reserved it.

He gave Volta a thumbs-up. "Four thirty Sat-urday."

She smiled. "He says the lesson is at four thirty. Okay, I'll tell him. No, I think you should do that. All right, I will. Don't hang up, I need to talk to Aunt Stacy. I love you to infinity plus one. Good night."

After getting a progress report from her sister-in-law, Volta hung up. "Emma says, and I quote, 'Thank you, thank you, thank you.' And I'm supposed to hug you."

"Is that so?"

"Yes. I told her she should wait and do that herself, but she says I should hug you right now because you're super-nice."

"Well, then, you'd better do as she says." Scott grinned. "I'd hate to have to report that you didn't follow instructions."

She slid her phone in her pocket and stepped closer, putting her arms around his waist and giving a little squeeze. She looked up at him, and her face changed from amused to something softer. She tightened her hold and he ran his hands over her back. She snuggled her head against his shoulder. "Thank you," she whispered.

"You already said that."

"That was from Emma. This is from me." She gave him one more squeeze and then stepped away. "But we'd better hit the road. We still have another two hours to go, and I'm already getting hungry."

"Me, too."

The sun was setting when they turned off the highway. They passed a barnlike building on the right with a big sign out front. "A brewery?" Scott asked. "In a town this size?"

"You've been out of the country too long," Volta told him. "Microbreweries are popping up everywhere. This is a good one."

"I could use a beer right now. Is it open?"

"No, but the restaurant where I'm taking you carries their whole line."

A few minutes later, Volta pulled to a stop to let a line of people cross the road. In front of them was a downtown that looked as though it had been lifted from a hundred-year-old photograph and colorized. Quaint timber buildings had wooden signs on their porches advertising the names of the businesses.

Volta pointed to a red plank building. "We'll have to pop in there tomorrow and meet the new mayor."

"The mayor hangs out in the souvenir store?"

"Yes. At least, the old mayor always did. I've heard the new mayor is a relative."

"Why, particularly, do we need to meet the mayor? Is this someone I need to win over to the idea of adding prenatal services?"

"Oh, I doubt the mayor has any interest in medical services." The little lines at the corners of her eyes told him she was up to something, but he wasn't sure what. "You'll still want to meet him. It's tradition."

"If you say so." That was why she'd been so valuable on this project, because she knew her way around the people and traditions.

Volta went past the downtown and parked in a grassy field next to a wooden building.

Judging from the rambling lines, it looked as though the building had grown from a small cabin in fits and starts over many decades.

They went inside, where a lively crowd chattered, but the hostess immediately found them a table and handed them menus. "Hmm. Salmon quesadilla bites," he said.

"Sounds like heaven," Volta agreed. She laughed. "Do you know the first time I ever had quesadillas were the ones you made for me?"

He remembered. They'd walked back to his place after an afternoon of snorkeling, and they were starved. She'd suggested grilled cheese, but he didn't have any bread, only tortillas. "As I recall, you liked them."

"I loved them. You started my lifelong addiction to cheese and salsa. Emma loves them, too. Quesadillas are her favorite snack."

The waiter came. Scott ordered the quesadillas, a cheeseburger and a craft IPA. Volta asked for chicken pasta and a raspberry blonde ale. After the waiter left, Scott said, "I thought you never drank while you were on shift."

"I'm officially off now, once Mike dropped us at the airport."

"Then how are you getting paid for tomorrow?"

She shrugged. "I'm not. But that's okay. I've

already got my hours in, so I've earned a full paycheck this month."

"You could have mentioned it." The waiter returned with their drinks and the appetizer. Scott waited until he left to continue. "I would have talked to your boss to authorize your travel time as part of the fee we're paying."

"We're in Talkeetna, drinking beer. I don't need to be paid for the privilege. Let's just enjoy it." Volta raised her mug. "To good times and quesadillas."

They'd certainly had plenty of both during their history. Scott clinked his mug against hers and drank. "This is an excellent IPA."

"Told you."

"Yes, you did. My patient this morning, the one with the stitches, says you should always listen when a smart woman gives advice."

"He sounds like a wise man."

"Not wise enough. His wife told him to wear a protective glove when he cleaned fish."

"I'll bet he will from now on."

"Count on it." He watched her bite into one of the quesadilla wedges. Her face morphed into an expression of bliss. She always looked that way when she ate anything involving cheese and peppers.

He'd wondered, sometimes, if the Volta he remembered was a fantasy. The woman who could make him laugh, and the very next moment make him think about something in an entirely new way. The woman who seemed to carry around her own special brand of sunshine, warming everyone around her. Did she really exist?

But here she was, eleven years later, as smart and funny as ever. Not that she hadn't changed. She'd grown and matured. Become more confident. Scott liked that, and he liked seeing her with her daughter. Motherhood had given Volta a whole new dimension.

The waiter walked by carrying a tray with a flat bowl of some sort of cheesy pasta. Volta laughed. "Remember when I tried to make homemade ravioli?"

"Oh, yes." He remembered all right. She'd tried to roll out the pasta by hand using a beer bottle since his apartment kitchen had no pasta machine or even a rolling pin. Then she'd carefully cut out circles with a glass, filled them with a savory mixture of cheese, spinach and sausage, and stuck another circle on top. But when it came time to boil the pasta, the circles didn't stay stuck and the whole thing erupted into a slimy stew.

"What a fiasco."

"It wasn't that bad." Scott smiled at the memory. "The sauce was good."

"The sauce was from a jar. I can't believe you actually ate that mess."

"Well, you'd spent all afternoon making it just because I mentioned I liked ravioli."

"The expression on your face when I set the plate in front of you." Volta laughed and shook her head. "You probably never looked at ravioli the same way again after that experience."

"I took a cooking class once in Italy, and the instructor showed us how to make ravioli. I think the problem was that you didn't have the right kind of flour, and that you tried to put too much filling inside the pockets."

"Probably. Have you taken lots of cooking classes?"

"No. Honestly, I almost never cook. That class was during a four-day vacation I took along with a colleague and his wife about five years ago. I haven't taken another one, other than a couple of days in Houston every year or two. In fact, last time I checked, I had almost six months of vacation banked."

"Gosh, you are a workaholic."

It stung a little when she said it, even though it was true. Especially because it was true. Scott remembered his stepmother throwing that word around a lot during the final months before she moved out.

Only once after they were gone did his father express regret. "I shouldn't have married her," he'd mused, as much to himself as to Scott. "I'm not the sort of man who can keep his work life separate from his private life." And then he'd turned to Scott. "You're the same. You're focused, and that's what makes you good at what you do. Men like us shouldn't be married."

He didn't add, "And they certainly shouldn't have children," but it was true. As a child, Scott had hardly known his father, and the situation hadn't improved much since then. During the three days Scott had spent in Houston before he came to Alaska, they'd only eaten two meals together. And his father had spent most of that time trying to sell him on the idea of coming into practice with him.

Maybe that was his way of trying to make up for the time he didn't spend raising Scott. Or maybe he just wanted more hands on deck. Regardless, Scott had no interest in becoming a sports surgeon with his father.

"Scott?" Volta had that look of concern on her face. "Are you okay?"

He managed a smile. "I'm great." And he was. He was in Alaska, sitting across the table from a charming and beautiful woman. Not sitting alone at a table in a grand house, picking at whatever dinner the nanny had fixed for him. That was all in the past. Their waiter brought their entrees and asked if they wanted another beer. "Sure," Scott told him.

"I'm still working on this one. Thanks." Volta shot him that dazzling smile and the waiter paused in the middle of gathering up the empties to smile back.

Scott couldn't much blame the guy. She was stunning. Scott picked up his cheeseburger and closed his eyes, breathing in the smoky, meaty aroma. He liked traveling around the world, trying all different types of food, but the one thing he always missed was American cheeseburgers. No one else seemed to do them quite right.

Volta laughed. "You look like you can't decide whether to bite it or kiss it."

He opened his eyes and grinned at her. "Maybe both. I haven't had a good cheeseburger in over a year." He took his first bite, reveling in the taste. "So good."

Volta watched him, amused, while she tasted her pasta. The waiter brought his second beer, inquired if they needed anything, and left them alone. Scott took another bite and set aside his burger so that he could wash it down with a swig of beer. "How's yours?"

"Try it." Volta scooped up a forkful of pasta and held it up for him.

Scott leaned forward and ate off her fork. "That is good. Not as good as my cheeseburger, though."

"Oh, wow. Is that an owl?" Volta pointed out the window behind Scott's left shoulder.

He turned to look but didn't see anything except the tiny yellow leaves of a birch limb brushing against the glass. When he turned back, Volta was nibbling at one of the sweet potato cilantro fries that had come with his burger. He grinned. "You could have asked. I'll share."

"It's more fun to steal them."

He was tempted to start nibbling at the other end of the fry and work his way closer to her lips, like the famous scene with the dogs eating spaghetti, but he managed to tamp down that urge. He did stick his fork into her pasta and swipe an olive while she was busy with the fry.

She laughed, and Scott realized laughter was one of his favorite sounds in the whole world. Well, not all laughter, just Volta's. There was nothing extraordinary about it, and yet if he heard a recording of fifty people laughing, he was sure he could pick hers out in seconds.

Once they finished their meals, the waiter

stopped by. "Could I interest you in dessert? Apple tart? Hot fudge brownie sundae?"

Volta shook her head, but Scott had seen that telltale lip lick when the waiter mentioned brownies. "Fudge sundae, please, with two spoons."

The waiter returned shortly with the decadent dessert, smothered with thick chocolate sauce and whipped cream. Volta sighed. "I shouldn't."

"But you will." Scott handed her a spoon.

"I will." She tasted the first bite and closed her eyes. "Heaven. Tomorrow I'll eat salad."

"Tomorrow can take care of tomorrow. Tonight, just enjoy."

After they'd finished dinner, Volta drove a few blocks away and stopped in front of an L-shaped two-story building made of pale logs. A wooden sign with a red cross hung over the railing of a front porch tucked into the bend of the house. A green window box was full of dead marigolds. Up above, a narrow balcony jutted from a gable wall, with a flower box full of purple and yellow flowers hanging from the railing.

Volta reached under the yellow leaves and plucked out a wooden daisy attached to a key. "Looks like Nate was a little overoptimistic about the last frost. He should have used pansies in both flower boxes." She took the flagstone path to the rear of the building. Scott followed her, carrying their bags.

A flight of stairs with metal grates for treads led up to a landing on the second floor. There was barely room on the landing for the two of them and their small suitcases. Volta unlocked the door, pushed it open and flipped on the switch.

A paper lantern lit up overhead, casting a warm glow across the room. A small kitchen took up one end of the room, with a table in the middle and a couch and two easy chairs in front of a corner fireplace. The vaulted ceiling was lined with tongue-and-groove cedar. The lack of dust on the end tables made Scott believe someone was regularly cleaning the place in the doctor's absence, although the air was a little stuffy.

Volta crossed the room and opened a pair of narrow French doors to let in the cool evening air. She turned and smiled. "Our home for tonight. What do you think?"

Our home. He rather liked the sound of that. "I feel like if I listen closely, I might hear cowbells and yodeling."

"Not likely. Huskies howling, maybe. You can take the bedroom." She walked through an archway near the living area into a hallway, opened a door, and removed a set of sheets and a blanket. "I'll sleep on the couch."

"I'll take the couch," Scott offered.

She shook her head. "Your feet would hang over the edge. I've slept on it before and it's just right for me." She spread the sheets onto the couch.

"Do you visit your friend here often?"

"No. Nate's an old buddy, but Minnie and I just met last summer. She let me stay with her while I helped at a local health fair. They dressed me as a vampire and had me taking blood samples."

She collected another set of sheets from the closet and carried them into a bedroom. The roof sloped sharply over a sleigh bed. Volta snapped a sheet to spread it across the mattress and tucked a corner in. Scott reached past her to move the pillows out of the way. A strand of her hair brushed his cheek, releasing the scent of plumeria and a million memories.

Volta turned her head, bringing her face just inches from his. Their eyes met and held for a long moment. "I, um…" Volta glanced at the bed as though trying to remember what she'd been about to say. "I'll get a blanket." She disappeared into the hall. Scott tucked the fitted sheet around the mattress and emptied his pockets onto the nightstand.

Volta returned a moment later. She laid the blanket on a chair and picked up the horseshoe charm lying on the tabletop among the spare change. "This was your mother's, wasn't it?"

"Yes."

"It's sweet that you carry it with you." She returned it to the nightstand and left him to finish making the bed. When he came into the living room later, Volta was standing outside on the tiny balcony. She tilted back her head and closed her eyes. Much like the pansies cascading over the railing, her delicate appearance belied her resilient nature. When he joined her outside, a spruce-scented breeze cooled his face.

He stood behind her, not touching her, but near enough to feel the heat of her body. Down below, twilight shadows and glowing windows made the town look as quaint and cozy as those Christmas snow globes people collected. Volta let out a deep sigh and leaned back against his chest. Almost of their own accord, his arms encircled her, pulling her close.

He rested his face against the top of her head, her scented hair soft against his cheek. Then she turned and reached up to cup her hand against his face. She raised herself onto her toes and let her lips touch his. The kiss was tentative, barely making contact. Almost as though she was afraid. Of what, he wasn't sure.

She drew back and in the twilight, he couldn't make out the blue of her eyes, but he could clearly see the softness of her expression, the curve of those luscious lips. She slid her arms around his neck.

The second kiss was anything but tentative. He brought her closer, slanted his head to bring the kiss deeper. Warm and enticing, it felt like coming home. And to a man without a home, that was the most amazing feeling in the world.

After a satisfyingly long kiss, she drew back just far enough to smile at him. "Scott?"

"Hmm?"

"Why did you come to Alaska? Really?"

"To find you," he admitted. "I told myself it was to make sure you were okay, but really I wanted to be with you again. Even if it was only for a little while."

She brushed a strand of hair from his forehead and then traced her finger along the edge of his jaw. "I'm glad." She let out a long sigh. "I may be sorry later, but right now, I'm glad you came." She snuggled her head against his shoulder, and he held her tight.

Behind them, the pale silver moon peeked from between the branches of the surrounding trees. It made its way higher, eventually rising above the level of the trees and into the sky. The air grew cooler. And still he held her.

Finally, she stirred. "It's late, and we have an early morning tomorrow. We'd better get some sleep."

"I suppose."

She popped onto her tiptoes to brush a kiss across his cheek and then squeezed past him into the living room, where she shed her sweater and pulled a few things from her suitcase. "Give me five minutes in the bathroom, and then it's all yours." She disappeared into the hallway.

He picked up the hooded sweater she'd been wearing and held it to his nose, breathing in the plumeria scent that clung to the yarn.

She returned, now dressed in loose pajama pants and a T-shirt. The pajama fabric was printed with moose, complete with canes and top hats, dancing their way across the lines of the plaid. He couldn't help but chuckle.

She smiled. "A gift from Emma."

"She has good taste."

"I know. You can't go wrong with dancing moose."

"A classic motif." He hung her sweater over the back of a chair.

Volta lay on the couch and pulled the covers up under her chin. "Good night, Scott."

He bent to drop a kiss on her forehead, made his way to the hallway and flicked off the light. When he looked back, he could just make out the shape of Volta's face, against the dark cloud of hair spread on her pillow. "Good night, Volta. Sleep well."

CHAPTER ELEVEN

Volta woke the next morning to the heavenly aroma of fresh coffee, and if she wasn't mistaken, vanilla. She opened one eye. Scott was perched on the coffee table beside the couch, waving a take-out cup under her nose. "Good morning, sunshine."

"Is that a vanilla latte from Duce Goose?"

"It is."

She sat up, accepted the cup and took a sip. "Mmm."

He picked up another cup from the table and drank from it. "This is good coffee."

Volta took another swig. "Any coffee I don't have to get out of bed and make is good coffee. This is bliss."

He grinned. "I brought you a muffin from the coffee cart. Or we can go out for breakfast and save the muffin for later if you'd rather."

"What kind of muffin?"

"Cranberry almond. I already finished mine. They're good."

"Yum. Gimme." She set her coffee on a

coaster. "I mean, yes, please, I'd like a muffin. It was thoughtful of you to bring me breakfast."

He winked. "It's okay. Emma isn't here. You don't have to set a good example." He stood and headed for the door. "I'll go for a walk around town while you dress."

"You showered? I didn't even hear you."

"Good, I'm glad I didn't disturb you. We're supposed to be at the clinic downstairs in forty-five minutes. Does that give you enough time?"

"More than enough." She could be dressed and ready to roll in less than a minute if necessary. Forty-five minutes to shower, dress and eat was luxurious. "Thanks, Scott."

"For what?"

"Breakfast. Setting up the meeting. Letting me sleep in."

"No problem. See you soon." He smiled again before slipping out the door.

Volta yawned and took another sip of her coffee. She loved, loved, loved vanilla lattes, but she seldom indulged in them. Too many calories. Too expensive. But Scott remembered how much she used to enjoy them. In Hawaii eleven years ago, coffee stands weren't on every street corner the way they were in Anchorage now, but he would regularly walk several blocks out of his way to bring her favorite coffee drink.

And now he was doing it again. Bringing her coffee. Letting her sleep. Taking care of her. She was so used to being the person who took care of everyone else, it felt rather odd to be the one taken care of. But in a nice way.

She lingered over the muffin and coffee, and then, after a glance at the clock, jumped into the shower. Fifteen minutes later, she'd finished dressing and was standing in front of the mirror, brushing her hair, when she heard the door shut.

"Volta?" Scott called.

"In here. I'm ready." She packed the brush in her bag and dragged it into the living room. He was leaning against the door, thumbing through a paperback book with a bloody knife on the cover he'd no doubt found at the used book store a couple of blocks away. Scott had always been a fan of old mysteries.

He looked up, letting his eyes roam from her toes to her face. He smiled, as though she'd made his day just by being in the same room. He set the book on the kitchen counter. "You look nice."

Volta glanced down. She wore plain khaki pants and a blue-green shirt. Maybe it was a step up from scrubs or the flight suit, but hardly runway fashion. However, the shirt was one her brother's girlfriend, Sabrina, had designed, with curved seams that followed her shape and buttons with an iridescent sheen like a mallard's head. "Thank you. Is Nate here yet?"

"I saw a rusty green Jeep pull up in front."

"That's him. Let's go."

Nate greeted them and hugged her like the old friend he was. Since he'd come in early before the clinic opened, they were able to talk uninterrupted for almost an hour. Scott got answers to all his questions and Nate had some ideas to offer, as well. Ten minutes before opening time, Nate's receptionist, Zoe, arrived and started banging around the office, opening windows and checking rooms.

"That's my cue. I know I have at least two people coming in as soon as we open, but if you have more questions I can try to find time for you later this morning."

"I guess we've covered it." Scott handed Nate a card. "If you have questions or ideas for me, I'll be in Anchorage another week or so, working on the report. Thanks for making time to talk with me."

"Sure. I appreciate your finding out what's needed first instead of jumping in and duplicating other efforts. It sounds like a good project."

The men shook hands. Volta hugged Nate again. "Thanks. And thanks for letting us use the apartment. I'll drop off the key with Zoe before we go. Give Brit my love."

"Will do."

She and Scott left Nate's office and stepped into the reception area. Zoe called, "Volta, hi. I thought you were coming in this afternoon."

"We were." Volta crossed to the window. "But we finished early and drove down last night. Zoe, this is Scott."

"I know. We talked on the phone when he was setting up the meeting."

"Zoe already gave me some good feedback about her experience with prenatal care," Scott explained.

Volta waited for them to exchange greetings and then asked Zoe, "How's everything? Is that baby crawling yet?"

"Crawling? He's walking. Only nine months old, and he's already into everything."

"Sounds like you have your hands full."

"You said it. So you're all finished with Nate? I don't need to schedule anything for later?"

"Nope, we're all done."

"What are your plans for the day?"

"We're stopping off in Willow on the way back to Anchorage," Scott told her.

"When?"

He consulted his notes. "Our appointment isn't until four. I thought I'd call and see if we can move it up."

"Or," Zoe said with a mischievous smile, "you could take advantage of being ahead of schedule and play hooky for a while. Roger is doing a preseason flight today to check out conditions and I'm sure he'd be willing to let you tag along."

"On the glacier?" Volta asked. She'd always wanted to do a glacier landing but could never justify the expense.

"Yeah. I'll give him a buzz, make sure it's still on." She pulled out her phone and walked away from the window to make the call.

Volta turned to Scott. "What do you think? You want to do a glacier flight? Or should we stick to business?"

"What kind of flight are we talking about, exactly?"

"Roger, Zoe's husband, is a pilot. He flies Denali climbers to base camp, but his main income is flying tourists to see the sights and land on the glacier. I've heard it's spectacular."

Scott grinned. "You really want to do this, don't you?"

"I'd love to, but you're the guy in charge. If we should move on down the road, we can."

He shrugged. "They're not expecting us in Willow until later and I don't even know if they could see us early."

Zoe came back. "Roger says he'd love to have you. Can you be at the airport in an hour?"

Volta looked at Scott. He nodded. "We'll be there," Volta told Zoe. "That gives us time to walk around downtown."

Zoe came from behind the reception window and crossed the room to click on the open sign and unlock the door. "Are you going to introduce Scott to the mayor?"

"That's the plan." Volta opened the door and held it for a man sneezing into a tissue to enter. "Thanks, Zoe. This should be great."

"Enjoy." Zoe waved goodbye before turning to the man. "Hay fever starting early, Peter?"

SCOTT HAD NEVER expected this assignment to include a glacier landing. He felt behind his ear to make sure the patch he'd applied before the flight was still in place. These patches were good for three days, so that should get him through this flight. The sun felt warm on Scott's face as he strolled alongside Volta on the way downtown. He reached for her hand and she gave his a squeeze.

Downtown was a relative term. Downtown Talkeetna was more like a grassy meadow with a ring of cabin-like buildings at the edges. Volta led Scott into what seemed to be a combination souvenir store and ice cream shop. It was empty except for a man sweeping the area next to the cash register. "Good morning. I'll bet you're here to meet the mayor."

Volta grinned at him. "Yes, sir. I've visited Mayor Buddy Jasper many times, but I haven't had the pleasure of meeting the new mayor."

"Mayor Tips isn't quite as gregarious as Buddy Jasper, but he's learning. Right this way." The man set his broom aside and led them toward the back of the store.

Scott looked at Volta and raised his eyebrows. "The mayor hides in the storeroom?" he whispered.

"You'll see," she whispered back.

The stepped up to an alcove, where a young brown-and-fawn cat lay sleeping on the seat of a chair. "Meet Mayor Tips. He served as Buddy's apprentice for a year."

Scott chuckled. "Mayor Tips, huh?"

"Duly elected in a completely official unofficial write-in election." He chuckled. "I'll leave you to get acquainted."

The mayor opened one blue eye and regarded them. Apparently deciding Volta was worth waking up for, he yawned, and then stretched, doubling the length of his body. He reached out with one back foot, and then the other. Finally, he stepped forward and rubbed his jaw against Volta's hand.

She stroked the length of his body. "You're so soft." The cat allowed her to stroke him twice more before rising onto his back feet and resting his front feet against her chest, demanding to be picked up.

Volta cradled him and moved closer to Scott. "Mayor Tips, I'd like you to meet Dr. Scott Willingham. He's in Alaska for work, but I told him he couldn't come to Talkeetna without meeting you." She leaned closer to the cat's head. "He's a pretty good guy, even though he's not from here."

The cat held a paw toward Scott. Scott gently took the paw between his thumb and forefinger and shook it. "It's an honor."

The cat closed his eyes in a condescending answer to Scott's greeting, and rubbed his head against Volta's shoulder. She smoothed the fur along his back. She'd always loved animals. Scott had been surprised when she'd said she had no pets, but he could see that her job schedule would make it difficult. Just like his.

Soon, she set the mayor back onto his chair.

"I suppose we'd better head out if we're going flying."

Scott bought a cat-shaped pewter brooch, figuring it was the least he could do to help the business that supported the town mayor and gave Volta so much pleasure. He pinned it to Volta's shirt. "There. Now you're official."

"Thank you." She smiled, admiring his gift.

They returned to the clinic to collect the car and their jackets. Volta drove them to the small airport and parked. Two men stood talking beside a red Beaver parked to the side of the runway. The plane rested on three wheels, but each wheel protruded through a ski. Volta waved, and the taller of the men waved back.

"Hi, Roger," Volta said as they approached. "This is Scott Willingham. He's a doctor with DEMA, in Alaska doing a study."

"Hi. Zoe told me about you." He offered his hand to Scott. Both men wore caps and shirts with the tour company logo. "I'm Roger Nelson. This is Tig Gustaf, another staff pilot. We're doing a trial run today to check out conditions before we start four-a-day landings next week."

Scott shook hands with both men. "This is a treat. I've flown in small planes, but I've never landed on a glacier."

"Glaciers are cool." Roger laughed at his own joke.

Tig groaned. "Do you say that to every single group you take up?"

"Aw, lighten up." Roger poked him with his elbow. "It's funny."

"Lucky you're a good pilot," Tig said, shaking his head, "because you could never make it as a comedian."

"Just get on the plane." Roger gave Tig a good-natured shove. He shot a grin toward Scott and Volta. "I have to practice my tourist talk."

Scott glanced over at Volta, who was chuckling under her breath. "Don't lose your cool," he whispered, which instantly made her snort with laughter.

"See," Roger told Tig. "Funny."

They loaded into the plane. Tig sat up next to Roger, leaving Scott and Volta their choice of the remaining back seats. They sat in the middle, beside the biggest windows, and put on their headsets. Once Roger finished his checklist procedures, they took off.

As soon as they cleared the trees, Denali and the other mountains loomed up ahead of them. They flew past the highway and spotted the cluster of lodges at the entrance to the national park. A gravel road led into the park, a faint line almost lost in a vast area.

A little further on, they flew over a valley. A milky river wound back and forth across the emerald-colored valley floor and disappeared between two peaks, one covered with snow and the other a peachy color. Behind the peaks, more mountains rose in shades of buff and purple and gray, all set off against streaks of brilliant green vegetation. Roger's voice came over the headset. "These are the Polychrome Mountains, so named because of the vibrant colors in the various, uh—" he paused for a moment "—rocks."

Tig's laughter came over the headphone. "Geological formations."

"That's what I said," Roger replied. "Rocks. And as we get further in, you can see several small glaciers tucked up in the steep-sided valleys here."

Scott spotted the telltale parallel lines of a glacier winding between two peaks below a vast snowfield. They flew over it and came to another wide valley.

Roger continued his spiel. "That boulder you see all by itself on the right doesn't seem too big, but it's actually about the size of a school bus. It's an example of a glacial erratic. See how it looks different from any of the rocks around it? That was because a glacier may have carried it a hundred miles or more before leaving it there."

Volta leaned across Scott's lap to see out his window. Her wide eyes and bright smile reminded him of how Emma looked at her birthday party. Volta flew over and around the Alaska wilderness for a living, and yet she still got excited about a flight-seeing adventure.

She pointed toward the lower slopes above the valley. Scott could make out a group of something, presumably animals, milling over a pass there. Tig validated his assumption. "There's a herd of caribou on your right at about two o'clock."

As they climbed higher, the mountains and glaciers became bigger. Tig pointed out the Muldrow Glacier, and the peaks of Denali and Foraker. "And there's Ruth Glacier, our destination."

The plane descended, flying between two rocky cliffs and following the Great Gorge, a steep section of glacier a mile wide. They passed over several huge crevasses before the skis touched down on the snowfields in the Ruth Amphitheatre. The plane slid to a stop, and Roger jumped out to open the doors and offer a hand to Volta. She hopped down, and Scott followed.

"It's amazing," Volta said, gazing across the expanse of the glacier.

Scott had to agree. It was easy to see from the air that glaciers were simply rivers of ice, flowing ever so slowly downhill. What wasn't apparent was that these weren't normal-sized rivers. The glacier was at least a mile wide.

"How deep is the ice we're standing on?" Scott asked.

"Twelve hundred meters, according to one measurement," Roger said.

Tig added, "To give you perspective, the tallest building in the world is a little over eight hundred meters, and the Grand Canyon is a little over eighteen hundred deep at its lowest point."

"What's that?" Volta pointed to a tiny structure in the distance.

"That's the Don Sheldon Mountain House. You know who Don Sheldon is?"

"A famous bush pilot, right?"

"Yes. He pretty much pioneered glacier landings. Anyway, he built that cabin in the sixties. Flew in all the materials strapped to the side of his Piper Super Cub or inside his Cessna 180."

"Wow. Now, that is a private getaway," Scott said.

"Walk around the glacier if you want,"

Roger said. "When we bring the tourists, we usually stay around twenty minutes."

Scott and Volta walked away from the plane. Even with their jackets, it was chilly walking over the snowfields, but invigorating. Scott captured a photo of the plane that had brought them in. He'd snapped a couple of exposures on his phone when something cold smashed against the back of his head.

He wheeled around in time to see Volta grinning while she packed another snowball. "Now you've gone and done it," he warned, tucking his phone inside his pocket.

She laughed and threw the snowball, but he deflected it. He scooped up a handful and ran toward her, packing it as he went. She squealed and ran, but he threw the ball and hit her in the middle of her back. Since she was wearing a down jacket, it probably hardly registered, but she spun around and fired off a snowball, hitting him in the shoulder.

She was scooping up another handful of snow when he caught up with her and wrapped his arms around her. "Oh, no you don't."

"Oh?" She twisted in his arms until she was facing him. Her face, inches away, was too tempting. He bent to kiss her. Just as their lips touched, she pressed the snow into the back of his neck.

"Oh, man." He brushed it out of his collar. "You don't play fair."

She laughed. "All's fair in love and war."

"And which is this? War or love?" he asked.

Suddenly she stopped laughing. She reached up to dust the snow away from his collar. "There. Did I get it all?"

"It's fine." Scott hated the awkwardness his question had caused. "Here, why don't you pose so that I can get a picture of you with the plane in the background?"

"We'd better join Roger and Tig. They're probably eager to get home."

It sounded to Scott more like she was the one eager to get home. Why mention love? It only made things worse. "Volta, last night—"

"Doesn't change anything. I get it."

Unfortunately, she was right. "I'm sorry I can't be the kind of man you need." The kind like her husband. Someone who was there for her every single day.

"I said I get it. You don't need to apologize." She started for the plane. "Come on, they're waiting."

He caught up to her. "Maybe we can get one of them to take a picture of us together before we go."

Tig and Roger were obviously accustomed to tourists requesting photos and suggested several poses with and without the plane. Once they'd finished, they loaded up and took off across the ice and into the blue sky.

Volta stared out the window, but she no longer had that look of wide-eyed wonder. Instead, her expression was pensive.

All's fair in love and war? If love were the least bit fair, he and Volta would be together. But he'd made his choices and she'd made hers. A couple of kisses on a balcony and a snowball fight on a glacier couldn't rewrite the past.

CHAPTER TWELVE

"Look. The leaves on the birches have gotten bigger, just in the three days we were gone. According to local lore, once the leaves are the size of a mouse's ear, it's safe to plant your garden." Why did she say that? Volta realized, even as the words came out of her mouth, that the observation was something only a gardener or Emma would be interested in. Ever since she'd made that stupid remark about love and war, nothing between them had felt the same.

But Scott dutifully looked at the trees while waiting for traffic to clear. "They're greener, too. I guess it's really spring."

"Yes. I'll probably plant tomorrow."

"Ah." Scott pulled the car they'd rented in Fairbanks up beside his car in the parking lot of Puffin Medical Transport, popped the trunk and transferred the suitcases. "I'll follow you to the rental car return and take you home."

Volta moved into the driver's seat. "That would be great, thanks."

She circled the airport and turned into the

rental car area. In her mirror she could see Scott. In another couple of minutes, she would get in the car with him. Ten minutes later, he would drop her off at home. And her part of the study would be done. It may have been a mistake, spending three days on the road with her ex. Every minute together had felt like old times. They still laughed at the same jokes, liked the same foods, noticed the same details.

It was almost as though they'd never been apart, at least up until she mentioned love and war. Why did she do that? Why bring up love? Love wasn't the answer, not in their case. Love was what had torn her heart in two once before. Because she'd loved him, and he'd loved her, but not enough to change his life plans.

Yet that was a long time ago, when Volta was only twenty. She'd learned more about love since then. Love wasn't a chain, binding people together. If you loved someone, you wanted their happiness, even if it meant sacrificing some of your own. Marriage and parenting had taught her that.

Sometimes she had to say no to Emma, because what Emma wanted either wasn't good for her or wasn't possible. Seeing Emma sad and disappointed did nothing for Volta's happiness, but it was necessary. Just like it was going to be necessary to say goodbye to Scott. Again.

The attendant zapped her car with the scanner. "All set. Thanks. Need a lift to the terminal?"

"No thanks." She made her way across the short-term lot to the parking area where Scott waited.

He looked up from his phone when she opened the door. "I would have picked you up."

"I didn't mind the walk. It felt good to stretch my legs." Volta waited until he'd started the engine and pulled out. "You think you have all the information you need for the study?"

"I believe so. After talking with all those people and visiting the bush, I have specific recommendations in mind. I only need to organize the supporting notes to demonstrate how the fund can do the most with the least." He merged with traffic before asking, "What are you going to plant?"

"I'm sorry, what?"

"In your garden."

And she thought he hadn't been paying attention. She smiled. "Sugar snap peas. Carrots. Leaf lettuce. Green onions. Zucchini. Sunflowers, because Emma loves them. Maybe radishes because they're quick. My rhubarb will be ready to cut before long, and my raspberries will ripen in August. I'm thinking of starting a strawberry bed."

"I like strawberry rhubarb pie."

"You've never met a pie you didn't like."

"True." He fiddled with the visor, blocking out the sun. "It must be very satisfying to watch something you've cared for grow and thrive."

Volta got the idea they were talking about more than gardening now. "It is satisfying. I like my job because it's rewarding to help someone in trouble, but raising something, whether it's a carrot or a daughter, is the most satisfying thing in the world. At least, I think so."

He glanced at her, a fond expression on his face. "You're a nurturer. You always have been."

Was she? Maybe that was why she'd been drawn to Wade. His ultimate goals were home and family. He'd loved what he called her nesting instincts, whether they involved painting the bathroom or growing herbs in the window over the sink. He would have been so happy when she told him she was pregnant. If she'd had the chance. "Thanks for letting me be a part of this project," she said to Scott. "I'm sure some real good will come of it."

"I feel the same. Your contributions were

invaluable. Thank you." He turned in to her neighborhood and slowed almost to a crawl. "I feel like I need to say something about last night."

"You already did, on the glacier. Remember?" The kiss they shared was one of those memories she planned to tuck away, one of those rare precious moments she could pull out now and then to cherish. Not something she wanted to dissect in a conversation. "Why can't we just leave it alone?"

"Because…" He pulled the car to the curb and turned to her. "Because I'm—well, *sorry* isn't the word because I'm not sorry. I'm glad we had that time together, and I'm glad we kissed."

"I'm glad, too."

He met her gaze. "Where do we go from here?"

"There is no we." She reached to touch his cheek, to smooth away the sadness in his eyes, and then drew her hand away. "I'm a mother now, and you said it yourself. You're not the kind of man I need. Not someone who'd be in my daughter's life in the long term."

"What if—"

"You know you're devoted to DEMA. You haven't had a vacation in five years, Scott. Yes, last night I fell for you all over again, but that doesn't mean—"

"You fell?"

"It doesn't change anything."

"Doesn't it?"

"No," she said, firmly. "It doesn't."

"What about my lesson with Emma tomorrow?"

"What about it? As far as Emma is concerned, we're coworkers and friends. No kisses, no promises. Emma has no idea I knew you before she was born, and she doesn't need to know. I appreciate the time you're spending with her, teaching her to ride, but last night notwithstanding, that's all it is."

"Understood." He drove the final two blocks before he turned in to the driveway. He fetched her suitcase from the trunk, and she tugged it along the sidewalk. "Volta?" His voice was soft.

"Yes?" she asked without turning.

"Last night, I fell, too."

Volta paused. She didn't want to watch him drive away. Quickly, she slipped through the side door via the garage.

Dropping her bag at her feet, she entered the kitchen, only to be almost bowled over by Emma launching herself into her arms. Volta laughed and hugged her daughter. The way

Emma was growing, she wouldn't be able to catch her like this much longer. Dressed in her pajamas with damp hair, Emma smelled of shampoo and toothpaste, all but ready for bed.

Volta gave her a big squeeze and set her on her feet. "Hi. How was the math test?"

"I got an A. Only one wrong answer."

"That's great." Volta turned to Stacy, who was pushing the start button on the dishwasher. "Thanks for staying with Emma. Did everything go okay?"

"Sure. We had fun, didn't we, Emma?"

Emma nodded. "We looked at pictures." She grabbed Volta's hand and pulled her toward the living room. "Come on, I'll show you."

The coffee table in the living room was piled high with familiar boxes and albums. When Hannah and Jim had sold their house and moved to a smaller place in Homer, they'd divided the family photos between Wade and Stacy, and it looked like Stacy had dug them all out of the bookcases in the hallway.

"Look." Emma picked up a book with the word *Memories* splashed across the cover. It wasn't one of Hannah's, but the scrapbook Volta had started the day she and Wade got back from their honeymoon. Emma flipped to a marked page about a quarter of the way through the book. "This is Daddy getting a trophy." The photo showed him with an enormous grin on his face, dressed in down bib and jacket with his goggles pushed up onto his forehead. He held the silver cup up over his head while the surrounding crowd cheered. Volta had decorated the page with snowflakes and a cutout of a trophy.

"That was when he won in the Arunka Open. He said it was one of his best races ever."

Emma set the book on the table and Stacy picked it up to examine the page.

Emma found another album. "Here he is when he was eight like me." Two pages were filled with photos of a birthday party. Wade was blowing out candles on a cake decorated with ninjas. Volta smiled. It looked exactly like something he would have chosen.

Then she noticed the girl in the background. Five-year-old Stacy was staring at her brother with rapt admiration as though blowing out the candles was a miraculous feat. Volta looked over at Stacy, sitting in the chair with the scrapbook in her lap. The expression on her face as she gazed at the picture of her brother with his trophy wasn't much different. He'd always been her hero.

To Stacy, Wade was larger than life. Nobody would ever be good enough for her brother.

Volta certainly wasn't. The sad thing was, Stacy was right. Volta wasn't good enough. She'd never given Wade her whole heart, because she'd already given away a piece of it before she met him. But she'd loved him the best way she knew how, and he'd told her over and over how happy she made him. He'd given her a daughter. And that alone would make her love him for the rest of her life.

The clock on the mantel chimed. Volta looked up. "Do you realize it's thirty minutes past your bedtime, young lady? Come on, I'll tuck you in."

"Okay." Emma gave her that half abashed, half proud smirk she always did when she thought she was getting away with something. She started up the stairs with her mother right behind her. "Is Dr. Scott still going to give me a lesson tomorrow?" she asked as they reached the landing.

"That's the plan." Volta shooed her into her room, tucked her into bed and reached for the book on the nightstand. "One chapter, and then right to sleep, okay?"

"Okay." Emma hugged her stuffed dog. "How much longer is Aunt Stacy going to be here?"

Volta looked up from the book. "I'm not sure. Why?"

"I just wondered." Emma snuggled deeper into her pillow. "I don't think she likes Dr. Scott."

"Why would you say that?"

Emma shrugged. "She said I didn't have to listen to him because he's not my daddy. Is that true?"

Volta was beginning to question the wisdom of leaving Emma with Stacy for three days. "He's teaching you to ride horses, just like your teacher at school teaches you to read and do math and things like that. If you didn't listen to people who teach you, how would you learn anything?"

"That's what I thought." Emma closed her eyes and listened while Volta read a chapter from the latest book Emma had checked out of the library, which was, of course, about a girl and a horse. It looked like they'd advanced a chapter or two while Volta was away.

As Volta finished the chapter, Emma was teetering on the verge of sleep. Volta kissed her daughter's forehead. "Good night, sweetie. I love you to infinity."

"Plus one," Emma murmured. "G'night."

Volta eased the door shut and walked downstairs. Stacy had disappeared somewhere. Volta gathered up an armload of albums and carried them to the hall, where she sat down to arrange them on the bottom shelf.

"You can't just hide him away in a drawer, you know." Stacy stood staring down at her with her hands on her hips. "And pretend he never existed."

"What are you talking about?" Volta slid two more albums into place.

"Wade. You just pack him away on a shelf while you go wandering around the state with your boyfriend. Does that guy even know you were married?"

"You know very well I was working." And kissing, but that was absolutely none of Stacy's business.

"I figured out why his name seemed familiar. He's the guy who dumped you in Hawaii. Were you having an affair with him while you were married to Wade?"

Volta rolled her eyes. "Stacy, you're delusional. First of all, Scott has been working overseas since he finished his residency in Hawaii."

"See, you know exactly where he was, and when. If you weren't having an affair, you were in contact with him. It's still cheating."

That did it. Volta stood up and locked her eyes onto Stacy's. She made the conscious decision not to yell. Instead she enunciated each syllable. "I'm going to make this perfectly clear. I never cheated on your brother. In any way. Ever." She took a step closer. Stacy eased backward. "Because you're Emma's aunt and she loves you, I'm going to give you a chance to apologize. Otherwise, you can pack your things and get out of my house. Think about that and make your decision while I bring in my suitcase."

Volta spun around and stalked into the garage. How dare she! Volta cheat? Never. Wade was devoted to her, and she would never, ever have done anything to hurt her husband.

Too bad Volta didn't believe in ghosts. If Wade's spirit had overheard what Stacy had accused her of, he would have put his sister in her place. But he wasn't here to fight her battles, so Volta was going to have to do it herself.

When she returned, Stacy was standing in the living room, staring out the window. Volta carried her suitcase upstairs, set it in her bedroom and peeked inside Emma's room. Emma was sleeping soundly. Volta shut the door and returned downstairs.

"Time's up. What's your decision?"

Stacy turned to face her. "I'm sorry." It didn't sound particularly sincere, but she'd said it. Volta remained silent, waiting for her to continue. Eventually, she did. "I know you didn't cheat on Wade. But—"

"Be very careful in what you're about to say," Volta warned. "Emma already told me you'd tried to undermine Scott's authority as her riding instructor. I'm not inclined to put up with a bunch of nonsense from you tonight."

"Her own daddy should be teaching her, not some guy you know."

"I agree. I wish Wade could be here with Emma. But he's not. And there's nothing I can do to change that."

Stacy's bottom lip extended like a stubborn child's. She blinked, hard. "It just seems like you don't ever think about Wade, after all he did for you. He paid for this house and your school. You wouldn't be here if not for him."

Half true. Her emergency response training expenses came from the savings her parents had set aside for her. Wade had made the down payment on this house, but Volta had been making the mortgage payments from her own salary for over eight years. The money from his modest life insurance policy was tucked away in an account to pay for Emma's college. But Wade did give her Emma. And Emma was everything.

"You're wrong that I don't think about him." Volta walked over to the coffee table and picked up a scrapbook still lying there. She flipped to a page of Wade at the top of the lift at Alyeska. "You know that expression that Emma gets on her face when she's about to climb to the very top of the monkey bars? Or go shooting down the sledding hill? Maybe you don't, because you're not around Emma all that often. But I see it." She pointed to the photo. "It's exactly the same expression Wade would get just before he started down a black diamond ski run. I see him in Emma every day. I couldn't possibly forget him, nor would I want to."

"I miss him." Stacy sniffed. Her lip quivered.

"I know." Volta ordinarily would have offered tissues and a hug, but she was not inclined to reward Stacy for her melodrama. Instead, she gathered up another load of memories and put them away.

After a moment, Stacy came into the hall, carrying the last two boxes of photos. "Are you really going out with the guy who dumped you?"

"How does that concern you?"

"I'll take that as a yes." Stacy shoved the boxes onto the shelf.

Volta sighed. "I'm not dating Scott. He's agreed to continue to help Emma prepare for the horse show until he finishes his stint in Alaska or her regular instructor returns, whichever is sooner. Either way, he'll only be in Alaska for another week or two, so let it go already."

Stacy opened her mouth and then closed it again. After a moment, she shrugged. "I got mint chocolate chip ice cream. Want some?"

"No, thanks. I'm tired." Tired of Stacy judging her. Tired of defending herself for things she'd never done. And tired of feeling guilty for not loving Wade enough. "I'm going to bed."

CHAPTER THIRTEEN

"Now, LET'S SEE a figure eight at a lope." Scott stepped back against the fence and watched Emma complete the maneuver. "Excellent form, but Butternut was a step late changing her lead. This time try to shift your leg positions a little earlier, okay?"

"Okay." Emma tried again. Scott was impressed with her ability to concentrate on the task at hand. He doubted many eight-year-olds were capable of this sort of focus. This time, the horse changed leads just as she crossed the middle line. Emma reined up next to Scott. "How's that?"

"That was perfect. Let's do it again."

He watched her work, his smile growing broader as she practiced, getting better and better. Her natural posture and form were quite good, and she had a light hand on the reins. Butternut was a fine choice for her, easygoing but eager to move.

Finally, he called a halt. "Great job. Give me

a minute to saddle a horse for me, and we'll go on a trail ride."

Emma's face lit up, but she hesitated. "Shouldn't we keep practicing for the show?"

Scott shook his head. "You've practiced enough for today. The whole point of the class is to demonstrate you have the skills to ride in the open and control your horse. And the way to get good at that is to do it."

"Okay." She nudged her horse forward to follow him to the barn.

When Scott had called Dr. Thomas to clarify something for his report, Bart had offered to let Scott borrow his horse. Actually, it was his daughter's horse, but she was away at college, and happy to let him ride. The horse turned out to be an old palomino gelding named Nugget, a placid fellow who was happy for the attention Scott offered. Scott had the saddle blanket on and was reaching for the saddle when Volta showed up.

"Sorry if I'm late. I got held up in the check-out line behind someone with seventy-six coupons, most of which were expired. Are you done with the lesson?"

"It's not time to go yet," Emma told her. "We were just going on a trail ride."

Scott looked at his watch. "I reserved two

mma nodded wisely. "You have to answer
en it's work, 'cause it could be an emer-
cy. Mommy's supervisor is named Bernie.
et him at the company picnic, and he made
a dog out of balloons."

'Really?" Scott would never have guessed
e head of Puffin Medical Transport made
lloon animals.

"He made a hat for one girl. And he tried
make an elephant, but it looked more like
rhinoceros because the trunk stuck up like
horn."

"I can see that would be a hard one."

They talked all the way home. Emma asked
all sorts of questions about horses, and what
animals he'd seen when he traveled, and his
views on sugar. "My grandma Jordan doesn't
believe in sugar, but my grammy Morgan takes
me to the candy store at the mall and lets me
pick out a quarter pound of whatever I want."

"What do you get at the candy store?"

"Sometimes chocolate and marshmallow
penguins. And sometimes peanut butter fudge.
But most of the time, I get chocolate-covered
macadamia nuts."

"Good choices." He and Volta had been both
especially fond of chocolate caramel macada-
mias when they'd lived in Hawaii.

hours for Emma today. Sorry, I thought I'd
told you."

"Oh." Volta tilted her head to the right, the
way she always did when she was thinking
through a decision.

"Don't make me go now," Emma begged.
"Butternut really, really, wants to go on the
trails."

"Butternut does, huh?" Volta chuckled.
"Okay. Well, I have frozen stuff I need to get
put away, so I'll go home, unpack the groceries and be back in an hour. It might take a few
minutes longer, depending on traffic. Can you
stay with Emma if I'm a little late?" she asked
Scott.

"I can bring Emma home," Scott suggested.
"I go right by your neighborhood on my way
to the hotel anyway."

"She needs a booster seat."

"I could transfer it to my car and return it
when I drop Emma off."

"Is that okay with you?" Volta asked Emma.

"Yes!"

Scott passed Volta his key fob. "Here. Why
don't you transfer the seat while I get Nugget
here saddled, and we'll ride by the parking
lot to collect my keys on the way to the trail-
head. Okay?"

"That would be a huge help. Thanks." She

leaned over to pat Emma on the leg. "Be careful and listen to Dr. Scott, okay?"

"I will."

Volta smiled. "See you in a while, then."

Scott enjoyed the trail ride. He reminded Emma about posture or positioning a time or two, but mostly he relished the opportunity to be with her. Volta was raising an amazing little girl.

Multiple trails twisted through the woods on the Anchorage hillside. At the suggestion of the stable manager, Scott had chosen the most open trails that had had a chance to dry out from the winter's snowpack, but they still had to cross through mud a few times.

He made sure they got back to the stables early to leave extra grooming time to remove the mud from the horses' legs and hooves. Emma was eager to learn all aspects of horse care. Once they had the horses stabled, they walked to the parking lot. Scott was checking to make sure Emma's car seat was secure when his phone rang. Work.

"Excuse me, Emma, I need to take this. I won't be long."

"Okay."

He closed the door and answered. "Scott Willingham."

"Hi, Scott. It's Hans."

"Hi," Scott greeted his boss. "morning for you, isn't it?"

"I'm at a conference in India, s as you'd think. We've had some vi so as usual, we're rearranging sc next month. Where are you on tha

"I've got all the interviews done need to write it up and deliver the re dations."

"How is it looking?"

"Good. I think they can make sig improvements with the resources th offer."

"How much longer will you need there?"

Scott considered. If he worked flat out, he could have the report written in two days or so. Probably another day or two to get the board together and report. But he wasn't inclined to p in sixteen-hour days. He'd promised Emma les sons, and he'd like to spend a little time out enjoying Alaska. "A week or so?"

Hans sighed. "I was afraid you'd say Okay. We'll work it out. Thanks, Scott."

"Sure. I'll let you know if some changes."

"Right. Goodbye."

Scott returned to the car. "Sorry. Th my supervisor."

"Mommy says life without brownies would be a tragedy."

He laughed. "Sounds like your mommy hasn't changed much."

"What do you mean?"

Scott realized his mistake. "Just that I noticed she likes chocolate."

"She always has M&Ms in her purse. She calls them her emergency rations."

Scott pulled into Volta's driveway and parked. A garden flat of assorted plants sat on the porch, next to a watering can.

"Oh, good," Emma said. "Mommy's planting the garden." She unbuckled herself, slipped out of the car and skipped around the side of the house. "Mommy, I'm home."

Scott followed Emma along the flagstone path running along the house beside a cluster of bright yellow daffodils. In the bed beside the path, spring shoots were making their way out of the ground, including several fiddleheads that would later uncurl into graceful ferns.

When they got to the backyard, they found Volta kneeling in a bed of dirt beside a wooden frame, holding a dibble in her hand. A trowel and a seed packet lay on the ground in front of her. Her hair was pulled back in a ponytail. Smudges of dark soil streaked across the pale blue of her shirt and one ran diagonally along her cheek. Nevertheless, she was gorgeous.

Volta smiled at him and became even more beautiful. "Hi. Thanks for giving Emma the riding lesson, and for bringing her home."

"I enjoyed it. We had a great ride today, didn't we, Emma?"

Emma nodded. "Butternut likes trail rides. And she likes it when I brush her legs with the soft brush to get all the mud off."

"What are you planting?" Scott asked.

"Snap peas."

"We put strings on the frame and the peas climb up real high," Emma said. "Can I plant some?"

"Sure. You make a hole to the second mark, like this, and then pull out the dibble and drop in a pea. Then make another hole this far apart. Can you do that?" She handed the dibble to Emma.

"Yes." Emma went to work. Volta stood and walked over to Scott. "Let me get that car seat from you. Emma, I'll be right back."

"Okay." Emma's attention was on the seeds.

They walked along the path to the front yard. "What are all the plants on the porch?" Scott asked.

"Pansies, lobelia, alyssum and fuchsias. Once I finish planting the vegetables, I'll put together some hanging baskets and container gardens."

"Sounds nice." Scott opened the back door and lifted out the booster seat. "Do you want to open the garage door and I'll put it in your car?"

Volta shook her head. "Stacy borrowed my car to go out with her friends." She took the seat from him and set it on the porch.

"Stacy's still here?" Didn't they say fish and houseguests stink after three days?

"Yep." Volta didn't sound happy about it. In fact, if he wasn't mistaken, there was a story there. But it didn't look like Volta was going to share it. She was probably eager to get back to her gardening.

"I'd better be going," he said. "Get some dinner and start organizing my notes."

"I have a casserole in the oven."

Scott looked up, surprised. Volta looked a little surprised herself. "Is that an invitation?"

She smiled. "Why not? It's Emma's favorite meal. Nothing fancy. Macaroni and cheese. Carrot sticks. Fruit salad for dessert."

"Sounds like a feast to me. I'm in."

She looked at her watch. "It will be done in ten minutes. I suppose I'd better pick up the garden tools in the meantime."

He used his thumb to brush away the streak

of dirt on her cheek. "Go wash up. I'll pick up your tools and bring Emma inside."

"I...okay. Come through the back door. There's a basket for garden tools in the mud-room."

Scott returned to the backyard, where Emma was still industriously poking holes. "Almost done?"

"Two more." Emma made two more holes, dropped in dried peas and patted the soil over them. "Now we need to water them."

"I'll get the watering can from the front porch," Scott offered. "Your mom says the macaroni and cheese is almost ready, so we need to hurry and clean up."

"Mac and cheese? Yum!"

Scott fetched the watering can, filled it at the spigot near the back door and carried it to the garden. At Emma's direction, he sprinkled water along the newly planted row. Simple as it was, there was something satisfying about the task, about the idea of starting a seed grow-ing. He could see why Volta liked to garden.

He and Emma collected the empty seed packet and the garden tools. Emma showed him a basket, where he set the dibble and trowel. The aroma of warm cheese wafted into the mudroom. They both washed in the mudroom sink before going into the kitchen, where Volta was setting another spot at the table.

"Good timing. Dinner's ready."

"Smells good." Scott sat down at the table with them. It was a simple meal, but delicious. While they ate, he and Emma filled Volta in on all the sights they'd seen on the trail ride.

"There were some tracks that might have been a wolf," Emma told her.

"Or a big dog," Scott pointed out.

"Or a wolf dog. Or a werewolf," Emma suggested.

Scott laughed. "A werewolf?"

"I saw it on a cartoon. But it wasn't real. Somebody put stuff on their big dog to make it look like a wolf and scare people away."

"Ah, sounds like cartoons are still borrowing from the classics," Scott said. "That happened to Sherlock Holmes more than a hundred years ago."

"Who's Sherlock Holmes?"

"You don't know about Sherlock Holmes?" Scott smiled at Emma. "Then you have a treat in store someday."

"He's a famous detective in books," Volta explained, "who lived a really long time ago."

"Did he have a horse?" Emma asked.

Volta grinned and shook her head. "I was

never too crazy about those stories. The author doesn't play fair with the clues."

"But Sir Author Conan Doyle changed the whole genre of fictional detectives. There weren't any rules when he wrote it."

Emma was looking back and forth between them. "And he wrote about werewolves?"

"Not exactly werewolves. Just a big scary dog. And only in that one story."

Once dinner was over and Scott had helped load the dishwasher, he'd run out of excuses to stay any longer. "Thank you for sharing your dinner. I suppose I'd better go back to the hotel and get my notes organized so that tomorrow morning, I can jump into writing the report."

"I'll walk you out. Emma, you need to find your spelling list. We'll go over the words before your bath."

"Okay. Bye, Dr. Scott. See you Saturday."

"Good night, Emma."

Volta followed Scott outside. "Saturday?"

"If it's okay with you. Butternut was booked tomorrow afternoon, but I reserved a spot Saturday morning at ten. Sorry, I meant to ask you first, but Emma was there when I made the reservation."

"Saturday is fine with us, but don't you need to be working?"

"I talked to my supervisor today and told him I needed at least a week, maybe more."

"A week." Volta made it sound like his last bit of freedom before an upcoming prison sentence. He couldn't disagree. "Are you sure you have time for this lesson Saturday?"

"I'm sure."

"Well, don't promise Emma any more lessons after that unless you're positive you'll be here."

"I won't make promises I can't keep. I understand what it's like to be a kid and have the adults in your life cancel."

"Okay," she said, but her expression was skeptical. Volta knew all about his relationship with his father, or rather the lack of one. It hurt a little to know she didn't trust him not to disappoint Emma. "Good night, Scott."

"Good night." He spotted the stable's newsletter lying on the porch where Emma had dropped it. He retrieved it and turned to give it to Volta. But she was already gone.

CHAPTER FOURTEEN

"NICE JOB!" VOLTA high-fived the girl who had just gotten three of five beanbags through the targets. She stamped her card with a smiley face, collected the beanbags and welcomed the next kid in line.

Today was field day at Emma's school, one of Volta's favorite volunteer activities. The kids looked forward to it for weeks, partly because of the games, and partly because it meant there were only two more days of school. It always started right after lunch.

Volta had almost been late because, as she was gathering up her bag, Stacy wandered into the kitchen, still in her pajamas. "Got any coffee?"

"Sorry, I washed the pot. You'll have to make more. Late night?"

"Yeah, went to a midnight movie with some friends. Haven't done that in years." She filled the pot with water.

Volta reached into the bowl where she kept her car keys. Empty. "Have you seen my keys?"

"Oh, I think I left them in my pocket. Just a sec while I start the coffee and I'll get them."

"I need to go now. Go get them and I'll make coffee." Volta had measured coffee into the pot and poured the water through before Stacy returned with the keys.

"Here. Say, yesterday when I came by to change clothes, I thought I saw that doctor driving out of the neighborhood."

"He brought Emma home after her lesson." Volta wanted to leave it there, but if Emma mentioned dinner, Stacy would think she was hiding something. "And to thank him for the lessons, I invited him to dinner."

"To thank him. Right." Stacy looked away, but not before Volta saw her eye roll.

Volta didn't have time to set her straight. "I'm late." She grabbed her bag and pushed through the door to the garage. Naturally, Stacy had left the gas tank almost empty, but Emma's school wasn't far away.

The kids had been vibrating with excitement when Volta arrived just in time to receive her assignment. Now, two hours later, they'd had a chance to run off some of their energy and were a little more mellow. The sky was beginning to cloud up, but the weather report said the rain should hold off until evening, thankfully, because the kids would have been sorely disappointed if they couldn't finish the day outside.

Volta handed her next contestant a beanbag. "Stand right here behind the line. Let's see what you can do."

A girl she remembered from earlier in the day dashed over. "Can I do the beanbags again?" she asked. "They're my favorite."

The boy's first throw missed. "Close," Volta said. "Try again." She handed him a second beanbag and turned to the girl. "Have you been to all the other stations yet?" Volta examined the girl's card. "Looks like you still need to do the Hula-Hoops first. Mrs. McElfray said once you've tried every activity once, you can repeat your favorites."

"Okay. I'll be back." She sprinted toward the Hula-Hoop area.

The boy sank his second throw. "I did it!"

"You sure did. You've got the hang of it now." She passed another beanbag. "Let's see you do it again."

He managed to make one more but missed the next one. The last bag landed halfway through the target, balanced on the edge. He looked dejected. "Just two of five."

Volta shook her head. "Are you kidding? You got a rim-bag. They're the hardest of all. They count double."

"Oh." He grinned while she stamped his card. "Good."

The next girl stepped up. "Are you Emma's mom?"

"Yes, I am." Volta tried to remember if she'd ever met this girl, but she couldn't recall. She handed her a beanbag.

"Does Emma really ride horses?" the girl asked as she made a half-hearted attempt at a throw. The bag fell short.

"Yes, she's learning to ride." Volta handed her the next bag, wondering where this conversation was going.

"I'm learning to play chess. My daddy is teaching me. Is Emma's daddy a cowboy?"

"No. Emma's daddy died a long time ago." Sometimes, when kids said things like this, Volta's heart ached over what Emma was missing. She was grateful for Leith, and for Emma's two grandfathers, but it wasn't the same as having a dad. The girl flailed her bag forward again, this time at least hitting the backboard. Her dad should teach her to throw. "Who's teaching Emma to ride? You?"

Volta passed another bag. "A friend of mine is teaching her. He knows a lot about horses."

"Is he a cowboy?"

"He's a doctor."

The girl shook her head. "Doctors don't ride horses. Cowboys ride horses."

Volta laughed. "Well, this doctor does ride horses, although maybe he's a little bit cowboy, too. You can be more than one thing. Like I happen to know your teacher, Mrs. McElfray, is also an excellent photographer. I saw her work at the Cabin Fever Festival last year. She won a ribbon."

The girl pulled her eyebrows together. "What are you?"

"I," Volta told her as she passed another bag, "am a flight paramedic, a mom, a volunteer, a gardener and lots of other things. What are you?"

"I'm just a kid."

"Oh, you're more than that. You're a student, for one thing. And a chess player."

"I guess." The girl lifted the beanbag awkwardly behind her shoulder.

Volta stopped her. "Try throwing it underhanded, like this." Volta demonstrated the motion.

The girl tried it, and the bag flew through the circle. "I did it!"

"You did. So you're a beanbag thrower, too. That's four things."

"Yeah." The girl tossed her final bag and

it, too, went through the hole. She grinned. "I am."

Volta stamped her card. "Okay, looks like you still need the hopscotch stamp. Go be a hopper."

There was no one waiting, so Volta took a moment to drink from her water bottle before she collected the beanbags. When she turned around, Emma was there. "Were you talking to Livy?"

"I don't know, which one's Livy?"

Emma pointed at the girl who had asked all the questions. "She doesn't believe I can ride a horse."

"She asked me, and I told her you were taking riding lessons."

"She says only cowboys ride horses. I'm not a cowboy but I can still ride a horse." Emma thought a moment. "I have cowboy boots, though, so maybe I am a cowboy. Or a cowgirl, at least."

Volta laughed. "I would think the defining criteria might be cows, but what do I know?"

"Cry-tear...?"

"Criteria. Never mind. Have you been to all the stations?"

"Yes, and I did the watermelon seed spitting contest twice."

Volta silently thanked Mrs. McElfray for not

assigning her to that station. "Want to throw beanbags again?"

"Sure." Emma lined up to throw.

Volta watched her sink all five. Emma was a natural athlete. She inherited that from her dad. Volta made a point of working out and staying fit, but she'd never been particularly coordinated. Emma got a lot of good things from her dad's genes. It was a shame he couldn't be there to see her.

Emma surveyed the field. "Maddy's at the Hula-Hoops. I'm gonna go do them again." Emma didn't wait for an answer before she darted away.

Volta watched her daughter wave at her friend and gallop across the field, her dark ponytail bouncing as she ran. Volta smiled.

AFTER SCHOOL, VOLTA stopped to fill the gas tank and pick up ground meat and a loaf of French bread. Once they got home, she drafted Emma to help her make meatballs. "Grammy Hannah and Grandpa Jim texted earlier and said they're stopping in Anchorage tonight, so I thought we'd make spaghetti for dinner."

"And garlic bread?"

"Of course, garlic bread. And a big salad."

"Are they staying long?"

"Only tonight. They said something about

driving north tomorrow." And hopefully taking their daughter with them. Even though Stacy had been really sweet with Emma, Volta had had just about enough of her attitude.

Volta heard a car door slam outside, but since she was up to her elbows in ground meat, she didn't bother to go look. A minute later, the kitchen door opened. Speak of the devil. Stacy looked over Emma's shoulder. "Hey, guys, what are you doing?"

"We're making meatballs," Emma told her, plopping the ball she'd rolled onto the cookie sheet.

"Cool. You're doing a good job." She patted Emma on the shoulder, but Volta noticed she didn't offer to help.

"Grammy and Grandpa are coming for supper."

"Yeah, they texted me. They want me to go with them to Hatcher's Pass."

"Are you going?" Volta tried not to sound too eager.

"Probably." Stacy yawned. "I'm going to take a shower. I hate washing my hair in that RV bathroom."

"Good idea. They won't be here for another two hours. You should have time to pack." Volta held her breath, afraid Stacy would renege on her intention, but she wandered up the stairs.

"Does Aunt Stacy have a job anymore?" Emma asked.

"Not at the moment."

"Maybe that's why she's sad."

Volta looked at Emma. "Aunt Stacy is sad?"

Emma nodded. "One time, while you were gone, I woke up and was thirsty, so I came downstairs." Volta knew about Emma's occasional bedtime thirsts, which usually meant she just needed an extra hug and to be tucked in again. "I saw her looking at those pictures and she was crying."

"Oh. I don't think it's a new sad. I think she just misses her brother."

Emma got a thoughtful look on her face as she rolled another meatball. "I don't remember Daddy, so I don't miss him, but I wish I did, and sometimes I wish I could have a daddy."

"I know, sweetie." Volta leaned across to drop a kiss on top of her head. "Sometimes I wish you could, too."

IT RAINED MOST of the night, but Thursday morning dawned clear and warm. Yesterday had been the last day of school. Summer might not officially start until June 21, but when school let out, summer was here as far as Volta was concerned. She sat on the stands at the arena and watched Scott and Emma work together. He was patient, but at the same time his coaching encouraged steady progress. Volta knew nothing about horses, but she could see that Emma's riding was smoother and more confident that it had been a week ago.

Scott had mentioned that he could only get an hour of horse time, so she wasn't surprised when he started winding down. A woman sat on the bench next to her. "She's doing very well. Is that your daughter?"

"Yes," Volta said, pleased to have another person verify what she'd observed.

"Your husband is a great coach."

"Oh, he's not my husband."

"Boyfriend, then. Is he available to take on more students?"

Volta decided her relationship to Scott was irrelevant to the conversation. "He's only in Alaska for work. He'll be gone next week."

"That's a shame. I was hoping Cait would be back after finals, but I hear she isn't returning for another few weeks. My older son has been working with his brother since she pulled out, but I was hoping to find a coach with more experience. I'm Linda Garcia, by the way."

"Volta Morgan."

"Volta?"

Volta made a face. "My dad's an electrician. Anyway, nice to meet you, Linda. Which one is your son?"

Linda pointed toward two boys and a spotted horse entering the arena. "There, coming through the gate." The boy riding the horse looked to be a year or two older than Emma. His teenage brother walked beside him.

Emma and Scott passed them on their way out. The older boy said something, and Scott stopped to talk with him. Meanwhile Emma smiled at the boy on horseback, and he smiled back. After a few minutes, Scott and Emma continued on to the barn.

Volta excused herself and made her way to the barn to watch Scott and Emma unsaddle and brush the horse. Once they'd finished, Emma fed the horse a carrot. "Bye, Butternut. See you soon."

Once they'd left the stall, Emma tugged on Scott's hand. "When is the next lesson?"

"Emma, Scott came to Alaska to do a job," Volta told her. "The job is almost over, so he'll have to leave in a few days. He can't keep giving you lessons."

"But the show is in two weeks," Emma protested. "And I have to practice." Volta hoped she didn't descend into whining. It didn't happen too often, but Emma was a kid and like all kids, she could be self-centered.

"I know," she told her daughter, "but Scott has other commitments. It's been really nice of him to spend his time teaching you, but he can't—"

"I'll be here at least until Friday," Scott interrupted. "Let me check with the office and see how much horse time we can get between now and then."

"But—" Volta started.

"Yesterday was the last day of school," Emma said.

"Emma—"

"Let's go see when Butternut is available," Scott said, and he and Emma strode off toward the office, leaving Volta to tag along. She should be annoyed at their high-handed tactics, but she was just happy that Emma would get a little more time with him. Happy that she would get a little more time with him. Which in itself was a warning sign, but she would deal with that later.

Scott removed an extraneous comma and pressed Save. It was done. Putting his recommendations into writing had taken him less than a week despite all the time he'd spent with Emma.

This morning, he'd done a final read and tweaked a word or two, but overall he was pleased with the result. The different people he'd talked to had given him a slew of ideas on how to improve prenatal care, but he'd been able to distill most of their suggestions down into a workable plan.

He called Ransom Goodman, the chairman of the Travert Foundation board. Ransom had started as a bush pilot with a single airplane service which, by the time he'd retired, he'd built into a prosperous aviation company. He and his wife were also experienced volunteers, both at the board level and hands-on.

They'd met once to talk about expectations before Scott started the study, and he'd been impressed at Leo Travert's choice to direct the foundation. Ransom was enthusiastic while remaining levelheaded, and most importantly, he was more interested in learning from the people in the field than in his own preconceived ideas.

"Scott, good to hear from you." Ransom's deep voice boomed over the phone. "How is it coming?"

"I've gathered information from a selection of health providers across the state, and I have some recommendations ready for you. I can send you the report, but I'd like to go over it with you in person if it's convenient."

"I would love to hear your recommendations. In fact, it would be best to get the entire board together so you can talk to us all at once. I'll schedule something ASAP, tomorrow or the next day, with any luck. We're eager to get started."

"I'll look forward to it."

"In the meantime, send me the report, and I'll get it out to the board members."

"I'll do that. Talk with you soon." Scott ended the call and checked his calendar. Today was Thursday. He had a one-hour lesson scheduled with Emma at eleven, and another tomorrow at twelve thirty. She was a competitor, focused like a laser on the upcoming show.

Scott halfway wished her instructor had never mentioned the show to her. Emma was coming along, but she wasn't quite ready, even for a beginner class. Could he have her ready in two more lessons?

Even if he could, if she couldn't ride for a week before the show, it would be difficult for her to keep the skills honed. The stable required supervision when a child Emma's age rode, and Volta wasn't qualified. Emma's original instructor hadn't returned. All she had was him.

Scott looked at his watch and did the mental arithmetic. If Hans was at headquarters, it would be around quitting time. If he was still in India, he might have gone to bed. Scott decided to take the chance. He dialed his boss's number.

"Scott. How goes it?"

"It goes well. Hope I didn't wake you."

"No, no. I'm back in London. I hope you're calling to tell me you finished earlier than expected. I could use you in Peru next week, if you're available."

"Sorry, no. I've done the paperwork, but I still need to meet with the board in the next day or two. Actually, I was calling about the possibility of taking some vacation time."

"Vacation? Who told you about vacation?" Hans laughed. Scott's tendency to bank his vacation was a long-running joke between them. "Oh, I see here you already took off three days to spend in Houston last month, which means you've only got five and a half weeks left this year. Plus, whatever you've banked over the years. When did you want to schedule this vacation?"

"As soon as I've met with the board of the Travert Foundation and turned over the report. I have some personal business here, and I'll need until after May 28."

"Personal business in Alaska? Would that

be salmon fishing? White-water rafting? Sea kayaking?" Hans chuckled. "Never mind. it's none of my business as long as you come back in one piece. Yes, I'll approve it. I was going to send Keenen to Guatemala, but I'll send her to Peru instead and backfill."

Backfill? Scott almost said he'd forgo his vacation and head for Peru, but then he thought of Emma's face when he'd agreed to more lessons. There were always people in need of medical care, always more need than they could possibly fill. Hans and his staff were wizards at getting the right people to the right places at the right time, and he wasn't worried. It was okay for Scott to take a little time off.

"Thanks, Hans. I'll send you an email once I've finished the project and check in next week about where you'll want me to fly next."

"Sounds good. Enjoy."

Scott slipped the phone into his pocket. Twenty more minutes before he needed to leave to pick up Emma and Volta.

He laughed to himself. Hans thought he was taking time off for some high-adrenaline adventure, when the thing he was most looking forward to was simply hanging out with his two Alaska girls.

AFTER WATCHING EMMA'S LESSON, Volta met her and Scott at the barn. Emma had decided Volta needed a closer relationship with the horse. "Butternut loves carrots," Emma told her mom. "If you feed her one, she'll like you. Hold your hand flat, like this."

Up close, the horse was even bigger than Volta had realized. That nervous streak inside her raised its overprotective head. If something went wrong with an animal this big—Volta stopped herself. It was okay. Emma wore her helmet, and according to Scott, followed all the safety rules. People had been riding on horseback for thousands of years. Emma would be fine.

As though reassuring her, the horse ever-so-gently lipped the carrot off her palm and chewed. Volta ran her hand down the horse's face, marveling at the soft hair. Butternut rubbed against her hand. What a sweetheart.

Scott loosened the saddle and lifted it off the horse. Emma picked up a brush and stepped on a stool so that she could brush the horse's back where the saddle had been. Butternut nodded her head, obviously enjoying the sensation.

Scott's phone chimed. He stepped outside the stall and looked at the screen. "Excuse me. I need to get this." He picked up. "Scott Willingham."

He stayed close by where he could keep an eye on Emma while he talked. "That's good news. What time tomorrow? One? Could you hang on, please, while I check my calendar?"

Tomorrow was Scott's last lesson with Emma, scheduled for twelve thirty. After seeing the schedule when they reserved the time, Volta knew the chances of rescheduling the lesson for a different time were slim. But Scott wasn't in Alaska to give riding lessons. He was here on assignment. Emma was focused on grooming the horse, not listening to Scott's conversation. She didn't realize he was about to pull the rug out from under her.

But Scott surprised her. "No, I'm sorry, but that won't work for me," he was saying. "I have another appointment that runs until one thirty. I could be there by two." He paused. "I understand. Sure, evening is fine. Seven. No problem. Thank you very much. I'll look forward to it."

He pocketed the phone and started toward Emma, but Volta put her hand on his arm and stopped him. "Thank you," she whispered.

He smiled at her. "Anytime. Say, I thought after we're done here, we might go for a walk by the creek. I was on the phone with DEMA this morning, and I have some news I think you're going to like."

"What's that?"

"I'll tell you as we walk. You game?"

"Anytime," she echoed him.

CHAPTER FIFTEEN

SCOTT WATCHED EMMA transition smoothly from a jog to a lope. She'd come a long way in the last two weeks. He was confident she was ready for the show tomorrow, especially after talking to the staff at the stable. He'd learned that in the beginner class, ribbons were awarded based on how well each participant executed individually, rather than in direct competition, and Emma was executing well.

He looked across the arena at Volta, who had settled in on the first row to watch. He waved, and she waved back, her smile reaching across the arena to tug on his heart. Two more days. That was all they had together. The day after the show, he was heading to Ethiopia, to a surgical clinic that specialized in birth injuries, where he would work for the next two weeks before moving on.

Leaving was going to be hard. Ordinarily, he would be eager to move on to his next challenge. While he left every assignment wishing he could do more, there was a sense of satisfaction that he'd given them his best and that he was leaving them better than he'd found them.

In many ways, that was true here. He'd discussed his recommendations with the Travert Foundation's board, and they were eager to take those recommendations and run with them, so he had accomplished his primary objective. He and Emma had been working together almost every day, sometimes twice a day, and in the time he had been coaching her, Emma had made great strides as a rider. He felt confident she would continue to improve. He could hardly wait to cheer her on at the show tomorrow.

But Volta. He wasn't leaving her life better than he'd found it. On the contrary, he had the feeling he was breaking his Hippocratic oath when it came to Volta. First do no harm. He'd harmed her once, and he was afraid he was going to do it again.

Not that he'd made any promises. They'd both understood, from the first day they met in Sparks, that this was a temporary assignment. She had been hesitant to let him get close, and yet when he'd asked for her help, she'd agreed to work with him, and the relationships she brought to the job had proved invaluable. It was the relationship between them that was difficult. He knew better, and she knew better, and yet they'd let these long-buried feelings surface once again.

He'd come to Alaska to make sure she was okay. He'd found a woman who was much more than okay. Despite the stones that life had flung at her, Volta was strong and brave and in charge of her life. And she was raising a daughter to be just as strong. It might hurt Volta when he left, but she'd be fine. Her character wouldn't allow for any other alternative.

Would he be okay? Occasionally, Scott wondered if he'd ever been okay. He could say without conceit that he was a more-than-competent doctor. He got along fine with the people he worked with. Often after spending a week or two working alongside him, the part-time volunteer doctors would invite him to stay in touch, or to stop by if he found himself in their hometown, but he never followed up. He had no close relationships. His father was practically a stranger.

Volta was the only woman he'd ever loved, and the moment he'd recognized that fact, he'd removed her from his life, as though her love was harmful to him. In fact, her love might have been the only thing that could save him.

But he'd made his decision. Now he had to live with it.

"Dr. Scott?" Emma was waiting for her next assignment.

He smiled at her. "You know what? You're ready. I think I'll saddle up Nugget and we should spend the rest of our time today on a trail ride. What do you say?"

A smile spread across her eager face. "Let's go."

VOLTA WAVED GOODBYE to Emma and Scott as they rode off on the main trail. He'd said they'd only be gone thirty minutes, so it wasn't worth leaving and coming back. She had a paperback in her purse, so she decided to sit on the bench near the parking lot and read until Emma was done.

On the way, she passed a woman who was flicking through her phone. The woman gasped. Volta turned back. "Are you all right?"

"Me? I'm fine. I just saw that they had a big earthquake in Samoa. I know someone who was going there. I want to make sure he's okay." The woman started punching numbers on her phone.

Volta leaned against the rail fence beside the parking lot and brought up the story on her phone. The Samoan earthquake was a magnitude 6.8, with the epicenter almost directly under a coastal city, and they had issued a tsunami warning. That didn't look good. If this was happening in Alaska, she would be on her way to the airport right now.

The woman finished her phone call and turned to Volta with a relieved smile. "He's fine, but he says he can't contact any of his friends in Samoa, so he's not sure if they're okay or not."

"I'm glad your friend is all right." Volta continued to follow the updates over the next half hour. The tsunami had materialized, almost thirty people had been reported missing, and power was out for most of the island. Roads were damaged.

Scott and Emma rode back up the trail. Emma reined to a stop in front of Volta. "Hi, Mommy. We saw two foxes playing together."

"How fun."

"Now we're going to groom Butternut real good so she'll be pretty for the show tomorrow. And Scott says I need to polish my boots."

"Good idea. You'll want to look your best for the judges."

Volta followed them to the barn. Scott unsaddled and ran a brush over his horse first, and then helped Emma unsaddle Butternut. He produced a bottle that looked much like the leave-in conditioner Volta used on Emma's hair. "I brought this shine dressing we can use on Butternut's coat to get her ready."

He squirted a little on a brush, and Emma went to work brushing it into Butternut's coat. "Pretty."

"Yeah," Scott stroked the horse's face. "She's looking good."

They moved to her neck. "You'll be there tomorrow, right?" Emma asked Scott.

"Sure I will."

"Will you be in the arena with me?"

"No, you and the others will be alone with the judge, but I'll be watching from behind the fence. You'll do great."

Emma smiled. They were working the tangles from Butternut's mane as Scott's phone chimed. When he looked at the screen he frowned. And Volta's chest went cold.

He stepped out of the stall. "Scott here. Where? How much damage? Helicopters? How about generators? Yeah, I understand. What time? Okay, I'll be ready."

He looked at her. She knew that expression. It was the same expression she'd seen on so many doctors' faces when they had to deliver bad news to the families of their patients. The same expression that had been on his face when he'd broken up with her. Calm and comforting on the surface. Only the tension in his jaw hinted at the cyclone of emotions whirling underneath.

"You have to go." She said it for him.

"I do. There's been an earthquake—"

"In Samoa. I heard."

"A maternity hospital has lost all power and has been cut off from the rest of the island. Two of the staff doctors are missing."

"When do you leave?"

"Two hours."

"But you can't go." Emma had slipped out of the stall.

"I'm so sorry," Scott told her. "If I could stay—"

"You promised."

Some of the color drained from Scott's face. Volta knew about all the broken promises of his childhood. "Sweetie, there are people in Samoa who need Scott right now," she said.

"I need him, too."

"I know. But they need him more. There's been a big earthquake, and people are hurt. They need a doctor."

A tear slid from Emma's eye. "I'll miss you."

"I'll miss you, too." Scott blinked as though he wasn't far from tears himself.

Emma flung herself against him and hugged

his waist with all her might. "Goodbye, Dr. Scott."

"Goodbye, Emma." He hugged her. "You're going to be an incredible horsewoman someday."

He turned to Volta, his eyes pleading for... something. She wasn't sure what. Maybe she couldn't hear his silent request over the sound of her own heart breaking. Again. He led her a few steps away where Emma wouldn't hear. "I'd stay if I could."

"I know."

"Maybe I can come back after—"

"No." It hurt to say it, but it was better this way. "We can't keep doing this. It's too hard on Emma. Too hard for all of us." She slid her arms around him. "Goodbye, Scott. Take your car. We'll finish with the horse and take a cab home."

He pulled her close. She could hear his heart beating, feel him draw air into his lungs and then release it in a long, slow breath. He leaned back, just far enough so that she could see his face. She tried to think of something to say, some final words, but nothing came to mind.

He looked into her eyes for a long moment, and then he kissed her one last time and walked out of the barn.

"COME ON, EMMA. Breathe in through your nose. One. Two. Three. Four. Now out, slowly." Volta glanced in the mirror at her daughter before the light changed and she had to return her attention to the road. The calming exercises weren't having much effect.

She'd never seen Emma so nervous, and they hadn't even arrived at the stables yet. Volta didn't know much about horses, but she'd been around other animals enough to realize Emma's anxiety could only upset the horse.

"I can't do it." Emma was almost sobbing. "Not without Dr. Scott. I need him here."

"Remember, the people at the stable said you're not in competition. You're only showing what you can do."

"But what if I can't do anything?"

"Emma." Volta used her best I-know-what-I'm-talking-about voice. "You've got this. Yesterday, Scott said you were so ready you didn't even need to practice anymore, right? That's why you took the trail ride."

"What if Butternut breaks gait?"

Volta had no idea what that meant, but it couldn't be that serious. "Then it happens, and life goes on. And you'll do better next time." Her phone chimed, signaling a message, but Volta ignored it.

She pulled into the parking lot and tapped her fingers on the wheel, waiting while a pickup and an SUV jockeyed over a parking spot. A glance in the mirror showed her that Emma hadn't yet given in to tears, but they weren't far away. Finally, the SUV conceded defeat and moved on to the rear of the lot. Volta followed and found a spot at the very end.

She opened Emma's door. "Come on."

Emma shook her head. "I don't feel good. My stomach hurts."

"All the more reason. Come on, sweetie. Get out of the car and we'll talk about it."

Emma unbuckled and slid onto the pavement. Volta wrapped her in a hug. "Listen to me. If you really don't want to be in the show, you don't have to. But don't forget, Grandma, Granddaddy, Leith and Sabrina are all coming to see you ride. You've worked hard to prepare for this and I think you'll be sorry if you don't participate."

"But…"

Volta guided her over to a bench and sat down beside her. "What's the very worst thing you can imagine happening today?" Volta didn't mean that literally, of course. With all the things she'd seen in her job, she could come up with all sorts of scary scenarios, but she trusted that Emma wouldn't be able to imagine them.

"I fall off, and everybody laughs."

Volta nodded solemnly. "What would you do if that happened?"

Emma thought for a moment. "I'd get back on the horse."

"So, even if the very worst thing happened, you'd know how to handle it. It sounds to me like you're ready."

"I guess."

Volta's phone chimed again. She checked the ID. Scott.

Tell Emma she's going to be amazing today. She's a born equestrian. I'm so proud of her.

Another text followed.

Got to go. Boarding in Fiji. Give Emma a hug for me.

"Look." She showed Emma the first text. "Scott sent a message for you."

"He did?" Emma leaned closer to the phone.

"See? Scott is a horse expert, and he believes in you. He says you're a born equestrian."

"Is that like a cowgirl?" For the first time today, Emma's voice was steady.

"Pretty much. So, you ready to cowgirl up?"

Emma giggled. "Okay."

"Okay. Let's go. Butternut is probably wondering where you are."

WATCHING HER RIDING that horse in front of the judge, Volta would never have known that an hour ago, Emma had been in meltdown mode. Volta's mom sat on the bleacher bench beside her, with Sabrina and Leith on the other side. Dad was standing at the fence, capturing everything with a video camera. They'd all cheered when Emma entered the ring. She must have heard because she gave a little smile.

There were five kids in the beginning class, including Linda's son. Emma was probably the youngest, and the oldest might have been eleven or twelve. According to the program, they'd all been riding for less than a year.

The judge had the riders walk their horses around the arena, and then change and walk the other way. Some of the horses tossed their heads and fidgeted when their riders turned around, but Butternut turned smoothly. Then the judge ordered them to jog, and later to lope. Several times during their maneuvers, one of the horses would drop from one gait to a different one. This always drew a collective sympathetic "aw" from the crowd, so it must have been a mistake. Emma managed to take her horse through all the gaits, even backing the horse up several feet when the judge asked. Volta applauded along with the rest of the crowd.

At the end of the class, the judge walked up to each of the children, spoke with them for a minute and presented them with a ribbon. Two were blue, and two were red. Emma was last in line. Whatever the judge said put a huge smile on her face. The judge asked her something else, and she answered eagerly. Then the judge handed her the blue ribbon, and Emma's smile grew even broader. Even though Dad was filming, Volta snapped a picture with her phone.

The judge gave an instruction, and the riders directed their horses to lope once more around the perimeter of the arena, while the audience applauded. Leith leaned forward to talk to Volta. "I'm impressed. She can really handle that horse."

"Look how tall she's sitting," Sabrina said. "Like a queen."

"I'm so glad," Volta's mom said. "When Russ said he wanted to get her riding lessons, I wasn't sure. But I knew you'd already agreed to send her to horse camp, so I figured individual lessons would help get her ready for that."

"They really did. Too bad her instructor had to drop out."

"Well, your friend Scott certainly filled in admirably. Where is he anyway?"

"He got called away. You heard about the big earthquake and tsunami in Samoa?"

"Oh, yes. That sounds awful. He's going there?" The concern in Mom's voice could have been for the people in Samoa, but Volta suspected some of it was aimed at her, as well.

She tried for a casual smile, but it felt tight even to her. "Yes. They've sent him to a maternity hospital. Some of their staff is missing, and they have no power, so they need help."

"Goodness." Sabrina clasped her hands together. "Those women must be terrified."

"It's a long way to Samoa," Leith said. "How long will it take him to get there?"

"I'm not sure," Volta answered. "He flew out of here last night. When he texted a couple of hours ago, he was changing planes in Fiji. I don't know any of the details, but presumably they'll fly him to whatever undamaged airport is the closest and helicopter in from there."

"That sounds a lot like your job," Sabrina said.

"I stabilize them, throw 'em on a plane and get them to the hospital. People like Scott are who I'm trying to get them to, so they can save their lives."

Emma and the others were filing out of the arena and another group was coming in. "Excuse me. I need to go get Emma."

Volta's dad, having filmed her all the way to the gate, was returning to the bleachers. "Tell her we're proud of her. She did great. We'll all go out for ice cream to celebrate later."

"I'll tell her." Volta made her way through the crowds to the barn, where the stable staff was busy trying to herd the kids into some sort of order. Emma climbed down off the horse, and one of the trainers led her away. Emma looked around the busy barn until she spotted her mother. She hurried over, holding up her ribbon. "I got blue!"

"I saw! That's great. Granddad filmed the whole thing, and he says after the show, he's taking us all out for ice cream."

"Peanut butter and chocolate?"

"Whatever you want. Don't you need to take care of your horse?"

Emma shook her head. "Somebody else is going to ride her next, so they took her to change her saddle. I'm all done."

"Well, then, let's go to the stands and show everybody your ribbon. We can watch the rest of the show."

Emma walked along beside her, surprisingly quiet. After a little while she said, "Dr. Scott isn't coming back, is he?"

"No. He's finished his job here."

"He was nice." Emma walked another step or two. "But I'm kinda mad because he said he'd be here for the show and he wasn't."

"You know why he had to go."

"I know," Emma said. "But I don't like people who make you like them and then go away forever."

Volta should defend him. After all, Scott had used his vacation days to stay and work with Emma, and he certainly couldn't be held responsible for an earthquake. But she understood Emma's feelings because she shared them. She didn't like people who made you love them and disappeared from your life, either.

You had to protect your heart. It was a lesson Volta had learned the hard way all those years ago in Hawaii, and yet she must not have learned it very well, because she'd gone and left it vulnerable again. She knew it would end this way and yet she'd let Scott slip back into her life, into her heart. And into Emma's.

She never should have let them spend time together. She should have realized that Emma wouldn't be able to resist growing attached to Scott. Yes, they'd made it clear Scott was only there temporarily, but a child Emma's age couldn't be expected to understand.

Emma had never had anyone important to her that she knew disappear out of her life before. A little piece of Emma's trust was gone, as well. And it was Volta's fault.

CHAPTER SIXTEEN

SCOTT YAWNED. HE hadn't gotten much sleep for the past two weeks, but they'd finally restored power and staffing to the maternity hospital. There was an old wives' tale that babies try to be born at the most inconvenient times possible, and often he wondered if it might be true. He'd personally delivered six babies in the first twenty-four-hour period after he arrived, two by C-section.

His response team included one other doctor, several nurses, and a handful of engineers who hooked up emergency generators and kept the incubators running and the lights on. The doctor was a volunteer who had left his ob-gyn practice in Kentucky to come help.

Scott's phone chimed. Huh. They must have gotten the cell towers working again. He scrolled through his messages, looking for nothing in particular. No, that wasn't true. He was looking for something from Volta, but it wasn't there. Did he really expect it to be?

He could have used the satellite phone to

check in with Volta and make sure she was okay, and to find out how Emma did in the show, but the sat phone was really for work communication and for the team to use to check in with their families. He had no family who cared where he was.

He'd thought of Volta and Emma lately. About how much he'd enjoyed his time with them. And then about the look on Emma's face when she realized he wouldn't be there for her show. That look was exactly why he'd made the decision not to marry or have a family. He knew the pain of being a parent's last priority and he never wanted to inflict that on a child. Or on a wife.

He lay down on his cot. After an eighteen-hour day, he expected to fall asleep immediately, but his mind wouldn't quiet. Alaska was a couple of time zones ahead, so Volta would be asleep now. Were the peas she'd planted up and growing yet? Had Emma found another riding instructor? Were they thinking of him when he thought of them? He grabbed his phone and typed out an email to Volta asking about Emma. And finally, he could sleep.

VOLTA WOKE AT the sound of her phone's chime. It only took a second to realize it wasn't the work phone but her private one. The numbers on the bedside clock read 1:11. Probably spam. She closed her eyes, trying to catch the last traces of her dream, but it was gone. She'd been having a lot of dreams lately where she was standing there with a group of people and they all suddenly disappeared, leaving her alone. She didn't need Freud to interpret that one.

She reached for her phone, to see who thought she needed to know about an "amazing one-day sale" at one in the morning, but it wasn't a business. It was Scott. Did he really think it was okay to maintain stony silence for two weeks and then just drop a line to her? She opened the message. He said he'd had no cell service or internet until now, so he couldn't contact her before. She probably should have realized that would be the case.

He asked about her garden, about how Emma did in the show, and about life in general. He mentioned delivering a lot of babies, and that power had been restored today. No complaints about working conditions, just checking in.

Now she felt all self-centered and whiny. The man was out there in the worst conditions, saving lives, and she was feeling neglected because… Because why? She'd told him to go and to not come back. If she should be mad about anything, it should be because he was emailing her now, not that he hadn't done it before.

She answered the email. Emma did fine, received a blue ribbon. No need to mention the preshow panic. The garden was fine. She was fine. Wishing him well. Signing off.

There. A perfectly polite email that asked no questions and left him no need to respond. There was absolutely no reason for Scott to contact her ever again. Because she and Emma and her garden and everyone and everything else in her life were flippin' fine. And if they weren't, it was none of Scott Willingham's concern.

CHAPTER SEVENTEEN

"SUCTION, PLEASE." SCOTT waited for the surgical nurse to clear the field. Ah, there it was. The tumor that had been causing his patient so much pain. A few minutes later the tumor was in a specimen tray, and he was closing. The specimen would have to be transported to a lab a hundred miles away to be checked, but generally tumors of this shape and position tended to be benign. Most likely, once Anu had recovered from the surgery, she was going to feel better than she had in years.

Anu was Scott's last surgery of the day. He was handling surgery this week in a DEMA hospital in Ethiopia that specialized in repairing birth injuries, but also provided other gynecologic surgery for women from all over the country. He'd worked in this hospital many times and was always struck by the resilience of the women who came to them for help. Anu, despite years of constant pain, was a grandmother and a leader in her community. Now that the source of the pain was gone, there would be no stopping her.

It was due to women like Anu that his job provided a great sense of satisfaction. But he was beginning to think job satisfaction wasn't enough. It wasn't a life.

The door to the second surgical room opened and Dr. Bradley Adams walked out. Brad had arrived three days ago. He'd been volunteering two weeks a year at this clinic for the past twelve years. He greeted Scott. "All done for the day?"

"Yes. Just finished."

"Me, too. Let's get some grub."

Scott accompanied him to the dining area. Most of the patients, at least the ambulatory ones, chose to eat here rather than in the wards. The short walk was good for them, as was the change of scenery. It was late, though, and most of the patients had returned to the wards. The two doctors made their way to the kitchen, where the smiling cook dished up hearty servings of spicy wat over rounds of injera, a chewy sourdough bread.

They thanked her and carried their meals to a table in the corner. Scott tore off a chunk of bread and used it to scoop up some of the vegetable stew and pop it in his mouth. Brad did the same. They spent a few moments taking the edge off their hunger before Brad spoke. "You know, I've tried to re-create this at home for my wife, but I can never get the spices right."

"I imagine it would be difficult. It's along the lines of curry, but not the same. Do you cook much?"

"Yes, I enjoy cooking. My wife and I take turns. Most workdays I keep it simple, but on weekends I like to try out new recipes. Some had been great successes, and others…" He winced. "Not so much. The kids have starting laying odds on whether a weekend experiment will be edible or not."

Scott chuckled. "How many kids do you have?"

"Four." Brad pulled out his phone and showed him a family photo. A dark-haired woman in a yellow dress held a toddler on her hip. A boy holding a soccer ball and two girls surrounded her. The boy and one of the girls looked much like the children of the patients Scott had seen today, as did the toddler. The other girl, smiling sweetly at her mother, had Down syndrome. All were laughing.

"You have a beautiful family."

"I'm a lucky man," Brad said, returning his phone to his pocket and scooping up another bite.

"Is your practice in Kansas solitary, or do you have partners?" Scott asked.

"I have four partners, which is why I'm able to do this. My partners are great about covering for me while I'm gone. One of them, Patricia Silva, also takes a leave to volunteer with DEMA, but she goes to Brazil. You're full-time with DEMA, correct?"

"Yes."

"That's fairly rare, isn't it?"

Scott nodded. "There are only forty full-time doctors in the organization, and twenty-eight of those are assigned to specific facilities. Only twelve of us are roamers."

"Are you married?"

"No."

"Still. It must take a toll, all that traveling."

People always said that. Scott used to reply no, he enjoyed the travel and meeting new people all the time. But now... "It's not easy. I've been at this for almost ten years now."

"Ten years." Brad whistled. "That's a long time to be away from home."

"I don't have a home."

"Then I feel for you. My home and family are everything to me."

"What about your work?"

"I enjoy my work. But it's secondary. It's not who I am."

"You have an ob-gyn practice. That takes a lot of dedication. Babies don't always arrive during office hours. That boy, the one who plays soccer. Don't you have to miss some of his games?"

"They all play soccer, and yes, of course I do. They understand that. My wife works mornings only, so she does most of the shuttling. She has a network of other parents who trade off for carpooling, and her parents live in the same town, so they sometimes help out. We make it work."

"Excuse me if this is too personal, but have you ever broken a promise to your kids? You said you'd be there and then you weren't?"

"It happens," Brad admitted readily. "I try hard not to make promises I can't keep. My partners and I take turns being on call. We run the practice so that the patients get to know all of us during their pregnancies, and they understand that they won't necessarily get their choice of doctors when it's time to deliver. But sometimes, an emergency comes up. My family understands that."

He used a hunk of injera to push a stray vegetable to the center of his plate. "My kids are the center of my life, but they're not the center of the universe. The sooner they realize that, the happier they'll be. That was one of the reasons I do this every year. When they're older,

I'll bring the kids along from time to time. My family makes me happy."

Scott chewed his bread and thought about that. When he was a kid, more than anything he'd wanted his father's attention. But he didn't need all of it, all the time. A little undivided attention would have been enough. He looked at the doctor sitting across the table from him. "You're a good man, Bradley Adams. You deserve to be happy."

Brad chuckled. "So do you, my friend. So do you."

Two weeks later, Scott was at DEMA headquarters in London, for his semiannual review. Hans tapped a stack of papers together and set them on top of a folder labeled with Scott's name. "So, how was the vacation in Alaska?" Scott thought of trail rides through the forest and running on the coastal trail. Of Emma's laugh and Volta's smile. He couldn't help smiling himself. "It was great."

"You've been back at work, let's see, six weeks now. How's it going?"

Scott started to give his usual response. *Fine, great, all is well.* But was it? "Okay," he temporized.

"Just okay?"

Scott shrugged. Hans waited for him to

speak, but when he didn't, Hans pulled another paper from the stack. "You've been with
us for, what, ten years now?"

"Yes."

"Do you know that the longest tenure for a
full-time traveling doctor we've ever had before
you was five years?"

"Was it?"

"Yes." Hans set the papers down and stee-
pled his fingers. "I hear you're not yourself
lately. That you seem distracted."

Scott frowned. "Who says that?"

"Does it matter?"

"I suppose not. Maybe I have been a little
distracted," Scott admitted, "but it hasn't affected my work."

"Not yet. But constantly moving from place
to place, working with different people each
time… It's stressful. The usual path is for a
doctor to move into that position immediately
after residency, to get a taste of what's out
there, and then, after a year or two, to settle
into a permanent spot somewhere. You know
that."

"I suppose I do."

"And yet, you've never settled. Do you know
why?"

Because that was who he was. Dr. Scott
Willingham: a man completely devoted to his

job, who never turned down an assignment. Who never allowed his personal life to interfere because he had no personal life. Just like his father. But in Scott's case, his dedication was providing medical care around the world. Wasn't that a good thing? "You need people like me," he protested.

"Yes, but we have other applicants. There's a very enthusiastic obstetrician who started yesterday, in fact. She's getting her physical and immunizations as we speak. You don't have to do this forever."

Scott gave a dry laugh. "I'm not sure I know how to do anything else."

"Then maybe it's time you learn. You're a good doctor, Scott. We don't want to lose you to burnout."

"I'm fine."

"Well, then, it's time to figure out the next stage of your career." Hans opened his desk drawer and pulled out a list. "We could use someone with your skill set in the clinic in Paraguay. Or …" Hans continued talking about the various possibilities around the world, but Scott had stopped listening. Hans was right. It was time for the next stage. Time for a fresh start.

"Do any of those options appeal?" Hans was asking.

"No."

"No?" Hans raised his eyebrows. "Time for you to settle down in one place?"

Scott nodded. "Consider this my resignation." He stood and offered his hand. "Thank you, Hans. It's been an amazing ten years."

Hans's gaze rose from Scott's hand to his face. He smiled. "If you're sure."

"I'm sure."

Hans rose and, ignoring Scott's outstretched hand, circled the desk to lay a hand on his shoulder. "Remember, if this doesn't work out, you'll always have a place with DEMA."

"Thank you."

"Will you be going into practice with your father in Texas?"

"Not even close." Scott grinned. "I'm heading to Alaska."

IT HAD BEEN surprisingly easy to arrange. When Scott called Bart Thomas, one of the doctors he'd interviewed in Anchorage, Dr. Thomas had immediately mentioned that one of his partners was about to go on maternity leave, and they needed a locum. Since Scott already had his locum license to practice in Alaska while he'd been on the study, it had been a relatively simple matter to apply for a ninety-day extension while the paperwork for permanent licensing went through.

After a successful first day at the practice, he drove to the hospital, where he only had one patient to see, a full-term new mom who had delivered yesterday and was eager to go home. He checked her, consulted with the nurses and signed her release papers, wishing her and her husband well on their new journey.

When he stepped out of her room, Dr. Thomas was at the nurse's station. "Scott." He waved him over. "We appreciate you filling in for Lindsey. How was your first day?"

"Good. You have a great staff."

"Yes, we do. Say, I wanted to let you know my daughter is taking summer courses instead of coming home, but she won't let me sell her horse, so Nugget is still available whenever you want to ride him."

"That's generous of you, Bart. I'll take you up on that offer."

"I'm sure he can use the exercise. Let me know if you need anything."

"I will. Thanks."

Scott handed off the release papers to the nurse and walked outside to his designated parking space. First day on the job: check. Temporary apartment: check. Car leased:

check. Now it was time to face up to the real reason he'd returned to Alaska.

He got into the car, pulled out his phone and called Volta's number.

She picked up on the second ring. "Scott? Are you okay?"

He supposed it showed the state of their relationship that her first assumption when he called was that something terrible had happened to him. "I'm great. How are you?"

"Where are you?" she demanded, ignoring his query.

"I am in the parking lot on the corner of Tudor and Elmore."

"You're in Anchorage?" She didn't sound overjoyed.

"Yes. Could I meet with you, please?"

There was a short hesitation. "I'm not sure that's a great idea. Why are you in Anchorage?"

"That's one of the things I wanted to talk with you about. Where are you?"

"I'm at Puffin headquarters."

"Are you on a mission?"

"No," she admitted. "Our team is second up."

"So you just need to stay within fifteen minutes of the airport, right? I could meet you at that coffee shop near headquarters."

"All right."

"Twenty minutes?"

"Fine."

He arrived in fifteen, but she was already there, stirring her coffee with a plastic stick. A second cup sat in front of the chair across from her. Her expression was hard to read. He took the other chair. "Hi."

"I got you a cappuccino."

"Thanks."

Volta watched him sip his coffee, her blue eyes unblinking. "Did the Travert Foundation bring you back to consult on your recommendations?"

He shook his head. "I've followed up with them and they're moving forward on the project. No, I'm here filling in for Lindsey Catlin while she's on maternity leave."

Volta tilted her head. "I'm confused. You're what?"

"Working as a locum in an ob-gyn practice here in Anchorage."

"Working as a locum? What about DEMA?"

"I resigned."

"Resigned? Why?"

"Because…because I love you." There. He'd blurted it out. He'd meant to explain it a little better and lead up to it, but that was what this was all about.

Volta didn't seem convinced. "What's love got to do with it?"

"Everything. After spending time with you and Emma, I realized traveling with DEMA wasn't what I want anymore."

She narrowed her eyes. "What do you want?"

"I want you, us. I want to be part of your life, yours and Emma's."

"Really." Her voice was flat. "You want to be a part of our lives, so you took a job as a locum in Anchorage."

"Yes," he answered immediately.

"Because you enjoy being with us."

"Yes." This time his answer was a little slower because that flashing light in her eyes was clearly a warning.

"Isn't that sweet? You want to take time off to play house in Alaska for a while, get Emma attached to you again, and then you'll go back to your job and leave us to pick up the pieces."

"I told you. I resigned."

"But one word from you and they'd put you right back on staff, wouldn't they?"

"Well…"

"Wouldn't they?" she demanded.

"Okay, yes. But I'm not going back. I'm here to build a new life."

"I want to believe you."

"You think I'm lying?" He'd quit DEMA and come all the way to Alaska. What more proof did she want?

"Only to yourself. You think you can give up your career—the career that demanded one hundred percent of your time and energy for ten years—without any regrets? Start from scratch?"

"I intend to try."

"You do that." She snapped the lid back on her cup and stood. "But when you've got it figured out, forget my number. Because I'm not in on this grand experiment, and I'm darn sure not going to get Emma involved. Fool me once, shame on you. Fool me twice, it's on me. Letting it happen a third time would be plain stupidity."

"Volta—"

"Enjoy your cappuccino. I need to get back to work." And she walked out of the coffee shop without another word.

CHAPTER EIGHTEEN

"CAN WE GET a dog?"

Not this again. Volta met Emma's eyes in the rearview mirror before the light changed and she pulled forward. "Still no. We've talked about this. With the sort of schedule I have, it wouldn't be fair to a dog."

"Sabrina would take care of it when you're working. She said so."

That didn't sound like something Sabrina would bring up without checking with Volta first. "When did she say that?"

"Yesterday, when her and Uncle Leith took me to the dog park with Tal and Boomer, I told them you said I could get a dog if somebody could take care of it while you were working. And she said she would."

"I did not say that."

"Yes, you did. You said we can't have a dog because you can't take care of it. But if she took care of it—"

"Emma, no. We're not getting a dog that someone else has to care for."

"But we keep Tal and Boomer sometimes, when they go on trips and stuff."

"Yes, occasionally. But not on a regular basis like work."

"But—"

"No." They'd arrived at the stables. "Come on. Len is waiting for you."

After using her most dramatic sigh to let Volta know she was being entirely unreasonable, Emma climbed out of the car. "Did you bring carrots? Len never remembers like Dr. Scott always did."

"Yes." Volta pulled a plastic bag from her purse. "I did."

They walked to the barn, where Emma's new instructor was waiting. Len seemed nice enough, but he couldn't generate the level of enthusiasm that Scott had. The two weeks of horse camp Emma was so excited about had been a minor letdown. She'd enjoyed riding with the other kids, but she complained that they were teaching the same stuff Scott had already taught her.

As they came to the trailhead next to the parking lot, Volta saw a man on a stocky palomino horse riding toward them. Emma saw him, too. "Look. It's Dr. Scott. He's here!"

Shoot. The last thing she'd wanted was for

Emma to run into Scott. "Come on, sweetie. We need to get to your lesson."

"But—" Emma started to say something. Then her mood seemed to deflate like a leaky balloon. "He's riding without me. I guess he doesn't want to be my friend anymore."

This was going from bad to worse. Should she confess to Emma that the reason Scott hadn't contacted her was because Volta had forbidden him to? Letting them spend time together would have been just asking for Emma to be hurt again, but was it fair to place the blame on Scott?

Scott spotted them and dismounted, leading his horse toward them. "Hi, Volta. Emma. I see—"

Emma raised her chin and walked past him. "Come on, Mommy. I need to get to my lesson."

Volta hesitated, wanting a word alone with Scott. "Go on ahead. I'll be right there."

Scott looked after Emma, his brown eyes sad. He turned to Volta. "I'm sorry. I didn't realize Saturday morning would be when Emma—"

"Yes, she has a regular schedule now. Ten thirty on Tuesday, Thursday and Saturday. I'd appreciate it if you'd avoid being at the barn at those times."

He nodded and looked toward the barn. "She's really upset with me for leaving before the show, isn't she?"

Volta blew out a breath. "Mostly, she's upset because she thinks you came back to town and didn't care enough to call her. That you don't like her anymore."

Scott's eyes narrowed. "You told her that?"

"No. That's what she assumed when she saw you." She had to set this right. "Don't worry. I'll explain later. She'll understand."

"I wish I knew how you were going to explain, because I sure as heck don't understand." He shook his head. "Never mind. I'll ride for another fifteen minutes to give Emma time to get out of the barn, so she won't have to endure my presence there." He swung up onto the horse's back and headed toward the trail.

"Scott?" Volta waited until he stopped the horse and looked back. "How is it going? Do you like the new job?"

"It's… I'm in an adjustment period, learning the ropes."

"Oh." Adjustment period. Right. Code for he hated it. The minute the doctor he was filling in for was ready to return, he'd be out of there. Just as she'd predicted. "Okay, well, thank you for giving Emma space."

He nodded and rode off. Volta slowly made

her way toward the barn. She was doing the right thing, keeping Scott away from Emma and out of their lives. Scott had spent his entire professional life traveling for DEMA. He might think he was ready for a change, but he wasn't going to settle down and join a practice in Anchorage. Not for long. Soon, DEMA would be calling on him, needing him for just this one emergency, and then another, and before long he would be back where he belonged, like some sort of superhero traveling the world and saving people.

At the barn, Len and Emma had Butternut saddled. Emma mounted the horse. Len reached for the bridle to lead her outside. "We're going to work on form in the arena the whole hour today," Len told Volta.

"Okay, thanks." Volta went to the bleachers on the far side to watch.

She tried to concentrate on Emma, but her thoughts kept returning to Scott. He'd looked so sad when Emma snubbed him, it was all Volta could do not to put her arms around him and assure him she'd fix everything. And she would, or at least she'd tell Emma the truth. But she couldn't fix the underlying issue, which was that Scott would be leaving again.

But what if he was ready to leave his old life and settle down in Anchorage? At the coffee shop, he'd told Volta he loved her. But he'd loved her before and that didn't stop him from leaving her.

The barn doors were visible across the arena, and the back end of a palomino horse was disappearing inside. Volta got up and slipped over to the barn. She found Scott in the stall, running a brush over the horse, who, judging by his half-closed eyes, was enjoying the massage.

She came to lean against the gate. "Hi." He acknowledged her presence without any show of surprise.

She watched him groom the horse for a few minutes before she spoke again. "Scott, I'm sorry I was so…" She trailed off, not sure how to end that sentence. He ducked under the horse's neck and began brushing the other side without answering her.

Maybe she should just leave. But she couldn't seem to walk away without knowing more. "You said you were in an adjustment period. What did you mean by that?"

"Why do you care?"

Good question. But she did care, whether she wanted to or not. "Look, I'm only trying to protect Emma's feelings. I do care how you're doing, and what challenges you're facing."

Scott lifted the horse's foot and did something to the hoof. "On one hand, it's nice to know what to expect mostly, day to day, and have all the best equipment right there in the office, and a lab in the same building. But..."

"But what?"

He let the horse set his hoof down. "Just little things. Like when we do an ultrasound, the tech gives the patient a printout in a cute little folder with duckies on the cover."

"What's wrong with that?"

He gave a half smile. "Nothing. It's cute. It's just... I'm not used to cute."

"What you mean is you don't feel like you're saving the world when you hand out a duckie photo cover."

Scott shrugged. "Maybe that's it. Not that I ever believed I was single-handedly saving the world—"

"But you single-handedly saved some babies and mothers that wouldn't have made it without you."

"And lost some, too." He patted the horse's neck. "But you understand this. You live in Anchorage. You could have been an EMT on an ambulance locally. Instead, you got flight-certified so you could help people who didn't have easy access to hospitals and ambulances."

"You're right. I do understand." Volta straightened the cuff of her shirt. "And that's why I think when this assignment is over, you'll be going back." She met his eyes. "Because that's the life you chose."

"What do I have to do to prove to you I'm serious about staying here? To make you trust me?"

"I honestly don't know." She wanted to trust him. She believed he was trying. But she wasn't willing to risk her heart, again, and she certainly wasn't willing to risk Emma's. "I just know that experience has taught me I'm better off steering clear of you." Volta looked at her watch. "Emma will be bringing her horse back in here in about ten minutes. Please be gone by then."

And this time, she was the one who walked away.

SCOTT STEPPED OUT of an exam room and into his office to jot a note about the patient he'd just seen. He glanced at the calendar. Today was Thursday. Emma would be riding this morning. He wished he could be there with her, or at least see her, but Volta was right. Until he was absolutely sure he could promise them forever, he needed to stay out of her life.

Last night, Lindsey had called to see if everything was going smoothly in her absence. He had almost been tempted to suggest she find another locum to cover the rest of her

maternity leave. After all, the whole reason
he'd come to Alaska was to be with Volta and
Emma. Without them, what was he proving?

As it stood now, he spent weekdays seeing
patients and went home to an empty apartment at night and on weekends. He had more
free time than he'd had since he was a teenager, but he was clueless about how to fill the
empty hours.

The nurse stuck her head in. "Patient in
exam room two. Michelina Norman."

"Thanks, Peggy." His mood brightened.
He'd seen Michelina twice before. At forty,
she'd already been considered high risk, and
then at twenty-eight weeks of pregnancy, she'd
developed gestational diabetes. Since then
she'd been coming in for weekly checkups.

One of the things he did like about this job
was getting to know his patients on an ongoing
basis, and Michelina was one of his favorites.
She had a smile for everyone, from the noisy
toddler in the waiting room to the doctor poking her with instruments. Her pregnancy had
been a complete surprise. She considered it a
miracle.

Scott knocked and entered. "Hello, Michelina. How are you today?"

"I'm great. Did you take advantage of the
sunshine this weekend?"

He smiled at her. She always seemed to be more interested in everyone else than she was about herself. "I went horseback riding on Saturday. How about you?"

"That sounds nice. I don't think I could climb onto a horse right now." She pointed to her bulging tummy and laughed. "But my husband and I had the whole family over for a barbecue. Don't worry, I didn't pig out on potato salad."

He checked her chart. "Your weight gain is healthy. How have your glucose levels been this week?"

"Good. I've taken to nibbling instead of meals."

"Great idea, both for your blood sugar and to avoid heartburn. Is the baby pushing on your stomach?"

"He thinks it's a soccer ball. I can't wait until he's born and I can take a full breath. Although I've been breathing easier the last day or two."

"Let's take a look." At Scott's request, she lay back on the table and he checked her abdomen. "The baby has dropped. You're getting close."

"That's good news. The nursery is ready. When do you think it will happen?"

"Soon. Which I'm sure you already suspected, since your due date is next week."

"I've been having more Braxton Hicks contractions."

"That's a positive sign. I'm on call this weekend, so if he decides to come, I'll be the one delivering him."

"Fingers crossed."

Scott smiled and moved on to his next patient in a better frame of mind.

ON SATURDAY NIGHT, Scott's phone woke him. More correctly Sunday morning, he realized as he answered. It was the hospital, calling to let him know Michelina was there and in labor. She was dilated to a six, so birth most likely wasn't imminent, but with her risk factors, he decided to head on over anyway.

With the streets almost empty, he made excellent time. He got scrubbed and gowned. When he walked into the room, Michelina was in the middle of a contraction, her husband holding her hand. "Hee hee. Ho ho ho," he chanted, as though casting an incantation to relieve his wife's pain. If only it worked like that.

The contraction must have eased because Michelina opened her eyes and grinned. She seemed thrilled to see him. "Dr. Willingham, you're here!"

"I couldn't miss the party." He introduced

himself to her husband while he checked the monitors. Her vitals looked fine. "How are you doing?"

"I've been better," she admitted, while her husband mopped the sweat from her forehead.

"I'll bet. Let me check your progress." Scott handled the exam. "You're already at a nine. You work fast."

"Here comes another one." She started to pant.

"You're doing great with your breathing. Don't push yet."

Two more contractions and she was fully dilated. Scott and the nursing team moved into position. It only took a few more contractions before the baby crowned. "Almost there, Michelina. You're brilliant."

But on the next contraction, the baby's head moved forward a fraction, and then reversed. Scott kept his voice calm but signaled the nurses. "Shoulder dystocia. Scalpel, please."

The nurse's eyes grew wider over her mask, but she handed him the scalpel. He made the incision. "Michelina, I want you to pull your legs toward your stomach, please."

A frightened whimper escaped, but Michelina complied, with the nurses guiding her legs in place. He pressed on her abdomen. For a long moment, nothing happened, but then he felt the rotation under his hand. He smiled behind his surgical mask.

The next contraction started. "There we go. One more push, and here he comes." The baby was in his hands. Breathing well, good color. His short delay didn't seem to have done him any harm.

Within minutes, he was cleaned and wrapped up and in his mother's arms. Tears of joy ran down her face. "He's so beautiful."

"Yes, he is," Scott agreed.

Michelina's husband kissed his wife's forehead and reached out to touch his baby, a smile of wonder on his face. This was a fortunate child, to be so welcomed, so wanted. Scott was honored to have played a part in bringing him into the world.

As Scott walked out to the parking lot, the sun rose over the mountain in an explosion of pinks and purples. Scott stopped to take in the beauty of a new beginning. It would be a fine day.

CHAPTER NINETEEN

BECAUSE SCOTT HAD been the on-call doctor the weekend before, he had Tuesday morning off. And for once, he knew exactly what he planned to do with it. The day dawned with hardly a cloud in the sky, which Scott took to be a good omen.

Volta had said Emma's riding lessons were at ten thirty. Scott managed to arrive at the stables at ten forty. He was walking toward the barn when he saw Volta coming toward him. She was looking down at her phone, so he was able to watch her for a minute without her knowing he was there. Today she wore a simple dress that swished around her legs as she walked. Her hair bounced on her shoulders. Whenever he stopped to watch her like this, she took his breath away.

She finished whatever she was doing on her phone, slipped it into the bag that hung from her shoulder and looked up to see him only a few yards away. Her feet slowed. "Scott. I thought we agreed—"

"I know. Emma. That's why I waited until her lesson started. I need to talk with you."

"I..." She looked around as though Emma might jump out from behind a bush any minute. "I was about to go grocery shopping."

"I'll go with you."

She looked as though she planned to argue, but suddenly she laughed. "Fine. You can push my cart. I'm going to the store on Huffman."

"I'll follow you."

Five minutes later, they pulled into the parking lot. Scott found a place three spots down from hers. When he got to her car, she handed him a stack of shopping bags. "Here. Carry these."

"Yes, ma'am." He took the bags and followed her into the store.

She consulted a list while he selected a shopping cart, and then she led the way to the produce section. "I need Yukon gold potatoes and fresh dill."

"Potato salad?"

She nodded. "My in-laws are coming for dinner tonight. Leith brought me some fresh salmon, so I thought I'd grill it."

"That sounds delicious."

"I'll need cabbage and carrots for slaw, too." She walked up and down the aisles, crossing items off her list. He pushed the cart, allowing her set the pace. She knew he wanted to talk.

She checked out and let him pack the groceries into the back seat of her car before she looked at her watch. "I need to pick up Emma in twenty minutes, which means I can give you fifteen to say whatever it is you need to say. Is that enough?"

It would have to be. "I saw a coffee kiosk inside," Scott said. "I'll buy you a vanilla latte while we talk."

That made her smile. He loved making her smile. They went inside, placed their orders and settled at an empty table nearby. Volta leaned forward. "So, what is this all about?"

"I delivered a baby on Sunday."

She nodded. "That's nice, but from what I can tell, you've delivered hundreds of babies."

"Yes." He grinned at her. "That's kind of the point. I've delivered hundreds of babies, on every continent except Antarctica. But this was the first baby I've ever delivered for a woman I've gotten to know."

"A friend of yours?"

"No, I'm talking about a patient. I've been her regular doctor for the last month and she trusted me, not as a last resort, but because she knew me and believed that I would take good care of her and her baby."

"And did you take good care of her?"

"I did. There were minor complications—

shoulder dystocia—but they're both fine. And I feel good about that. You said I'm trying to save the world, but maybe I was going about it wrong. Instead of trying to fit in as many patients as I possibly can wherever they may be, I need to develop relationships with my patients. I want to concentrate on one patient at a time."

She reached across the table to squeeze his hand. "I'm happy for you."

The barista dropped off their drinks. Volta closed her eyes and inhaled the aroma of coffee and vanilla. "Irresistible. You know all my weaknesses."

He hoped so. "Patients aren't the only relationships I want to build." He looked into her blue eyes. "I know I've hurt you, but I'm asking for another chance. Just a little time together to prove I can be the man you need me to be."

She paused, sipping her coffee. "Not with Emma. Not yet."

He nodded. "All right. But is there a way to see you alone?"

She stretched her fingers in that exercise she did when she was thinking. "Tonight after dinner, Emma is having a sleepover with her grandparents in their RV. I could meet you for a drink."

"Name the place."

"Moose's Tooth in midtown? I'm not sure when. I'll have to text you."

"I'll be waiting."

DINNER WITH HANNAH and Jim passed in dog years. Stacy was there, too. Volta had hoped she would have gone home to Utah by now, but she seemed content to hang out with her folks.

"How's the job search going?" Volta asked her as she passed the coleslaw around the table.

"Slowly," Stacy admitted. "I've applied for two jobs in Salt Lake, but I haven't heard back yet. I sent in a resume for one here in Anchorage yesterday."

"You're thinking of staying here?"

"Maybe. It depends." She looked at Emma. "I'd get to spend more time with my favorite niece." She held up a hand. Emma giggled and high-fived her.

Jim and Hannah talked about their travels and made plans for popcorn and a movie in their motor home with Emma tonight. They were finishing their dessert when Emma mentioned the baby loons in the park one block over, and Jim declared they should walk over and see them. Volta almost groaned aloud at the delay.

But finally, Emma was buckled next to Stacy into the back seat of the car her grandparents towed behind their RV. Her backpack, sleeping bag and stuffed dog, Rufus, were stowed away in the trunk. Volta waved goodbye and waited until they were out of sight before she pulled out her phone and sent a text. They're gone. Are we still on?

Scott answered immediately. On my way.

Fifteen minutes later, Volta made her way from the parking lot to wait with the crowd at the entrance of the most popular brewpub in Anchorage. Maybe it was a mistake trying to meet Scott there. Maybe it was a mistake to try to meet Scott at all, but here she was.

Hardening her heart when he'd said he loved her was the hardest thing she'd ever done. But for Emma's well-being, and her own, she'd had to say no. No, he couldn't be a part of their lives, only to disappear again, leaving a gaping hole. But seeing him today, excited at his epiphany over patient care, had loosened her resolve. He was trying so hard. The least she could do was listen.

A sudden touch against Volta's back made her turn, and he was there. Scott bent down to brush his lips across hers, the casual kiss of a longtime lover. He was assuming a lot, but the happiness the kiss provoked made it hard to disapprove. Before she could react, the party of eight in front of them moved aside to wait for a table. Scott urged her forward to talk with the hostess.

"Table for two, please." They were in luck. The hostess gathered menus and asked them to follow right away. As they passed by a row of booths, Volta heard her name called. Mike, the pilot, waved at her. He was sitting with his wife and another couple. Volta and Scott greeted them briefly before following the hostess, who was tapping her toe, waiting to guide them to a table tucked away in the corner.

Once the hostess had gone, Scott chuckled. "So much for a clandestine meeting."

Volta shrugged. "Apparently I'm not much good at choosing secret rendezvous locations. But it doesn't matter. Emma is with her grandparents at the campground, and it's not as though she and Mike run in the same circles."

The waiter came to take their drink orders. After he left, Scott opened the menu. "I've heard great things about the pizza here. What should I order?"

"You haven't had dinner?" It was almost nine.

"I wasn't sure when you would call. The Santa's Little Helper pizza sounds good."

"You never could resist a jalapeño."

"Why even try? Would you like an appetizer?"

"No, thanks. I might have a bite of pizza if you'll share."

"With you? Always."

The waiter returned with their drinks, poured the beers and took Scott's order. When he was gone, Scott lifted his glass. "To happiness."

"I can't argue with that." Volta clinked her glass against his. "Happiness for all."

They both sipped their drinks. Scott set his down. "Tell me about Emma. How was horse camp?"

"On one hand, she enjoyed being around horses and horse people all day. But most of what they were teaching, she already knew. It's my fault for signing up for the beginner's session, but at the time I registered her, I didn't know Mom and Dad were going to give her private lessons, and I sure didn't know you would be tutoring her."

"That's too bad. I take it she's back to lessons?"

Volta nodded. "There's a new guy named Len. He's no ball of fire, but he seems to be teaching her what she needs to know. Cait, her original instructor, is supposed to be back soon."

They chatted some more, and the waiter brought the pizza. Scott picked up a piece and took a bite. "Oh, this is good. I can't remember the last time I had pizza with jalapeños."

"Maybe you should indulge more often."

"Maybe I will." He met her eyes across the table. "It's taken me a long time, but I'm finally figuring out I don't have to sacrifice everything that makes me happy in order to help people. And nothing in my life has ever made me happier than you."

"Scott—"

"It's okay. We'll take it slow. I realize I'm going to have to prove myself to you. It's going to take some work to find my place, but I'm determined. You'll see. Here, try a bite of this." He held the slice for her and let her nip off a bite.

Then he set the slice on his plate and leaned across the table. "You have some cheese right here." He ran his thumb over her chin. Then he smiled and leaned further to brush her lips with his own.

Something flashed. Volta turned to see Stacy standing there, looking at the image on her cell phone with a self-righteous look on her face. Stacy didn't bother with preamble. "I thought you said he was leaving town."

Volta didn't flinch. "He came back."

"No kidding." Stacy turned to Scott. "Girl in every port, or do you think she's special?"

Without pausing, she answered her own question. "Because if you do, you're mistaken. She's a sponge. No loyalty at all." Before he or Volta could answer, Stacy turned and flounced away.

Things were about to get ugly.

VOLTA DIDN'T LEARN just how ugly until late the next morning. After a sleepless night, she was busying herself pulling chickweed from the flower bed on the side of the house when Jim and Hannah's car pulled up with Stacy in the driver's seat. She opened the back door, and Emma spilled out, tears flowing down her face. Emma was not a crier. This was serious.

Emma ran to Volta. "Were you kissing Dr. Scott?"

"Sweetie…" Volta reached out to her, but Emma shrugged off her hug. "Tell me."

Stacy followed, carrying Emma's things, looking smug. "Let's go inside, Emma. The three of us have stuff to talk about."

"No. We don't." Volta snatched the items away from Stacy. "Emma and I need to talk. You need to leave."

"But Emma wants—"

"I'll take care of Emma." Volta rested a hand on Emma's back and nudged her forward. "Go in the house, sweetheart. I'll be right there."

Emma grabbed her stuffed dog and dragged herself through the front door.

Stacy glared at Volta. "Who do you think you are?"

"I'm Emma's mother and this is my house. And I'm telling you to go away."

Volta turned on her heel and marched inside, locking the dead bolt behind her with an audible click. She could hear Stacy muttering something and then the slam of a car door. Volta sucked in a deep, calming breath. Now, where was Emma?

She found her in her room, sprawled across her bed. Emma lifted a tearstained face toward her mother. "You did, didn't you? Aunt Stacy showed me a picture."

"Yes, I kissed him. Emma, Scott's here because he wants to be with us. I told him he couldn't see you anymore until—"

"I don't want to see him. Ever."

"Why?"

"Because he's bad. He promised he'd be there for the show, but he broke his promise. He works in other places far away. I don't want you to get married again."

"Who said anything about marriage?"

"Aunt Stacy. She showed me the picture of you kissing him. Please don't marry him,

Mommy." The tears were flowing like Thunderbird Falls in the spring. "I don't like him."

"Shh, it's okay, sweetheart." Volta pulled her into a hug. "I'm not going to marry him."

"Promise?" Emma demanded. "Promise you'll never marry him?"

Volta stroked her back. "I promise I'll never marry anyone you don't want me to marry. Okay?"

Emma sniffed. "Really?"

"Really." Volta passed her a box of tissues. "I love you to infinity, Emma."

Emma paused and blew her nose. Finally, in a small voice she replied, "Plus one."

Volta squeezed her tight.

CHAPTER TWENTY

VOLTA WAS ALREADY at a table when Scott walked into the coffee shop, the same table where he'd met her before just after he arrived in town. Her face was pale. Even the blue of her eyes seemed duller than usual. He took his seat and reached across the table for her hand. "Are you okay?"

"I'm sorry, Scott." Volta licked her lower lip. "I considered calling, but I feel like I should say this face-to-face." She met his eyes. "It's over."

"I don't understand." Scott pushed his hair back from his forehead. "Why?"

"It's Emma. Just the thought of us together sent her into a panic."

"But Emma likes me. We get along fine."

"Apparently, she took it harder than I realized that you had to leave her before the show." Volta shredded the napkin on the table in front of her. "She doesn't trust you."

"Did you tell her I wasn't avoiding her by choice? That I wanted to see her when I came back and only stayed away because you asked me to?"

"I did. I explained that I didn't want you spending time together until I was sure. But when I said that, she cried even harder." Volta blinked away a few tears of her own. "You should have seen her, Scott. She was so upset at the idea that I might marry you."

He frowned. Something didn't add up. "Did you mention marriage? I thought the plan was to take it slow."

"I didn't. Stacy must have put the idea into her head. But it's clear Emma is never going to accept you." She reached for Scott's hand. "It's not going to work. I thought we could be together, but we can't. We need to break it off now, before it goes any further."

Those were almost the exact words he'd used when he broke up with Volta eleven years ago in Hawaii. He'd never realized just how inadequate they were…*before it goes any further*? He'd given her his whole heart. How much further could it possibly go?

He wanted to debate with her, to point out the unreasonableness of the decision. The three of them belonged together. Everything he felt inside said so.

But Volta was a mother. She put the well-being of her daughter before her own happiness. And she was convinced Scott wasn't good for Emma. How could he argue with that?

Icicles formed inside his chest. Eleven years ago, Scott had made the biggest mistake of his life when he broke up with Volta. He'd thought fate was giving him a second chance here in Alaska. Apparently, fate was laughing at him.

THE NEXT SATURDAY MORNING, Scott lay in bed, staring at the ceiling, wishing the phone would ring to summon him to work. Not very likely, since he wasn't on call this weekend. What did people do when they weren't working or traveling, and they had no friends or family?

He rolled out of bed and started coffee and toast, which were pretty much the extent of his cooking skills. He hadn't had a kitchen to practice in since he was a resident, and he'd spent most of his waking hours then at the hospital. Or with Volta.

Why did every thought lead back to Volta? It was over. She'd said it; it was done. No matter what he thought, what he believed, it took two to make a relationship, and Volta was out. Regardless of what he wanted. He poured coffee into his cup.

His first sip burned his tongue, and he set the cup down with a bang, splashing coffee all over the counter. He grabbed a paper towel to wipe it up. When he turned back, smoke rose from the toaster. This pretty much summed up the state of his life right now.

After dumping the charred toast and the paper towel into the trash, Scott went to shower and shave. Sunlight twinkled through the glass-block window of his bathroom, so at least it wasn't raining. Maybe horseback riding would improve his mood.

But Saturday was Emma's lesson day. Scott checked the time on his phone. Emma's lesson started in twenty minutes. If he gave her a ten-minute head start, he could take Nugget out on one of the secondary trails for a couple of hours without any danger of running into her. The instructors only took kids on the main trails, where there was more traffic and less chance of running into something unexpected.

Riding was a good idea. Nugget perked up his ears when Scott came into view. He saddled the horse and rode him out into the sunshine and along onto a twisting trail that roughly paralleled the main trail on the far side of a ridge. He rode at a steady walk, listening to the rhythm of hooves clomping against the earth.

Scott had been riding for about twenty minutes when a high-pitched neigh sounded, followed by a scream. Nugget startled, but Scott reined him in and lay a calming hand on his neck. Something was crashing through the brush, coming toward them. Nugget danced backward. Suddenly a huge brown shape burst out of the bushes directly in front of them and dashed onto the trail. Scott got a glimpse of the bear's face just before Nugget reared and whirled. It took Scott a couple of minutes to regain control. By that time the bear was long gone, but Nugget still shook with fear.

"Help!" The voice was faint, carried on the breeze. It seemed to come from the same direction where the bear had emerged. The woods were too dense and steep to ride in that direction, so Scott swung down from the saddle. The gelding shied and, before Scott could tie him, he took off like a shot. Scott dove into the brush, easily following the trail of broken limbs and trampled vegetation left by the bear. He climbed to the ridge, where the voice became clearer. "Help! Please!"

He scrambled down the slope and through the woods to the main trail. A young woman dressed in the green shirt all the riding instructors wore held on to the bridle of a terrified bay mare. "Are you all right?" Scott called.

"I am, but my student's hurt," the woman told him. "Butternut threw her when she saw the bear." She pointed toward a tangle on one side of the trail.

"Is it Emma?" Scott raced to where she was pointing. Emma lay there against a tree stump. Her arms and legs were tangled among the brush, her left arm at an alarming angle. At least she was wearing her helmet. "Emma, sweetheart, can you hear me?"

"Um." She opened her eyes, dark against her uncharacteristically pale face. "Dr. Scott?"

"It's okay, sweetie. You fell off your horse, but we're going to take care of you."

She reached for her left abdomen with her good hand. "My stomach hurts."

"We'll take care of that, too."

The riding instructor leaned in. "Is she okay?"

Scott ignored the question while he felt below Emma's ear for a pulse. Rapid but strong. "Did you call for help?"

The instructor held up her phone. "No bars. It's a dead spot."

"What's your name?"

"Cait."

"Okay, Cait. I'm a doctor. I'm going to stay right here with Emma. I want you to ride to a high point and as soon as you get a signal, call 911. Tell them we have a broken arm and possibly spleen damage. Do you understand?"

"Yes," she squeaked.

"Good. Then go back to the trailhead so you can lead the emergency responders here. While you're waiting, call Emma's mother and someone at the stable to make sure Butternut and Nugget made it back okay. Do you understand, Cait?"

She nodded, her eyes huge.

"Good. Go on then."

She swung onto her horse's back and took off at a gallop. She probably shouldn't have ridden that fast on this trail, but this was an emergency. Scott turned his attention back to Emma.

"Does it hurt anywhere else, sweetie?"

"My head feels all dizzy." She started to sit up, but he stopped her.

"Just lie still."

"I'm scared."

"I know. Here." He reached into his jeans pocket and pulled out his mother's charm. "Take this. It's my lucky charm."

"It's a horseshoe." She grasped it in her hand.

"Yes, and it's very special," Scott told her. "You hold on to that. The paramedics will be here soon. They'll carry you out on a litter, like a queen or princess. Then you'll get to go in an ambulance to the hospital and they'll get you all fixed up, okay?"

"Will Mommy be there?" Her voice trembled.

"Absolutely, Mommy will be there. Your mommy loves you."

"To infinity," Emma murmured.

"Plus one," Scott declared.

Emma gave a tiny smile.

The welcome sound of footsteps and voices soon carried through the woods. A minute later, the EMTs arrived. Scott helped them secure Emma to the backboard and carry her to the ambulance.

Scott spotted Cait in the parking lot. "Did you reach Emma's mother?"

"She's on her way."

"Send her directly to the ER," Scott called to her. "I'm going with Emma."

In the back of the ambulance, Scott held Emma's hand while an EMT started an IV.

"Dr. Scott, am I gonna die?" she asked in a small voice.

"Nope," he assured her. "You're going to have a cast on your arm, some colorful bruises, and probably a really cool scar, but you're going to be fine."

"Can I have a pink cast?"

Scott chuckled. "I don't know, sweetheart, but I'll be sure and ask."

At the emergency room, he stepped back to allow the staff to whisk Emma inside. Volta rushed in through the glass doors, her eyes wide in panic. She spotted Scott and ran to him. "Where is she?"

"Being examined. I think she's got a ruptured spleen, so depending on how severe it is, she might need surgery. Broken arm. Other than that, bumps and bruises."

"No head trauma?" Her voice was controlled, but Scott heard a tremor of fear. More than one doctor had mentioned to him that sick and hurt children were even scarier for medical professionals because they knew what could go wrong.

"She was wearing her helmet. The EMTs used a neck brace as a precaution, but I saw no signs of spinal damage. She'll be fine."

Volta's face collapsed, and tears gushed from her eyes. Scott wrapped her in a hug. "Shh. It's okay."

She sobbed. "I was so scared."

"I know." Scott rubbed his hand up and down her back. "But you'll want to be calm and smiling in a few minutes when you see Emma, so get it all out while you can."

"Mrs. Morgan?" a nurse called.

Volta straightened and sniffed. "Right here."

"Emma's ready to see you."

Volta looked up at Scott. "Will you stay?"

"As long as you need me. I'll be right here."

She gave him a little smile and grabbed a tissue from the box on a table before following the nurse through the double doors.

Scott found an empty chair and settled in to wait. After what seemed like hours, but was actually sooner than he expected, a nurse gave him a message. Emma was being prepped for surgery. Could he please come?

After getting directions from the nurse, he took the elevator to the fourth floor and found Volta alone in a waiting room. She seemed almost as small as Emma, huddled in a chair. When he stepped into the room, she looked up, and the relief on her face made him glad he was there. She hurried to him, and he pulled her into a hug.

He held her for a long time before she spoke. "You were right. The spleen is damaged. The CT scan looks like a tear, but it was bleeding heavily, and they decided laparoscopic surgery was the best bet. She's in there now."

"How are you holding up?"

"I'm okay. It's just…"

"Scary. I know."

"The surgeon has a good reputation. They're going to set her arm, too, while she's under."

"I hope you told them Emma wants a pink cast."

Volta gave a laugh. "She told you that?"

"Yes. She's going to be okay, you know."

"I know." She stepped back but grasped his hand and tugged him over to the chairs.

"Have you called your family?" Scott asked.

"They're on their way. Unfortunately, my parents went with Leith and Sabrina to an auction in Soldotna this morning. Sabrina said there were some antique dresses she wanted to see—she's a designer—and Mom's always up for that sort of thing. They invited Emma and me along, but Emma didn't want to miss her riding lesson…" She trailed off, no doubt wishing she'd insisted Emma skip riding today.

Scott squeezed her hand. "How about her other grandparents?"

"They didn't answer. Probably fishing somewhere. I left a message."

Scott nodded. They lapsed into silence, but she held on to his hand. Her eyes never strayed far from the double doors leading to the surgical theater. Across the hallway, elevator doors opened and Volta's parents rushed into the room. She jumped up and hugged them, and then hugged her brother and his girlfriend. She updated them on Emma's condition.

"They said it would be a fairly simple surgery. We should hear something soon."

Scott touched Volta's shoulder. "Now that

your family is here, I'll get out of your way," he whispered.

"Could you stay?" Her eyes were pleading. "Until she's out of surgery?"

"Of course." He would sit here until the end of time if Volta wanted him to.

The rest of the family looked mildly surprised at Scott's presence, but they were too concerned about Emma to ask many questions of him. Finally, the doctor stepped out and pulled his mask down. His smile told the story.

"She's fine," he told Volta. "It was a small tear. She should heal quickly. Dr. Laghari is setting her arm now."

"Emma wants a pink cast if possible," Scott said.

The doctor chuckled. "I'll pass along the request. Emma will be in recovery shortly," he told Volta. "Someone will be out to take you to her. Just you for now."

Volta nodded. "Thank you, Doctor."

The surgeon patted her on the shoulder, nodded at everyone else and went back through the doors.

Volta faced Scott and reached for both of Scott's hands. "Thank you. Thank you for taking care of her and thank you for taking care of me."

"Anytime. If you need me, call. I'll be there."

She smiled at him. "I know."

VOLTA SMOOTHED EMMA'S hair back from her forehead and smeared a little lip balm onto her lips. She'd woken from anesthesia just long enough to reassure everyone, and promptly fallen back asleep. They'd since moved her from recovery to a hospital room. Now she was beginning to stir once again.

"Mommy?" Her voice was rough.

"Hi, sweetie." Volta offered a cup of water with a straw.

Emma sipped the water and looked around the room, obviously confused.

"You're in the hospital. Do you remember falling off your horse?"

Emma's eyes grew wider. "There was a bear!"

"I heard that."

Emma took another sip. "Dr. Scott was there."

"Yes." When Cait told her that a doctor who had been riding nearby was going with Emma in the ambulance, Volta had somehow known it was Scott. And the thought had comforted her.

Emma looked down at the cast on her arm. "It's pink. I told Dr. Scott I wanted pink."

"He remembered."

A tap sounded at the door. "Hey, looks like someone woke up." Emma's granddad came into the room, carrying an enormous stuffed lion. "How are you feeling?"

She squealed and held out her arms. "Is that for me?" Emma was back to being Emma.

The family followed him in and gathered around Emma's bed. Emma hugged the lion and, in answer to their questions, told her story. "Cait and Sunny were in front of me and Butternut on the trail, when this bear ran out right between us and he was so big! Butternut was scared and tried to run away, and I fell off. And then Dr. Scott was there. I asked him if I was gonna die, and he said no and I asked if I could have a pink cast and he said maybe."

Volta's dad suppressed a chuckle. Mom smiled and touched the cast. "It looks like you got your wish."

"Yeah." Suddenly Emma's eyes opened wide. "Is Butternut okay? The bear didn't eat her, did he?"

"Butternut is fine." Scott walked into the room, carrying a sparkly pink gift bag. Volta tensed. What if Emma panicked at Scott being here, the way she had when Stacy brought her home last week?

But Emma grinned. "Hi, Dr. Scott."

"Hey there. I checked with the stables. Butternut ran straight back to the barn, and they took care of her. The bear is gone, too, as far as anyone can tell. You probably scared him away."

"Tell Butternut I'll be back real soon."

"I'm not sure about that," Volta hedged. Her first instinct after this disaster was to keep Emma and horses as far apart as possible, but she realized that wouldn't go over well. At least the cast bought her some time. Maybe she could get Emma immersed in a safer hobby by then. Like knitting. Although those needles could be sharp.

"Here." Scott distracted Emma by handing her the bag. "In case you get bored."

Emma's eyes lit up. She pulled out tissue paper and then a horse-themed activity book, a pack of colored markers and a clipboard. "Thank you."

"You're welcome. I'm glad to see you're feeling better." Scott patted her on the head, smiled at everyone and withdrew.

Emma enjoyed the family's attention, but before too long her eyelids began to droop. Volta decided it was time to send everyone home. "Let's let Emma get some sleep."

The nurse checked on her a couple more times. The doctor came by before he left for the evening. After examining Emma, he motioned for Volta to join him in the hall. "She's doing very well. I'll be by in the morning, and assuming there are no complications, I expect I'll release her then."

"That's great. Thank you." Volta went back in and settled into the recliner beside Emma's bed. Emma had fallen asleep again, still hugging her new lion. Her dark lashes spread against her cheeks, which were paler than usual but still pink. Her chest rose and fell, rose and fell.

Sometimes, when Emma was a baby, Volta would sit and watch her breathe like this, marveling at this tiny, miraculous person. She'd thought then that it wasn't possible to feel any greater love than she felt for her daughter that day. She was wrong. As Emma grew, so did her love.

Volta must have fallen asleep as well, because the next thing she heard was the nurse's footsteps. She smiled at Volta and handed her a bag. "Emma's things."

"Thanks."

The nurse recorded Emma's vitals and padded out. Volta checked the bag. Shoes, clothes and something else. A tiny charm. The horseshoe that had belonged to Scott's mother.

Emma's voice. "Mommy?"

"I'm right here, sweetie." Volta set the charm on the table. "Do you want a drink?" Emma nodded, and Volta held the cup for her to sip.

"Dr. Teva says you can probably go home tomorrow. But you'll need to stay in bed for a while to heal."

Emma spotted the horseshoe and picked it up. "Dr. Scott gave this to me."

"When?"

"When I was hurt. I was scared, and he gave me his lucky charm."

Volta smiled. "Did it make you feel better?"

"Yes." Emma waggled the charm back and forth so it caught the light. "Will Dr. Scott come see me at home?"

"Um, I'm sure he will if you want him to. Do you?"

Emma nodded. "He's nice."

"Yes," Volta agreed.

Emma pulled her eyebrows together, as though she was solving a difficult riddle. She turned the charm over and over in her hand. After several minutes, she cleared her throat as though she had something momentous to say.

"Mommy?"

"Yes?"

"You can marry Dr. Scott if you want. I can stay with Grandma while you're gone. Like Nick."

Nick was Emma's classmate, who lived with his grandmother while his mother was stationed overseas on military assignment, but that didn't explain why Emma would think she was leaving. "When I'm gone? What do you mean, Emma?"

Emma tilted her head. "Dr. Scott works far away, in Africa and places like that. So if you marry him, you'll go away, too. That's what Aunt Stacy said."

Stacy! No wonder Emma had been in such a panic. Stacy had her convinced her mother was going to desert her over a man. "Aunt Stacy is full of—um—she's mistaken. Scott did have a job traveling all over the world, but now he's working right here in Anchorage."

"Really?" Emma seemed thrilled. "He's not going away anymore?"

Volta hesitated. Scott had said he was here to stay, but that was when he'd believed she would welcome him back. Since then, he'd had a lot of time to reconsider. His current hitch as locum probably wouldn't last much longer. Was he staying or going?

"What matters is that I'm not going any-where. No matter what might happen between Scott and me, I'll always be your mommy, and I'll be right here with you. I'll still have to spend some nights working, like always, but I'm not going away, no matter what Stacy might have told you. Okay?"

"Okay." Emma stroked her hand over the pink cast. "Are you going to marry him?"

"I don't know, Emma. We'll have to wait and see."

CHAPTER TWENTY-ONE

VOLTA HEARD THE familiar step on the front porch, and her heart fluttered. When she opened the door, Scott stood there his hand up, ready to knock. He grinned. "Have you developed clairvoyance?"

"Just good hearing. Come in."

He stepped inside. "How's our patient?"

"Becoming impatient. Keeping her in bed is a challenge."

"That's a good sign. You say she wants to talk with me?"

"That's what she says. She won't tell me what it's all about, but she insists she needs to see you." Before taking him upstairs she added, "I have some interesting information to share with you as well, but I'll let you talk with Emma first."

"I have something I'd like to discuss with you, too, but we can save it for later."

Volta led him up the stairs and to a room at the end of the hallway, and then stood back to let him go first. Emma was sitting up in her bed with a book on a tray in front of her. She looked up and a broad smile crossed her face. "Hi, Dr. Scott."

"Hi, Emma. How are you feeling?"

"Better. Have you seen Butternut?"

"As a matter of fact, I have." Scott sat in the chair beside Emma's bed. "I stopped by the stables Sunday evening to make sure she and Nugget didn't have any aftereffects. They're both fine. Cait and the others were asking about you."

"They sent a card," Volta told him. Emma had loved getting mail. Volta still wasn't completely sold on letting Emma continue riding.

"Butternut didn't mean to buck me off." Emma threw a meaningful glance toward Volta as she talked to Scott. "She was just scared of the bear."

"You're right," Scott said. "She didn't mean for you to get hurt."

"Today is our lesson day. She probably misses me."

"Probably," Scott agreed.

"Next time you see her, tell her I'll come visit soon."

"Emma, we talked about this," Volta said. "You're going to be in that cast for at least six weeks. No riding with a cast."

Emma's bottom lip started to protrude in

that mutinous look, but Scott distracted her, pointing at the book she was holding. "What are you looking at there?"

"It's that book you gave me." Emma smoothed the page. "I'm supposed to find the difference between these two pictures, but they look the same to me. Do you see it?"

He studied the pictures. Volta looked over his shoulder. A man and a little girl were riding double on a horse. Everyone looked happy, even the horse. Emma was right, the two photos did look identical. Volta couldn't find a difference.

Scott was quiet for a long time before he said, "Ah, look down by the saddle horn."

Emma looked. "He's wearing a ring in one picture! And it's a horseshoe, like the one you gave me. Horseshoes are lucky."

Scott smiled at her. "Yes, they are."

Emma reached for the tumbler of water Volta had left on her bedside table and gulped it down. "Mommy, may I have more water, please?" For some reason, the request sounded like a line from a play.

"Sure." Volta took the glass from her, planning to fill it in the bathroom beside Emma's room.

"I want cold water. With ice."

"With ice?" Emma never wanted ice. Water

in Anchorage was plenty cold straight from the tap.

"Yes, please." Emma gave her the innocent look that meant she was anything but. She obviously wanted Volta out of the room while she talked to Scott.

"Okay, I'll go all the way downstairs to bring you water with ice."

"Thank you, Mommy."

"Scott, since I'm going downstairs anyway, would you like something to drink?"

"I'm good. Thanks."

"All right, then." Volta could hear them whispering as she walked down the hallway. In the kitchen, she dumped in some ice cubes, filled the glass with water and headed back. She considered trying to sneak up so she could eavesdrop, but decided that wasn't sporting. Instead, she clumped up the stairs.

"Well, will you?" she heard Emma asking as she approached the door.

"I'll talk to your mommy," Scott answered. "About both of those things."

Volta stepped into the room. "Here's your cold water with ice."

Emma took a little sip and smiled angelically. "Thank you." She set the glass on the nightstand and yawned, lifting her arm and her pink cast over her head in a theatrical stretch. "I'm sleepy. I think I'll take a nap right now."

"Well, if Emma's tired, I suppose we should go downstairs," Scott said. "Maybe I could get some of that special cold ice water down in the kitchen." He winked at Emma.

She winked back, the little faker. "See you later, Dr. Scott."

"You bet. Enjoy your nap, sweetheart."

"What was that all about?" Volta asked when they were downstairs and she was filling a glass with ice water. She set the drink on the kitchen table in front of Scott.

He chuckled. "Thanks, but I was kidding about the water. I'll tell you what Emma and I talked about, but you said you had something to tell me. You go first."

Volta sat next to him, reclaimed the glass and took a sip. She then put it down on the table again. "Emma told me why she was in such a panic when Stacy showed her the picture of us kissing." She explained to Scott what Emma had told her after she woke up from surgery. "…and Stacy had Emma convinced you were trying to steal me away and leave her behind."

"You've got to be kidding me." Scott looked outraged. "Why would Stacy do that?"

"To drive you away. Because I was married

to her brother, and she doesn't think I should be with anyone else."

"But he's been gone, how long?"

"Almost nine years."

"Nine years," Scott repeated. "They must have been close."

"Stacy's always admired him, but they didn't really spend much time together. After he died, she built him up in her memory until no real person could ever measure up."

"But what does that have to do with you?"

"She blames me for his death. He died in an avalanche and she insists I could have stopped him from going on a trip with his friends. Since I didn't, she thinks I should spend the rest of my life doing penance."

"She told you this?"

"Some of it. Wade's parents came by yesterday to visit Emma. Luckily for Stacy, she got a job interview and her parents had dropped her at the airport because if she'd come here, I would have lit into her."

"I'd liked to have seen that."

Volta chuckled. "Anyway, I told Hannah what Stacy had done, and she was not happy. She told me Stacy had tried to sell her on the idea that if I got involved with you, you'd try to keep Emma from spending time with her and Jim because you would be jealous of her father's family. Hannah just ignored her."

"I would never do that," Scott said. "I never got to know my maternal grandparents or learned much about my mother, and I've always regretted it. I would want Emma to spend time with her grandparents. Although I'm having doubts about this aunt."

"I'm way past doubts, but I'll take it up with Stacy someday in the future. Right now, I've got enough on my plate." She shuddered, shaking off all the ugliness of Stacy's treachery. "Okay, your turn."

"My turn." He let out a breath. "First of all, I'd like your advice about something."

She grinned. "I've always got an opinion."

"Good, because I need one. The Travert Foundation contacted me yesterday. They've taken most of my recommendations. The plan is to set up a plane with everything you'd find in a well-equipped practice in Anchorage, including an ultrasound machine, and do the rounds to the villages to give prenatal care to the pregnant women there. They want to hire two obstetricians who would take turns flying out every other week." He paused. "They want me to be one of them."

"That's fantastic."

"Is it? A terrific program, I agree, and it

would help a lot of women who need better prenatal care. And it would be ongoing, so I'd be able to establish a relationship with the patients. But it would mean being away every other week. I promised myself that I would never become my father, a man who neglects his family in favor of his job. That's why I shied away from the idea of family for so long." He took her hand. "I want to be there for you and Emma. Every single day."

Didn't he see? "Scott, do you think I'm a good mom?"

"You're a fantastic mom," he answered without hesitation.

"Even though when I'm working a shift, Emma has to stay with her grandparents or her uncle?"

"But she loves spending time with your family. Besides, you only work eight shifts a month, and you call her a couple of times a day, and when you're not working you volunteer and spend time with her, and—"

"And the job you're describing is so different, how? If you alternated weeks, weekdays I assume, you'd spend, let's see, ten or eleven days a month traveling? And what would you do with the other twenty days?"

He grinned. "If I have my way, I'll spend them with you and Emma."

"So, is this the part where I give my opinion? Because I am heartily in favor of that idea."

"What about things like starting your car in the mornings?"

She laughed. "I have a heated garage now. I don't need someone to start my car. I need a partner, someone to talk things over with. Someone who loves me."

"Oh yeah?"

"Yeah."

He squeezed her hand. "That segues nicely into the next two items on the agenda. Emma's requests."

"Requests, plural?"

"Yes."

"I suspect at least one of them has something to do with horses."

"You guess right. She wants me to convince you that as soon as the cast is off, she should be back on a horse."

"I don't know, Scott. She had surgery. People die falling from horseback."

"People die in small plane crashes, too, and yet you and I are willing to risk it, because we believe in what we're doing. Yes, I realize it's not the same thing, but riding is important to Emma, and she's good at it. My opinion is that we should do what we can to keep her safe, like insisting on helmets and nixing steeplechasing, but that we should allow her to continue. Of course, it's your decision."

"What is steeplechasing?"

"It's a cross-country horse race over various types of jumps. Big jumps."

"Ugh. No steeplechasing." Volta took a breath. "Leith and I talked about this bear. He says the riding trails around the stable are along ridges, while bears tend to hang out near the creeks, especially during salmon season. It's not likely that Emma would come across another bear riding there. But still—"

"You're nervous."

"I am. But you're right. If this is something Emma really wants to do, my fear shouldn't be what holds her back." Volta laughed. "But don't tell her yet. I don't want her trying to convince me riding with a cast is a good idea."

"I won't. Now for the second part of Emma's agenda." He grinned. "It seems she's in the market for a new daddy, and I'm in contention."

"Oh, my gosh, she said that?" Volta felt her cheeks growing warm.

"She did. I was suspicious the two items were related, but she assures me that even if I can't convince you to let her ride anymore, she still wants me. That's high praise in my estimation."

"I'd have to agree."

"The question is, do you want me?"

"Hmm." Volta pretended to consider it. "As I recall, you're not much of a cook."

"No. But I'm great at picking up vanilla lattes and finding good restaurants."

"And you're prone to motion sickness."

"Only if I forget my patch."

"And you don't seem to know much about gardening."

"Not a thing. But I have a strong back, and if you hand me a shovel and point, I'll dig."

She got up and set the water glass in the sink. Without turning, she commented, "On the other hand, you are a very good riding instructor."

"Yep." He stood and scooted the chair under the table.

She faced him. "And you're a doctor. I suppose that might come in handy on occasion."

He grinned. "You never know."

"And you're a good kisser."

"Good?" He looked offended.

"Oh, you think you're better than good?"

"I do."

"Maybe you should prove it."

"Don't bet I won't." He locked eyes with her, a cute teasing smirk on his face, and took a slow step forward. Volta smiled. He touched her cheek and ran his finger slowly along her jaw to tip up her chin. His lips brushed hers in the lightest touch and pulled away.

"That's it?"

"Just warming up." He gathered her in his arms as his eyes sought hers once again. He held her gaze as his face drew closer. And closer.

Her mouth tingled with anticipation. Finally, their lips met and she closed her eyes. As his mouth pressed against hers, a bubbly sensation started in her chest and spread throughout her body until she felt as if she could float away like a helium balloon. She eased into him, and he pulled her tighter, deepening the kiss. Anchoring her to him.

After a long moment, he drew back far enough to see her face. That playful smile had returned, but he was breathing fast. He raised an eyebrow. "Well?"

"Yes." She returned the smile. "I think we could find an opening for a man with your qualifications. What sort of job title did you have in mind?"

"I'm quite partial to the title of husband," Scott answered, and before she could reply, he kissed her again.

"Did you talk to her?" A hopeful voice broke in. Emma was peeking around the corner of the kitchen door. "Are you gonna be my daddy?"

"Hey, you," Volta said, waving her forward. "You're supposed to be in bed." But she opened her arms in invitation.

"I was thirsty." Emma giggled and allowed herself to be hugged.

"Daddy. I like that title, too." Scott wrapped his arms around them both. "And I'm highly qualified. Do you know why?"

"Why?" Emma asked.

"Because I love you—" he dropped a kiss on Emma's head "—and you—" he brushed a kiss across Volta's lips "—to infinity."

"Plus one," Emma said.

Volta smiled at her future husband. "Plus two."

"Infinity plus infinity." Scott laughed. "That's how much I love my Alaska girls."

* * * * *

For more great romances in the Northern Lights series from Beth Carpenter, visit www.Harlequin.com today!

Get 4 FREE REWARDS!

We'll send you 2 FREE Books plus <u>2 FREE Mystery Gifts.</u>

Love Inspired® Suspense books feature Christian characters facing challenges to their faith... and lives.

FREE Value Over $20

BETTY NEELS COLLECTION!

Buy 3 and get **1 FREE!**

Experience one of the most celebrated and beloved authors in romance! Betty Neels will delight you with her signature brand of storytelling: happy romances, memorable couples and timeless tales of lasting love. These classics have been combined in 2-in-1 books for your reading pleasure!

Get 4 FREE REWARDS!

We'll send you 2 FREE Books plus 2 FREE Mystery Gifts.

FREE Value Over **$20**

Both the **Romance** and **Suspense** collections feature compelling novels written by many of today's best-selling authors.

YES! Please send me 2 FREE novels from the Essential Romance or Essential Suspense Collection and my 2 FREE gifts (gifts are worth about $10 retail). After receiving them, if I don't wish to receive any more books, I can return the shipping statement marked "cancel." If I don't cancel, I will receive 4 brand-new novels every month and be billed just $6.74 each in the U.S. or $7.24 each in Canada. That's a savings of at least 16% off the cover price. It's quite a bargain! Shipping and handling is just 50¢ per book in the U.S. and 75¢ per book in Canada.* I understand that accepting the 2 free books and gifts places me under no obligation to buy anything. I can always return a shipment and cancel at any time. The free books and gifts are mine to keep no matter what I decide.

Choose one: ☐ **Essential Romance**
(194/394 MDN GMY7)
☐ **Essential Suspense**
(191/391 MDN GMY7)

Name (please print)

Address _____ Apt. #

City _____ State/Province _____ Zip/Postal Code

Mail to the **Reader Service:**
IN U.S.A.: P.O. Box 1341, Buffalo, NY 14240-8531
IN CANADA: P.O. Box 603, Fort Erie, Ontario L2A 5X3

Want to try 2 free books from another series? Call 1-800-873-8635 or visit www.ReaderService.com.

STRS19R2

Get 4 FREE REWARDS!

We'll send you 2 FREE Books <u>plus</u> 2 FREE Mystery Gifts.

Harlequin® Special Edition books feature heroines finding the balance between their work life and personal life on the way to finding true love.

FREE
Value Over
$20